The Siren Saves The Billionaire

USA TODAY BEST SELLING AUTHOR
KRISTEN PAINTER

THE SIREN SAVES THE BILLIONAIRE:
Nocturne Falls, Book Thirteen

Published in the United States of America.

Welcome to Nocturne Falls, the town that celebrates Halloween 365 days a year. The tourists think it's all a show: the vampires, the werewolves, the witches, the occasional gargoyle flying through the sky. But the supernaturals populating the town know better.

Living in Nocturne Falls means being yourself. Fangs, fur, and all.

Custom-aquarium specialist, Undrea Seeley, is supernaturally good at creating made-to-order fish tanks for her customers. Probably because she loves what she does. And because she's a mermaid. She also loves living in a town where she can be herself. Well, the version of herself everyone thinks she is. But then, who isn't harboring a secret, right?

Tech billionaire Ethan Edmonds is an open book. Hard not to be when the media follows your every move, something they've done pretty much since he made his first million at seventeen by selling an app he'd created. Now he's sold his biggest company for an even greater profit and he's ready to disappear a little. At least enough to focus on a project that has nothing to do with money and everything to do with helping people.

But when his self-appointed fiancée decides he needs a majestic centerpiece aquarium in their new home, she has no idea things are about to spring a leak. Ethan has never met a woman like Undrea and is instantly captivated by her free spirit and fun-loving ways.

Undrea understands his attraction to her, however. It's driven by magic she can't control, but she's still determined not to harpoon his relationship, despite her growing feelings for him. Then she realizes there's something fishy going on and it seems Undrea's not the only one hiding her true identity.

Saving Ethan from the dark forces out to get him could mean revealing the truth she's been trying to hide. But will that secret sink them both or will she sacrifice herself to protect the man she's fallen in love with?

For all the water babies
who'd always wished they'd had a tail.

Enjoy!

1

Late nights and early mornings were a girl's best friend. At least when that girl wanted a little privacy to take a swim in the lake.

Privacy that was necessary, because said girl was also a mermaid.

By the light of the moon that still shone bright in the early morning hours, Undrea Seely went to her usual spot by the lake. She'd been coming here for about as long as she'd lived in Nocturne Falls. And although some of the area around the lake had begun to be developed in the last few years, there was quite a bit of it that remained forested and unspoiled except for the path that wound around it. Farther out, there was a road too, but in most places the trees and underbrush were thick enough to create a screen. The fog rising off the water helped, too.

The path was a popular walking, biking, and running trail for many of the locals, and since the new development had begun, tourists had started coming out here as well. Especially since they'd added paddleboat rentals at the other end of the lake where the shops and businesses were.

The paddleboats were quite a draw. Shaped like dragons, the boats came in black, green, and purple. The tourists adored them, judging by how often the boats could be seen tooling around the lake during operating hours.

But it all made privacy a little harder to come by.

Even more reason to be here before the birds were up.

She stepped off the path and walked toward the large rock formation near the shoreline. There were a few young trees and some bushes clustered around it in such a way that they formed a natural wall. It was the perfect place to shed her human trappings.

She stripped down to a simple one-piece black bathing suit, then folded the rest of her clothes into a neat pile. Her swimsuit would shift with her when she changed forms, like the clothing did for all the shifters she knew. It was part of the magic built into their systems and a rather convenient one.

With a quick look around to make sure she was alone, she left her things behind and walked into the water.

The feeling of sinking into the water, of having it lap around her, was unlike anything else. Winter or summer, cold or warm, being in the water was her equivalent of coming home. Her safe place.

That didn't mean she missed her underwater life.

She didn't. Her life here in Nocturne Falls was about as perfect as she could want. She waded in deeper.

Sure, a little more male company might be nice now and again, but that would come. Eventually, the right merman would move to town and that would be that. Besides, she was in no rush to tie herself to that kind of anchor.

Not that married life wouldn't be great. She saw that in her parents and in her married friends. But she wasn't there yet. Her mom said it was because she hadn't met the right guy. Maybe so.

The water was past her knees now, but the urge to shift had hit her as soon as she'd broken the surface. Legs were great for being on land, but nothing compared to the power and speed of moving through the water with a tail.

Hers was as beautiful as any other merfolk tail she'd ever seen. Granted, she was biased. It was *her* tail, after all. But the glimmer and shine and iridescence never got old.

She waded deeper in until it was safe enough to dive, then she did, shifting as she arrowed through the water and taking a deep gulp of it so that she could breathe, which was made possible by the gills behind her ears.

She swam forward in the same position for another few moments, then rolled over onto her back and flicked her tail once to propel herself farther.

She was about four feet under now, but even in the dark, her eyes could make out the sprinkling of stars still visible in the early morning sky above her. As for visibility below the surface, the moon shed enough light to allow her to see underwater. Didn't matter if only a sliver of light filtered through; her eyes used it.

Too deep, however, and she'd eventually be unable to see. The lake only had those kinds of depths in a few places, none of which she'd be visiting today.

As she swam, she noticed something new. The current. Not long ago, on the commercial area on the far side of the lake where the shops and such were, a waterwheel had been installed near one of the natural springs as part of an eco-project to generate electricity.

It seemed like that wheel had added a new current to the lake, a subtle one, for sure, but she could feel it. Maybe not so subtle in some places.

Diving deeper, she passed schools of shiner minnows drifting amongst the aquatic plants that stretched toward the surface. Deeper still, she passed bass and sunfish, redhorse and darters. A few good-size trout zipped along, headed for the surface and whatever bug breakfast they might find in the early hours.

Near the bottom, crayfish scurried away under rocks, not hiding from her but from a large catfish shuffling by.

But the fish weren't why she was there. She had plenty of aquariums if she wanted to see those.

No, she'd come to the lake to swim. To be a mermaid. With another powerful pulse of her tail, she sped through the open water. If she didn't shift back to her true form every so often, she could lose the ability altogether.

It wasn't hard to know when it was time. When she'd been on two legs for too long, an ache would start. Once it began, there was no stopping it. And the longer she stayed out of the water, the more the ache grew.

Thankfully, accessing water wasn't hard. Any body of water would do the trick. Even a bathtub, in a pinch. For that reason, she'd made sure that the house she'd bought had a tub. A big one. She'd also set up a television in there because she spent a lot of time in that tub, especially in the winter months, when most outside water sources were frozen over.

She had a koi pond in her front yard, but she'd put that in. There had already been a sunken spot in the yard there, so it was probably deeper than it needed to be, but the koi were thriving. She'd yet to take a dip in it herself, however.

A pool would have been great, but not a necessity. Besides, she'd been fortunate to find a house in the hills, and that house wasn't too far from the creek that fed the falls. Above those falls, a short ways up, was a natural pool.

If not for the amount of people it attracted in the summer months, it would have been an ideal place for a swim. She'd thought about talking to the family that owned Nocturne Falls, the Ellinghams, about registering as one of the town's characters. Being a character was easy. It basically meant that a supernatural would publicly take on their true form under the guise of pretending to be that character to entertain the tourists.

The tourists, of course, assumed the character was done with makeup and prosthetics. Really, *really* good makeup and prosthetics.

Lots of supernaturals did it. That was the beauty of living in a place like Nocturne Falls, a town that celebrated Halloween every day of the year. You could be yourself, your *real* self, and the tourists thought it was part of the show.

Sure, there were some downsides to the tourist part of the town, but Elenora Ellingham, the grandmother of the three men who, along with her, owned and operated the town, had taken a very special precaution years ago.

She'd had a powerful witch, one enigmatic Alice Bishop, bespell the waters of the falls so that anyone who drank from them would be unable to see the truth of what was right in front of them. That was the same water that fed the reservoirs that served the whole town. It was pretty much impossible *not* to drink the water.

And so, Nocturne Falls had become a haven for the supernatural. As well as a money-making tourist destination, which made everyone's life a little easier.

As far as Undrea knew, the town didn't have an active mermaid. She could probably slip into that role pretty easily. Especially now that the lakeside was being developed.

But then, she didn't need a second job. She had her own enterprise, Tanks A Lot, that supplied and set up custom aquariums in people's homes and businesses.

She also maintained those aquariums for many of her customers as well. She did pretty well with it, too. She wasn't going to be buying a yacht anytime soon, but she didn't need a yacht, either.

Yachts were for folks without tails.

With a smile, she swam faster, exhilarated by the sheer speed she could achieve in the wide-open expanse of the lake.

That was another reason she liked the lake best. It was big, and she could swim fast, dive deep, and at this wee hour of the morning, go undetected.

But already the moon was sinking in the sky. Her time to swim would soon be over, and not just because of the sun's rise. She should have come sooner, she knew that, but she had a meeting about a potentially huge job today, and she couldn't afford to be tired from being up crazy early.

That job, if she got it, would be the setup and installation of the biggest aquarium she'd ever done. It might even bump her into a new tax bracket. It was that major. And it would be that expensive. She couldn't wait to see the house the tank was going into. Today would be her first visit.

The woman who'd hired her definitely seemed like she was going to be one of those super picky types, but weren't the uber wealthy all like that?

Undrea wasn't worried. No one knew fish and aquariums like she did. Not around here, anyway. Maybe not in the entire state of Georgia.

She bobbed to the surface, content to float. Already the sky was turning a soft pastel lavender at the eastern edge as the sun inched towards the horizon. Not that she could see the horizon because of the trees, but the sun was definitely rising. She wasn't ready to give up floating just yet, though. Not with how wonderful the water felt.

Reluctantly but for her own safety, she shifted back to her human form. She had to get out soon and get ready for the day, but she didn't want to. Not yet. And because she could still breathe water in her human form, she rolled over and floated like that, face down, watching the fish swim.

It was one of her favorite pastimes, whether through lake water or aquarium glass.

Some were curious, darting up to nibble her fingers as she let her arms dangle. Being a little ticklish, she laughed, and bubbles carried the sound away.

She could almost sleep like this, just floating and watching the fish and drifting in the current. It was that peaceful. There was no more comfortable position to be in than lying in the water. No mattress compared, that was for sure. And she couldn't do it in her tub because there just wasn't room.

The longer she floated, the heavier her lids got. Would a quick nap be so bad? She'd still make her appointment on time. But she couldn't sleep on the surface. She knew better than to risk being seen.

With a little kick of her legs, she descended below the waterline, then let her eyes close as sleep tugged at her and the kind of dreams that only happened in the water filled her head.

2

The smooth, paved path disappeared under Ethan Edmonds's feet as he followed it through the forest surrounding the Nocturne Falls lake. The air was crisp, the scenery beautiful, and the sky just beginning to lighten with the rising sun.

All in all, a wonderful start to his day. Too bad he loathed running. Well, maybe loathed was too strong of a word, but running sure wasn't his favorite thing. That much was certain. He did it anyway. Obviously.

He did it for two reasons. One, because running felt like a necessity. Like it was the only real way to balance the long, sedentary hours he spent on the computer. And since there was no changing what he did for a living—not immediately, anyway—he had to find a way to make sure he didn't turn into an unhealthy blob of a human, atrophied from too much time spent sitting.

Oh, he'd tried both a treadmill desk and a standing desk, but they required a part of his brain to focus on that activity while still working. Maybe he just wasn't good at multitasking, which seemed accurate because when he was at the computer, all he wanted to do was concentrate on the project in front of him.

Not trying to stay upright while the floor moved underneath him. Or didn't. Either way, it seemed that keeping himself upright used the same parts of his brain he needed for active, analytical thinking. Work just didn't get done.

The second reason was that for the last two years, he'd been having episodes where he'd come to after having blacked out. Which was the reason for the stupid monitor programmed into his smart watch. He never remembered having the episode or anything leading up to it, either. So far, every doctor he'd been to was clueless as to the cause of them. But several had suggested he get more exercise.

And so on a regular basis, he laced up his trainers and headed out, for the other thing he probably didn't get enough of. Fresh air.

Yes, saying he loathed running was too strong a statement. Sometimes, it wasn't that bad. But most mornings, his internal monologue was all about self-motivation and convincing himself not to stop, to keep going, keep moving, to reach his goal for that run.

It took some doing too. Usually.

Today wasn't quite as bad. Actually, it wasn't bad at all. There were no people to dodge, like in the city. But also maybe because this was his first run on this new trail and there was so much to look at. At least now that the sun was coming up and he could see his surroundings a little better.

As an early riser, getting a head start on the day made him happy. By lunch, he'd usually accomplished more than most people had even thought about.

Which was why it made sense to get his run done first thing. It also gave him some anonymity. He snorted softly. The fact that anyone knew who he was still seemed bonkers to him, but landing on the cover of several business and tech magazines hadn't helped.

In his mind, he was just a geek, a techie whiz kid who'd developed a few pieces of software and a little tech that someone else had wanted to buy for the kind of money that didn't seem real.

At seventeen, he'd sold his first app for a little over a million dollars. That had also been his first taste of celebrity. Such as it was.

Of course, he wasn't a kid anymore. Thirty-six wasn't old, but it wasn't kid status either. Which was part of the reason Nina was pushing him to get married. He knew that.

She'd been subtle about her desire to get married. Mostly. But ever since his latest company, Blnk, had been bought out, her hints had become bolder.

His running app, also on his smart watch, chimed in with his pace and distance. Half a mile done, two and a half left to go.

He supposed Nina would make a fine wife. She was smart, pretty, and incredibly well put together in a kind of hip way that the camera loved. More than that, he knew the odds were slim that she was after his money. She had her own and stood to inherit even more. She was a trust-fund baby, from a wealthy, untouchable New England family, the Hascoes.

Old stock was how his mother described the Hascoes. Although his mom didn't seem to care too much who he married or when he took that step, so long as he was happy.

Nina always looked like she'd just stepped off the glossy cover of a magazine. Every hair precisely in place, impeccable clothing, and with an air of perfection that seemed almost superhuman at times.

He, on the other hand, sometimes wore the same T-shirt two days in a row. Or forgot to shave. And seemed to perpetually need a haircut.

He pushed his glasses back on the bridge of his nose. He couldn't help it. Those things just weren't as important to him as whatever project he was working on. Which was currently a ceramic ion exchange membrane with a solar-powered self-cleaning attachment that he hoped would revolutionize desalinization processes. If he could get it to work.

If he could—no, *when* he could, he planned to donate the technology to the countries that needed it most, the countries that could benefit from clean water and had access to the sea. For those countries, it might change everything. They might even be able to resell the sea salt that would be a byproduct of the water cleaning.

Which would just be a bonus. For them.

After all, he no longer needed the money. Not after selling Blnk, the software that allowed a person or company to temporarily disappear online.

Sweat dripped down his back, even in the cool spring air. He didn't mind. That was the only reason he was out here, to sweat and get a workout that would make up for the rest of his inactive day.

He only had one earbud in today, too. Most of the time he listened to music, another love of his, but this was a new path and he wanted to be aware of his surroundings on his first trip around the lake while still being able to hear his running app.

Truth be told, the jury was still out on Nocturne Falls. It seemed like a nice enough small town, but he hadn't lived outside of a big city since he'd left home for college. He thought he wanted this kind of change. But he wasn't sure just yet.

One thing was for certain. His money went a lot further here than it did in any of the big cities he'd come to love.

His new house was proof of that. Four thousand square feet of space. In New York, that would have cost him more than he wanted to think about.

But the hustle and bustle he'd thought he should get away from now seemed…too far away. Even with the tourist industry this town supposedly had, it didn't seem that busy. Not like what he was used to. Although he hadn't exactly immersed himself in Nocturne Falls.

The truth was, in the week he'd been here, most of that time had been spent setting up his office with his computer workstation and sound system.

He knew he had to give this place more time. And he would. But if he didn't feel more at home here in a month or so, he'd have to give serious thought to returning to another of his big-city properties. At least for a few weeks.

He had to feel connected to the world or he feared he'd lose touch with the hum of it all. And that hum, that buzz, that cosmic vibration or whatever someone might call it, was what kept him inspired. What moved him to create the next new thing.

Without that vibrancy, he worried his drive would disappear. And without that? Life would be pointless. And then he might as well marry Nina. He laughed and shook his head. She wouldn't like that sort of thought one bit.

The movement of shaking his head made him catch sight of something in the water. He slowed his pace, trying to see better in the dim morning light. The shadows from all the trees didn't help. Neither did the fog lifting off the water. He looked closer.

Something had surfaced.

He stopped altogether.

Not something. *Someone.*

A woman. Face down and not moving, except for her long, coppery-blond hair, which floated around her like some strange kind of water weed.

Without a moment's hesitation, he ran for the lake, pulled off his glasses, and dove, but he had a feeling he was going to need the police more than the paramedics. There didn't seem to be any signs of life.

He lost sight of her as he swam. Maybe the current had moved her?

Or maybe she'd gone under.

He gulped a breath and sank down to look, but there was only enough light to see a few feet around him. Wait, there she was to the left of him. Still floating.

Definitely dead. Her arms dangled lifelessly from her body. She must have come out here for a swim and something had gone terribly wrong. His heart sank at the thought of such a tragedy.

He surfaced, took in another breath, and paddled toward her, trying to figure out what his plan should be. Check to make sure she was dead? But then he probably shouldn't touch the body after that. In case this was a crime scene.

It wasn't. Was it? Because he didn't want to do anything to screw up a thing like that.

But she had to be dead. She'd been face down too long. Probably just an accidental drowning. Small towns didn't have a lot crime.

Gingerly, he took hold of her arm and turned her over. Thick strands of hair covered her face. He moved a few of them, enough to see her face. She was extraordinarily beautiful. And didn't seem to be breathing.

Instantly, he put his mouth on hers and did his best to do CPR while also keeping them both afloat and swimming for shore.

It was almost light enough to see clearly now. Maybe someone would come by to help. Another jogger.

Then the woman in his arms moved. She gasped a second later, her eyes blinking open. They were the most stunning sea green. "What are you doing to me? Get your hands off me, you creep."

"I—"

She shoved him away, causing him to go under.

He bobbed up again. "I wasn't doing anything to you. You were drowning."

"I was not. I was swimming."

"I am not a cree—ma'am, you were floating face down and definitely not swimming."

She frowned harder. Which didn't make her any less beautiful. Then her eyes widened, she gasped, and a split-second later, she disappeared down into the water like she'd been pulled under. He was looking at her, and then she was gone. It happened that fast.

The water rippled as if she'd kicked hard. A little trail of eddies moved across the surface in the direction of the other shore for a few feet, then even those swirled away.

He stayed there, treading water and watching. She never came back up.

He stayed a little longer, kicking like crazy to hold his position, waiting for her to reappear. She had to. But she never did.

Then he started to shiver in the cold water and decided it was time to get out.

He swam back to shore, no longer certain of what had just happened. He knew he'd seen a woman with hair like spun copper and eyes like the deep sea. He knew he'd briefly had his mouth on hers. And that her lips had been soft. And warmer than expected.

He knew she'd disappeared with a speed and suddenness that didn't seem possible. And that she hadn't reappeared, which also didn't seem possible.

Beyond that, he couldn't be sure of anything else.

He walked out of the water, dripping wet and utterly confused. He picked up his glasses from the grass where he'd dropped them. This was one of those things probably best kept to himself. He pulled off his T-shirt and wrung it out.

But something told him that getting that woman out of his head wasn't going to be an easy feat.

3

How had that happened? How? Undrea took a quick look around to be sure the coast was clear, then dashed out of the water to where her clothes were stashed.

She got dressed as quickly as she could, but pulling clothes on over damp skin wasn't easy. Because of that, she'd just worn terry-cloth track pants and a jacket here. They were easiest to throw on over her wet one-piece.

At least he'd just been a tourist. Some overeager fitness maniac who had to get a run in at the crack of dawn. And then decided to save a drowning woman.

Drowning.

As if.

She snorted and rolled her eyes at the same time, almost making herself fall over. She wasn't the most graceful thing on land right after she'd been in her mer-form for a bit. It took a minute to get her land legs back, as it were.

She squeezed the water out of her hair, twisted it up and clipped it into place, then fished her keys out of her jacket pocket and headed for her truck.

There was only one explanation she could think of for how she'd ended up at the surface and close enough to be spotted from shore.

The new current in the lake. It had floated her to the top and right into that tourist's line of sight.

That rather attractive tourist. But that was beside the point. Like *really* beside the point.

The most unthinkable part of the whole thing was that he'd kissed her. Sort of. Was it really a kiss if it was actually CPR?

It was still his lips on hers. Did that qualify? He seemed human, though, and that could be a problem. At least he'd be gone soon enough. That was the best part about tourists. They were temporary. And any effects he might feel would be gone in forty-eight hours.

So long as…there wasn't any further contact. Or something like that. Honestly, if it was CPR, it shouldn't even count. She really ought to know, but it had been so long, and it wasn't like she had a handbook she could flip through and find the answers.

She also wasn't about to call her parents. She rolled her eyes. That would not go well. They already weren't thrilled with her living in this town amongst so many uprights.

The only saving grace in her parents' eyes was that Nocturne Falls had a good number of supernaturals.

This was crazy. Why was she thinking about her parents? Enough was enough.

It wasn't a kiss. That very mistaken and equally handsome tourist had just been trying to save her. That was it.

End of story. She was never going to see him again anyway.

She tried to shake it off. This was not the morning she'd intended on having, obviously, but she could not let it throw her. Today was a big day. She had a major client to impress. She needed to be on her game.

She nodded as she unlocked her truck and opened the door. "That's what I need to think about. The job. Not whatever happened in the lake. That was nothing. The job is all that matters."

She got behind the wheel. "And now I'm talking to myself. Perfect."

She spent the ride home focusing on a safe topic. What to wear. Simple was probably best. Khaki pants and a Tanks A Lot polo shirt. That would be easy and professional.

But this was a *big* job. Would they expect her to dress up?

She hoped not. Her closet basically had two modes. Work. Or party time at Insomnia, the nightclub in town for supernaturals. It was one of her favorite spots to hang with her girlfriends on the weekend. She tended to let her wild, mermaid side out to play on those occasions.

But showing up in a slinky green sequin slip dress

and gold platform heels wasn't going to cut it with a client.

Khaki pants and work shirt it was.

As soon as she got home, she went straight for the shower. She'd set her coffee to brew when she'd walked out the door for the lake, so there was a full, hot pot waiting for her in the kitchen when her shower was done.

Even so, she lingered under the water. Happily, the urge to shift was gone. She'd be good for a bit now, although there was no telling how long she'd be good for. The need to shift wasn't a regularly scheduled thing like the wolves with their full moon.

For merfolk, these things had more to do with emotions. They were creatures of the water, after all, subject to the ever-changing tides. And emotions weren't really that much different.

A couple of great, smooth, stress-free weeks and Undrea might not have to shift at all. Unless she wanted to, of course. A week where everything went wrong, and she'd find herself chin-deep in her tub with her tail flopped over the end before that week was up.

She just had to listen to her legs. They were her barometer.

She wrapped her hair in a towel, her body in a robe, and went out to the kitchen. Breakfast was two strawberry Pop-Tarts spread with peanut butter, a tin of sardines on the side, and a large coffee with hazelnut creamer and three sugars.

Merfolk had admittedly weird palates and exceptionally high metabolisms. After that swim, she needed to refuel in a big way. There was a good chance she'd have a granola bar in the truck, too. And for lunch, she'd be at Howler's Bar and Grill. Ordering whatever was on special, usually, because Bridget didn't skimp on the serving sizes.

Although Undrea sometimes added a side of anchovies. Amazing what they did to the flavor of a cheesesteak. Or a chef salad. Or meatloaf. She knew they weren't most people's go-to add-on, but those people were mostly uprights.

Undrea turned on the television and ate while she watched a little morning news show. Not much of interest but she figured she'd better know what was going on in the world in case the client made small talk.

Undrea didn't want to appear uninformed, despite the fact that she stayed off of social media altogether.

After the meeting, she'd head to her office, which was attached to the warehouse where her team built all the custom tanks. And this was definitely going to be a custom job. She really hoped she got it.

Work was good, and the tank maintenance contracts kept the lights on, but a big job like this might mean bonuses for her team. Which would be awesome. They worked hard, and they deserved to share in the rewards.

From the brief the client had given her over the phone, Undrea couldn't imagine how this job couldn't be big. The woman had talked about a dividing wall aquarium between the living room and the dining room.

An entire wall.

That was going to take some serious construction know-how. She had Aaron Rigby for that. He was a former Navy SEAL who'd gotten his degree in engineering and would make sure the tank build was sound, but what about the house itself? She might have to hire someone to confirm whether or not the floor could take that much weight.

If it couldn't, maybe she could talk the client into something smaller but still showy. A lot of these big jobs really were about managing expectations. People wanted big, impressive tanks, but rarely did they understand how much other equipment that took. Equipment that wasn't meant to be seen but was still very necessary to keep the fish healthy and alive. Undrea wasn't going to cut corners when it came to that.

This was her business and her reputation. There was only one way to do a job. The right way. Dead fish and murky water made no one happy.

That didn't mean she had any intention of missing out on this job. It just meant she was going to have to go about securing it the right way.

Which usually meant helping the client see that their vision might not be the best thing for the space.

Wouldn't be the first time.

She finished getting ready by drying her hair into its natural waves, then added a little makeup and jewelry and slip-on sneakers. In case the client was weird about people wearing shoes into the house, those were easy to get off and still cute.

Weirder things had happened than being required to take her shoes off in a client's home. This was Nocturne Falls, after all.

She hesitated. Was this client a supernatural? She had no idea, and merfolk weren't always so great at telling who was what. Human, sure. But other supernaturals? Not so much. She'd just have to watch for any telltale signs.

And if she wasn't sure, she'd ask. Not the client, but one of her friends who was a supernatural. Like Bridget Merrow, who was the wolf shifter who owned Howler's, or maybe Mattie Sharpe, the Celtic witch who kept bees that made the best honey around.

Mattie's mead wasn't too bad either. And she was one of Undrea's besties.

That reminded Undrea that she still needed to see if everyone was up for Friday girls' night at Insomnia.

Undrea had a feeling after this week, she was going to need it.

She drove to the address the client had given her. It was up in the hills like she was, but farther up. Where the big houses were. Like where Van, the dragon shifter, and his Will-o'-the-Wisp wife, Monalisa, lived.

All of the houses in this area were big. This one seemed to be no exception.

She wound up the driveway, but she could already

see the tip of the home's chalet-style roof through the trees. And when the rest of it came into view, it was hard not to stare.

The entire front of the home seemed to be glass. She parked and got out, trying not to gawk.

It looked like a small ski resort. Minus the lift. And the snow. And the crowds. Okay, it only looked like a ski resort because of the building. Nothing else. But still. It was very impressive.

She felt underdressed, but there was no helping that now. She grabbed her portfolio and the folder she gave to all potential clients and walked straight up the steps to the front door.

She pushed the doorbell. She could hear the chimes playing in the house. The tune sounded oddly familiar, but she couldn't place it.

A woman in a body-hugging black knit dress and tall black boots answered the door. Her hair was cut in a short, modern shag and dyed an impossible shade of plum that made her green eyes seem to glow. Chunky silver earrings and a matching bracelet completed the look. "You must be Andrea. From the fish store."

"Undrea from Tanks A Lot, yes, that's me." She stuck her hand out. "Are you the one who called?"

"I am." The woman stepped back without shaking Undrea's hand. Maybe she hadn't noticed. "Come in. I'll show you where we'd like the tank."

We. She'd used that term on the phone too, but Undrea wasn't clear if that "we" referred to her partner, her child, her parent…no idea because she hadn't specified. "Great."

Undrea followed her through the house. It was spectacular. Simple, clean lines with a kind of post-modern fifties vibe that felt both retro and space-age new.

Undrea suddenly wanted to redecorate her entire house in the same style. "Groovy place. I really love it. A tank would look awesome in here."

She meant that too. Tanks added life and color and interest to spaces like nothing else could.

The first floor seemed to be the main living area with the kitchen, dining room, maybe some guest rooms, and who knew what else, with more rooms upstairs, all set around a balcony that overlooked the big center room. A light was on in one of the rooms upstairs, but from Undrea's angle, she couldn't tell if there was anyone in there.

The woman stopped and gestured to a space on the floor. "Right here."

Another yard or two, and the floor descended a few steps to a sunken sitting area with a large stone fireplace and chimney breast that went all the way up to the vaulted ceiling. It was a beautiful spot. But Andrea already knew the tank the woman wanted wasn't going to work.

"The garage is under this space, isn't it? Which means there's no crawlspace where piers can be added." Undrea opened her portfolio to the notebook and slipped the pen from its loop so she could jot things down.

The woman made a face like she hadn't understood the question. "Piers?"

Andrea nodded. "I'll need to know how much load these floor joists can hold. I'm sure your builder can tell me. Or whoever built this house. How tall did you want this tank to be?"

The woman raised her hand up, keeping her palm flat towards the floor. "About here."

Undrea wrote down six feet. "And about how long?"

The woman glanced at one side of the room, then the other, took a few steps out and stopped. "About to here. People have to be able to walk around it, obviously, to get to the seating area."

Undrea wrote down eight feet. Then did a quick calculation. "Yep. Definitely going to need to know more about this floor."

"Why?" The woman's groomed brows arched.

"Because you're talking about a nine-hundred-gallon tank. Approximately. That's almost seventy-eight hundred pounds for just the salt water. Add the acrylic or glass surround, the base, the fish, coral, sand, and equipment on top of that and…" Undrea gestured like the rest was obvious.

Maybe it wasn't, though, because the woman kept staring at her.

"Just saying," Undrea added. "It's going to be very heavy."

"I see. Well, maybe the floor can be reinforced?"

"That's what we need to find out. I have an engineer on my team who can help us make sure everything is sound, but we'd definitely need to talk to the builder too."

"How soon can you have all of this done?" She smiled. "I'd like it to be ready for our engagement party."

"Oh, I see." Undrea smiled. So the *we* she'd spoken of was her partner. "Congratulations."

"Thank you."

"When is the party?"

The woman's smile faltered. "It's, uh..." She glanced upstairs. "Soon."

"Can you give me an actual date? Just so I know what the time frame is. A week? A month? A—"

A man walked out onto the balcony and looked down. "What's going on now?"

The man was incredibly handsome. And except for his glasses, dry clothes, and dry hair looked exactly like the tourist who'd tried to save her life earlier.

Undrea's pinkie toe on her left foot began to ache.

This was not a good sign.

4

Ethan stared down at Nina, but a second later his entire being focused on the woman beside her.

The very beautiful, living, breathing, *dry* woman beside her. Could she really be the same woman he'd tried to rescue at the lake? The one who'd just disappeared into the water? He wasn't sure.

At least he couldn't be until he'd had a closer look. But then how many women could there be in this town with that spun-copper hair? He jogged down the steps. Bowie, his Sphynx cat, ran down after him.

As soon as he hit the ground floor, he knew. It was her. He'd never forget that mouth. Or those eyes. But he didn't want to say anything. Didn't want to embarrass her. He'd just pretend this was their first meeting. It would be weird to explain to Nina anyway, especially since he'd hidden the fact that he'd come home wet, knowing how she'd freak out.

Nina had a fear of open water because of a

childhood incident. That was as much as he knew and as much as she'd ever said.

But the woman from the lake was as beautiful as he remembered, which was good, because he'd begun to believe that she was some kind of early morning apparition and that he'd imagined the whole thing. Clearly, he had not.

He realized that he was just standing there, staring. "Hi."

She looked at him like he was about pull a rug out from under her. She blinked, eyes wide, then swallowed. "Hi."

Bowie sat down directly in front of her and stared up at her.

She glanced down and seemed to take a moment to process what she was seeing. "Your cat is wearing a sweater."

Ethan nodded. "He is. Since Bowie is basically naked all the time, he gets chilly." Today's sweater was a black and white Fair Isle pattern knitted by Ethan's mom. She'd decided Bowie could very well be the only grandchild she might ever have, so she'd figured she should spoil him as best she could.

He'd gotten quite the collection of sweaters over the years.

The lake woman continued to stare at Bowie. "He is pretty naked." Her gaze grew slightly more focused. "Are his eyes two different colors?"

"Yep," Ethan answered. It had taken Nina almost three months to notice that. But then, she wasn't really a cat person.

"Cool," the lake woman said. "Is that why you named him Bowie?"

Ethan smiled at how smart and clever the lake woman was. Nothing more attractive than a clever person. Except perhaps a kind one. "You know David Bowie?"

"Sure, I mean, who doesn't, right?"

She suddenly became more beautiful.

Nina cleared her throat, reminding him she was still standing there. As if he'd forgotten. He turned the conversation back to the main topic and pushed his glasses up. "So you're, uh, the aquarium specialist? Nina thinks we need an aquarium here. That it would be a great feature for parties and stuff."

"I am. And I'm sure it would be. Aquariums can also be wonderful for relaxation." The lake woman stuck her hand out. "I'm Undrea, by the way."

"*Un*-drea?" He shook her hand.

She nodded, smiling. "Yes, exactly like that."

"Cool name. I'm Ethan."

Nina sighed. "So. What's the next step?"

Undrea looked at her. "I'll take some measurements, draw up a preliminary sketch and give you an estimate based on all of that. We do need to talk about fish, however."

"Fish?" Ethan asked. "Don't you provide those?"

She glanced at him again, nodding. "I do. But I need to know what sort of activity level you want in your tank. A big showpiece fish? A ton of schooling fish? Or those that tend to be more solitary? Or for instance, if you're a night owl, you might prefer nocturnal species. And then there are the invertebrates and the corals. Should you choose to go that route."

He frowned. "That sounds...complicated." Which wasn't an issue. He could do complicated. But this wasn't anything he knew a lick about.

She smiled, a beautiful sight. "It is, but you don't have to worry about all that. It's my job. You just give me an idea of what you want and I'll make it work. Of course, I'm getting a little ahead of myself. It remains to be seen if this floor is structurally sound enough to support the weight of such a tank or if it needs to be reinforced."

"Right." He nodded. "That's probably step one."

"It is. And if the floor can't, then there are two options."

"Oh?" Nina asked. She had her arms crossed, with her hand on her chin and that elbow resting on her opposite hand.

He knew that pose. She was either bored or bothered. Or both.

He had a pretty good guess which one this was.

"Yes," Undrea went on, rightfully oblivious to the shift in Nina's mood. "We can either have the floor reinforced like I said or go with a smaller, more conventional setup. A tank will still be possible. It just might be a different sort of tank than what you're imagining."

"I see." Nina gave a quick, tight smile. "I look forward to your findings. Thank you so much for coming by."

"Um..." Undrea's brows pinched together. "I still

need to do measurements." She pulled a small tape measure out of her pocket and showed it to Nina as proof.

"Oh." Nina exhaled like she was bored with it all. "Fine, go on then."

Arms still crossed, Nina walked over to Ethan. Bowie, however, followed Undrea, apparently convinced the tape measure was a toy.

Nina took her hand off her chin so she could use her finger to draw little circles on his shoulder. "How about a hike later? It's gorgeous outside."

"I guess I could. So long as it's not a long one. I went for a run already." And a bit of a swim, which Nina would have hated. Thankfully, his smart watch was waterproof enough that it had survived. But clearly Undrea didn't share Nina's fear of water. His gaze slipped to Undrea again.

Nina exhaled loudly. "I wish you'd woken me. I would have gone with you."

That was *why* he hadn't woken her. He liked that alone time.

He also couldn't imagine what she would have made of the whole woman in the water situation. Lady in the lake? Girl in the gully? No, gully wasn't a synonym for—

"Ethan, are you listening to me?"

"Hmm? Yes, sorry. You know how it is when my mind gets working." Nina never would have jumped in to help, he knew that much.

"Yes, I do."

She just didn't need to know what it was working

on. He made himself focus on her. "What were you saying?"

That earned him another sigh. "Just that we should go into town for lunch. You've been working too much, and you said yourself that you wanted to see more of the place you'd moved to."

"True. I did say that." He nodded. "Okay, let's do lunch. Hey, we could go out to the lake afterwards. They have paddleboats. Really cool ones."

Nina made a slightly horrified face. "No."

Soft laughter brought his attention back to Undrea again. She must have crouched down to measure the floor, because Bowie was now sitting on her shoulders and she was still hunched over, unable to get up.

Or at least unwilling to get up and dislodge the cat.

"I'm so sorry." Ethan went over to help.

"It's okay," she said. "He's just being friendly, aren't you, kitty cat?"

"Too friendly." He picked the cat up. "Bowie, dude, you can't climb on women like that."

Undrea snorted. She straightened as soon as Ethan removed the purring feline.

Bowie immediately headbutted Ethan's chin, which got him some scratches on the head. "Sorry again. If you need to charge me extra for interference, I understand."

"Nope, all good." She was still smiling. Then she reached out and gave Bowie a little pet. "He's so soft. I wasn't sure what he'd feel like. Kind of velvety."

"He's very soft."

"He's the most interesting-looking cat I've seen."

"I'm kind of allergic to cats, but the Sphynx is a fairly hypoallergenic breed, so that's how I ended up with him."

"I bet a cat like that is expensive."

"They can be, but he came from a Sphynx rescue."

Bowie planted a paw on Ethan's head and started grooming his hair with a tongue bath.

Undrea laughed. "He's funny. Is he always like that?"

"You mean lacking a sense of personal space?" Ethan nodded, grinning. "Yes."

"How about you hold on to him until I get these last few measurements?"

"I'd be happy to." He took a few steps back to let her finish.

She looked at her tape, wrote down some numbers, then closed her portfolio and put the tape measure back in her pocket. "Okay. All done."

Nina's phone rang. She took the call, holding up a finger as if to say she'd just be a moment even as she walked off to find some privacy.

Undrea shrugged. "I have everything I need for the preliminary stuff."

"Can I walk you to your car?"

She hesitated. "Sure."

"Great." He put Bowie on one of his many cat trees and opened the door for her.

She went out ahead of him, then he followed, quickly closing the door before Bowie joined them.

He wanted to say something about the lake but wasn't sure if he should.

At the bottom of the steps, she turned. "About this morning. I'm sorry I called you a creep. I was startled and—"

"No, you had every right. I shouldn't have assumed that you were…"

"Dead?" She snorted. "Sorry about that. That must have really freaked you out."

"It did. But maybe not so much as you suddenly being alive. Which I'm super glad about, by the way."

"Thanks." She looked extremely amused.

He took advantage of her good mood to ask the question that was plaguing him. "How do you hold your breath so long? And how did you just disappear into the water like that?"

"I'm an amateur free diver. That's what I was doing in the lake this morning. Practicing. It kind of puts me in a zoned-out mental state, which is why you startled me."

"Sorry about that. Free diving, huh? That's really cool."

She opened up her portfolio and pulled out a business card. "Here. In case you have any questions about the tank before I get back to you. Or if you decide what kind of fish you want."

"What kind of fish would you put in the tank?"

The question seemed to catch her off guard. "There are so many right answers."

"Dream tank. What do you fill it with?"

"Dream tank? Money's no object?"

He nodded. This was easily one of his favorite conversations to have with people. What they'd do in a certain situation if money were no object. Answers that surprised him were rare but worth it. "Right."

"Well… I'd have to say jellies, but that's a selfish answer."

"Jellies? Jellyfish?"

She nodded.

"Why is that selfish?"

"Because they're pelagic—"

"Open ocean."

"Yes." She smiled like she hadn't expected him to understand that. "They aren't suited to tank life. I mean, sure, people keep moon jellies, but they rarely live more than a year, and that's with ideal conditions. Which are nearly impossible. You have to maintain a very particular and constant water flow, for one thing. But they're so beautiful."

"If not jellies, what then?"

She grinned. "I already have that tank."

"What is it?"

She shook her head. "I'll tell you after you decide what you want. I don't want to unduly influence you."

Nina walked out onto the balcony above them, still on the phone. She stared down, frowning.

He sighed. "I should go. I'll give the fish some thought." But he'd also be thinking about her. How could he not? He could have kept on talking to her. She was smart and interesting in so many ways. Different, too. There was something about her he couldn't quite put his finger on.

"Okay," she said. "Again, call or email if you have any questions or concerns. I'm always available for my clients. I know fish can be a big decision."

"Thank you."

With a nod, she slipped past him and got into her truck. It was a marine blue F250, and somehow it was both a surprise and completely fitting that she drove such a beast.

He watched her go for a few seconds, then jogged back upstairs.

Nina was just hanging up as he walked inside.

"Everything okay?"

"Just my mother, checking to see how we're settling in." She glanced toward the door. "Maybe the tank is a bad idea. Seems like it's a lot more complicated than I thought."

"Are you kidding? I think it's one of the best ideas you've had."

Her eyes rounded. "Really?"

"Absolutely. I love the idea of having a saltwater aquarium while I'm simultaneously developing this desalinization membrane. It's genius."

She smiled. "Well, then. Full speed ahead."

5

Breathlessness wasn't a feeling Undrea could ever say she had truly experienced before. After all, she could breathe air *and* water. In fact, breathlessness had never actually happened to her.

Until now.

Until Ethan.

"So much for not seeing him." She exhaled. "Oh my cod. I'm in trouble." She stared at the road ahead as she drove and tried not to think about all the weird, squishy, *magical* feelings whirling around inside of her. "Serious trouble. That was not CPR. That was definitely a kiss. At least the universe thought it was, because I am *screwed.*"

She should go to her office, but she needed to talk to someone first. In person. Not on the phone, not via text. She needed live and face-to-face.

And that person was Mattie Sharpe.

Thankfully, she lived close by. Near the vineyards,

which was convenient because her bees were especially good at pollinating those vines.

Ten minutes later, Undrea pulled into the gravel drive of Mattie's English-style cottage and climbed out of the truck. The garden around Mattie's cottage was always beautiful, no matter the time of year, but in the spring like it was now, with everything budding and blooming, the garden was on the verge of amazing.

She was a talented Celtic witch but also a very talented gardener. The two pretty much went hand in hand when your witchy gifts were earth-centric.

Undrea knocked on the door.

It opened a second later. "Come on in," Mattie called from inside the cottage, too far away to have been the one who'd opened the door. But then that was usually Blueberry's job these days. Mattie had to do something to keep the imp busy.

Undrea walked in. "Sorry to come by unannounced."

Mattie wiped her hands on a red gingham towel before tossing it over her shoulder. "You weren't unannounced. The bees told me you were on your way. What's bothering you?"

Undrea took a deep breath and thought about where to start.

Blueberry, the tiny imp who lived with Mattie, guarded her bees, and generally got up to mischief, flitted past to sit on her shoulder. Mattie's brows shot up as she took a good look at Undrea. "Uh-oh. I can already tell it's not a what that's bothering you. It's a who. What's his name?"

Undrea sank down into a chair at the kitchen table. "Ethan. And it's worse than you can imagine."

"Wait. This feels like it requires tea. Let me get that started." The burner under Mattie's kettle flared to life. She got two cups and a tin of loose tea out while the water heated. "All right. Go ahead. From the beginning."

So Undrea did. At the very beginning. The lake.

Mattie busied herself with measuring the tea and adding a plate of cookies to the table and didn't interrupt until the word CPR came out of Undrea's mouth. Then she looked over her shoulder and scoffed. "I'm sorry. CPR?"

"I'm sure that's what he meant it to be, but..." Undrea shook her head. "I have a distinct feeling the universe is looking at it differently."

"Based on?"

"Based on the weird squishy feelings I got from being around him just now. Which all boils down to this being bad. Very bad."

As the pot began to whistle, Mattie poured water over the leaves in the smaller pot so the tea could brew, then brought the pot to the table, put it on a trivet and sat. Blueberry flew down to perch on the lid. He was about the size of a hummingbird, with a bright green body and crystalline wings reminiscent of a dragonfly's. Mattie gave him a small piece of shortbread cookie, which he held with both hands and began to nibble enthusiastically, spewing crumbs everywhere. He had the table manners of Cookie Monster.

Mattie looked at Undrea. "Explain."

Undrea took a breath. "You know how I am the thing that I am? The thing that no one else knows?"

"Right." Mattie nodded. Blueberry finished his cookie and flew off to the window. Mattie poured tea into their cups.

Undrea drizzled honey into her cup and stirred. "Well…the magic of my kind says if a man kisses a woman like me, voluntarily, that I have no choice but to fall in love with him."

There was more to that legend, but Undrea didn't want to believe it was true. Or that she was capable of such things.

Mattie sipped her tea. "And that's a problem why? Is he mean? Cruel to animals? A serial killer? It didn't sound like he was any of those things from what you've told me so far."

Undrea leaned in. "I don't want to fall in love with him because he's not available. He's *engaged*. And I am not a homewrecker. Besides that, his girlfriend is a little scary. She's one of those perfect supermodel types that looks like she smells something and it's you."

"Pffft." Mattie seemed unimpressed with Nina. "Does the kiss make him immune to your, you know, *gifts?"*

"No. So there's that, too." Undrea took a deep breath. "The rest of that whole thing about how I'll have no choice but to fall in love with him ends in me doing what my kind is famous for."

Mattie grimaced. "You *are* in a spot of trouble."

"Thanks for your brilliant observation, Mats. The ache in my pinky toe is a pretty good indicator of that."

Mattie snorted. "Are you having any urges to, you know, control him or whatever?"

"Nothing like that. Yet."

"That's good. What do you want from me? I can help. I just need specifics."

"I need to not fall in love with him." She frowned. "Which I think is already happening. He's amazing. He has the coolest cat, too. One of those hairless ones. You know the kind?" She drank some of her tea to keep from saying more.

"Hoo boy. You're already talking about his cat. I'd say the falling in love part is definitely happening. How long did you talk to this guy that you think he's amazing? And that his cat is cool? Girl, you are headed down a slippery slope and you are wearing Crisco booties."

Undrea stared at her amusing friend. "Can you help me or not?"

"I can, but it'll take me a minute. I'm just not super versed in merfolk ways." Mattie frowned as she sipped her tea. "Why can't you just ask your parents what the rules and regs are on this?"

"Because if I'd paid attention in school I'd know them, and also they already think I'm pushing my luck living amongst the uprights. Do you know what they'd do if I said a man had accidentally kissed me? My father would be here by nightfall, trident out and ready to do battle. Well, not battle. But ready to force Ethan to marry me or whatever happens in a situation like this. Or worse, to cart me off back home to live with them." The horror.

She shook her head. "They can't know. We have to handle this in house."

Mattie nodded. "I had a feeling that would be your answer. Okay, I need to do some research. See what the books say. If I can even find the books that talk about this. Then I'll figure out how to reverse this sort of event." She turned her cup slightly. "You think you can hold off from being completely head over heels for a few days?"

"I hope so, but then I thought I was never going to see him again too. And really, if I can stay away from him for forty-eight hours, then all of this goes away. Or maybe that only applies after the first contact." Undrea rolled her eyes. "It could be that the forty-eight window is gone now that I've seen him again. Or that it's restarted. I really don't know."

"You should have paid more attention to the old legends."

"Yeah, well, I wasn't going to live that life, so I didn't see the point. I was a little preoccupied with what living on land was going to be like," Undrea continued. "Anyway, not seeing him is no big deal now. I told them it would take a few days to get the estimate together. I'll just tell them it's taking longer than anticipated. However long it takes."

"Good. Try not to see him or talk to him. If you have to communicate, do it by email. You know how sight and sound can work with these magical entanglements. Especially sound, in your case."

Undrea nodded. She knew. They could intensify any magic already in play. "I can do that."

"Perfect." Mattie put her hand on Undrea's. "We'll get you through this. If we have to, we'll call in the whole crew."

"We might need them." Undrea drank the last of her tea. "But I was sort of hoping to avoid that level of humiliation."

"Hey, it's not your fault that of all of the lakes in the world, he just happened to show up in yours."

Undrea cut her eyes at her friend. "Your sympathy is overwhelming."

Mattie laughed. "At least he's cute. I'm assuming he's cute?"

"Handsome as all get-out." Undrea looked at the time and suddenly got to her feet. "I'd better get to work. My employees are going to think I've moved in with the new client. Thanks for listening."

"Anytime. I'll get to work on the research and see what I can find out." Mattie stood up and hugged her.

Mattie smelled of beeswax and flowers. Undrea hugged her back. "Talk to you soon."

"Be well."

"I'll do my best."

"And tell Aaron I said hi."

With a smirk, Undrea nodded and left.

By the time she got to her office, she was feeling better. Mattie would figure something out. She always did. And if she couldn't, then they'd call in the crew, like she'd suggested.

The crew being Pandora and Marigold Williams,

two of their more conventional witch friends in town; Willa Iscove, fae stone and metal worker; Bridget Morrow, the werewolf who owned Howler's; her sister-in-law, Ivy Merrow; Roxy St. James, a human who could now shift into a panther thanks to some very special magic; Tessa and Jenna Blythe, the valkyrie sisters; Imari Zephara, the genie; Caroline Linzer, another feline shifter; Delaney Ellingham, one of the newest vampires in town; and Monalisa Tsvetkov, the Will-o'-the-Wisp who'd recently married Van, the dragon shifter.

Ivy, Delaney and Monalisa weren't regulars, though. Both Ivy and Delaney had young children who kept them busy. And since Ivy was married to the town sheriff and Delaney was married to one of the town owners, they had all kinds of extra stuff going on.

Monalisa and her husband spent a good deal of time in Las Vegas.

It was just a fact that they were all growing busier with each passing day. They almost all had husbands or boyfriends and lots of work to do. Some had kids, adopted or otherwise.

Mattie, Imari, Caroline, and Undrea were some of the last truly single women in the group.

And while Undrea sometimes hung out with Greyson, a roguish vampire she'd become friends with after installing a tank at his place, even he'd become less available since finding his soulmate in Kora, the daughter of the reaper who owned Insomnia.

Of course, they did get a lot of free drinks when they went to Insomnia now.

As dear as all of those women were to her, the idea of them knowing what had happened to her didn't sit easily. She especially didn't want Greyson finding out.

Mostly because it felt like there was too great of a chance of her secret accidentally being revealed. Having Mattie know was one thing. But having all of them know?

What if they looked at her differently? The women might not. But Greyson probably would. She wouldn't blame him, either. And what if one of them slipped up and let her secret spill? Would she still be allowed to live in Nocturne Falls?

She sucked in a breath. That wasn't something she'd considered. She might be asked to move. Or told to move.

Holy cowfish. Was that possible?

She supposed she could always go talk to Delaney about it, seeing as how she was an Ellingham. But if Undrea told her, then Delaney would have to tell Hugh, her husband, and if he knew, what was to keep his entire family from finding out?

No, Undrea couldn't tell anyone else. Her parents had always warned her that her secret could be her undoing in the world of the uprights.

She pulled into her spot at the warehouse office space and parked. She turned the truck off and looked at the front door of her business. Her employees might even leave if they knew who they really worked for, and then were would she be? They were all human, except for Aaron.

Without a team to get her jobs done, her business would collapse, and then she might as well go home to her parents.

Shaking her head, she got out of the truck and went inside, determined to get past all of this.

"Morning, boss."

"Morning, Whitney." Undrea picked up her mail from the inbox on Whitney's desk. Whitney was the newest hire, a young woman with a love of fish and knack for organization that made Undrea giddy. "How's it been so far today?"

"Quiet. Amanda and Curtis are out on maintenance. Aaron's in the warehouse working on that Parker job. How was the new client?"

"Good." Not a lie, but not the full truth either. But Whitney didn't need to know all about that. "If we get that job, it's going to be the biggest one we've done yet. I'm just not sure it's going to work out the way they want it to."

"Floor issues?"

Whitney was such a smart woman. Undrea loved a fast learner. "Yep, you nailed it. The tank is going to be a beast. It's going to take Aaron and a serious conversation with the builder to work this one out."

"I hope you guys can make it happen."

"Me, too." She looked through the mail. Bills, mostly. "Anything else?"

"The live rock for the Parker job came, as well as the fish from Bright Ocean Breeders. There was a shipment in from Blue Marble, too. Aaron's acclimating all of it."

"Okay, I'll go out and have a look. Then I'm going to answer emails and hopefully take Aaron to lunch so we can talk over this new job."

"What about phone calls?"

"Put them through."

"You got it."

Undrea went into her office, dropped the mail on her desk, fed her beta fish, Poseidon, then went out to the warehouse. Aaron was at the quarantine tanks, getting their new stock acclimated to the water. Aaron Rigby was one of her very first hires. And while he was most definitely an engineer, he was also a fish guy. Literally and figuratively.

And while that might have made them a match, they'd figured out pretty early on that they were only compatible as friends, which was fine. Aaron was a shifter of the water dragon variety, sometimes called a leviathan, a nessie, or a sea serpent. It helped having an employee who understood what it meant to be more than you seemed.

His true form had probably contributed to his outstanding service as a Navy SEAL.

"Hey, Aaron. Mattie says hi."

He glanced up and smiled. "Does she?"

Undrea nodded. It was obvious the two liked each other, and yet they didn't do anything more than exchange greetings now and then. Whatever that was about. "How does the new stock look?"

"They look great. These basslets are amazing."

"You can't beat them for color."

"That's for sure."

She came over and crouched down to look at all the new fish, still in their shipping bags but submerged in the tank water they'd be quarantining in. Aaron had set up the drip lines, too, so that water from the tank they were about to be placed in could slowly mix with their bag water. It was important to acclimate them properly to avoid shock. "Hello, little fellas."

"How'd the visit go?"

She looked up. "Great, but I don't know about the floor."

"That big of a tank, huh?"

"Nine hundred gallons, roughly."

He whistled. "*Big* tank. We'll figure it out."

"I was hoping we could do just that at lunch."

"Sure." He grinned. "Meatloaf today, I think."

"That sounds great." She straightened. "I could use some comfort food."

He hooked his thumb over his shoulder. "I'll grab my tablet so I can sketch out a few designs while we eat. When you're ready."

"Perfect. I need about forty-five minutes to look at email."

"And I still need to sort out this live rock. Yell when you want to go. Don't forget to look at those sketches I put on your desk."

"Will do." She went back to her small office, fired up her computer and logged in. The sketches from Aaron looked perfect, as always. Her inbox wasn't as easy to get through. Half a dozen client emails, a handful of supplier emails, and a few industry newsletters, which was about standard.

She was just about to open one of the newsletters when another client email arrived.

From Ethan.

6

She didn't want to read it. But at the same time, she'd never wanted to read anything quite so much in her life.

She rolled her eyes. The magic had already gotten its hooks in her. She might as well have been in fifth grade, eager to find out if the cute boy in the row behind her thought she was cute too.

Oh, this was bad.

Emails were harmless, she reminded herself. And he was her potential client. She couldn't very well ignore an email from him.

She still stared at it for a long, long minute before clicking on it.

Dear Undrea,

I'm very glad our second meeting went better than our first.

She smiled. It had gone better, that was for sure. And she was glad about that, too.

I've done a fraction of the research I need to do, but I can already tell I'm going to want the full kit. Fish, coral, anemones, and whatever other inverts you think would work. If I'm going to do it, might as well do it up right, don't you think?

Looking forward to our next meeting. I think Bowie is too.

All the best,

Ethan

She read it three times, which was ridiculous because there was no hidden meaning. Nothing to read between the lines for.

She hit reply and typed out a quick response. *Thanks for the input. I'll take all of this into consideration as I plan your tank. I'm also glad our second meeting went better than the first. Tell Bowie I said hi.*

—Undrea

Was that too cute? Telling the cat she said hi? But no, he clearly adored that animal. And Ethan had brought him up in the original email, so the response was warranted.

She read her answer a few more times. Added the word "new" in front of tank. Then deleted it. Then added "Talk soon!" as her closing sentence.

And finally hit send.

It was only then she realized he hadn't mentioned Nina once. His cat, yes. His fiancée, no.

Was that a sign of anything? Or was she just losing her mind over an upright that just saw her as *the aquarium specialist?*

But Ethan didn't just see her that way, did he?

Although maybe that was exactly how he should see her. And the only way he should see her, because that's all she was ever going to be. Sure, they could be friendly. That was how she treated all of her clients. They might even become friends. After all of this magic nonsense was behind them. That happened with clients, sometimes. Becoming friends.

Roxy was an example of that.

But Roxy hadn't been a handsome, sexy man currently engaged to someone else when Undrea had met her. That was a whole different kettle of fish.

She put Ethan and his email out of her mind. She'd answered him. That was all she needed to do.

With laser focus she went through the rest of her inbox, answering questions, making note of a supplier's sale she wanted to take advantage of and forwarding two customer questions to Whitney to handle.

Then she grabbed her purse and keys and headed for the warehouse to get Aaron for lunch. She needed to keep focusing on work. That would get her through this. And if she kept doing that, before long, Ethan's job would be behind her and so would this whole stupid kiss thing.

She hoped.

What was it about Undrea? She was wedged into Ethan's brain like a complicated equation that needed solving. Although he had a feeling she could never be solved, and therein lay her appeal.

Try as he might to focus on the ion membrane, his thoughts kept returning to her. The way she looked. The fascinating color of her hair. How she smelled of the ocean in the best possible way. The light in her eyes when she talked about something that excited her. The color of those eyes.

Bowie hopped up onto his desk, sat on the plans for a small community center that Ethan was considering funding, and meowed at him.

"Yes?" Ethan said. "Can I help you?"

Bowie lifted his foot, then put it back down.

It was clear the cat wanted attention. Ethan grinned. "Hey, dude, I was kind of looking at those plans."

Bowie stared as if to say he knew better.

"Okay, well, I *was* about to look at those." Ethan scratched under the cat's chin. "What do you need? Some attention, huh? Or are you trying to get treats out of me?"

"Ethan?" Nina called up. "Are we going or—?"

Nina's open-ended questions were really questions that didn't need answering. They were her way of passive-aggressively telling him what to do. It was cute. Sort of. Now they didn't seem quite as cute as they had once been.

"Yes. Coming," he yelled back downstairs. He gave Bowie another rub on the head. "I have to go out.

I'll be back soon. Then we'll have some play time, I swear."

He grabbed his jacket and headed down.

Nina smiled at him as he descended the steps. "Ready for lunch?"

"Sure. Where are we going?"

"I found a spot in town that's supposed to be very popular with locals. It's called Howler's Bar and Grill."

"A bar and grill?" His brows went up in a teasing way, but it was a surprising choice for her. "You really are branching out."

She laughed, looking pleased with herself. "I'm embracing my new hometown."

"You are. I give you points for that." She was the one who'd found Nocturne Falls and sold him on it as one of the upcoming small towns to live in.

He felt bad for thinking she'd been passive-aggressive earlier. She'd just been trying to get him moving. He knew that. He also knew how easily he could go down rabbit holes with his work and disappear for hours.

How else was she supposed to motivate him? He smiled at her. "You look very pretty, by the way."

"Thanks." Her smile turned sly. "As pretty as your new friend?"

He made a face. "My who?"

"Don't play coy with me. I saw the way you were flirting with her."

"Are you talking about Undrea?" This was new. Nina definitely had a jealous streak, but he hadn't seen it in a long time.

She pressed her fingers to his chest and smiled. "You liked her, didn't you?"

"I did. But I like a lot of people. Especially intelligent ones. Didn't you like her?"

Nina blinked at that as if she hadn't expected that question. "She was…fine. I didn't really give it that much thought." Then her fingers pressed a little harder. "But you were definitely flirting with her."

"Was I? Because if that's how you perceived it, I think that's more about you than me. I was just having a conversation." Had he been flirting? He wasn't sure. Flirting felt deliberate. He'd just been enjoying Undrea's company.

Maybe that was flirting.

He didn't know. Didn't care. And he was done talking about it. "Are we going to lunch or—?"

She smirked at him as she picked up on the way he'd phrased the question. "Yes."

He drove, and as he did, he tried to pay close attention to his surroundings, to really take in this new place he'd moved to. It was nice. Beautiful, really. The hills were dotted with homes. A lot were traditional log cabins, but some were like his, built in the chalet style.

They were all sizes too, from little weekend retreats to—

"Wow." Nina leaned forward to see the massive home and property up ahead. "I've heard about this place. It's the Ellingham estate. It's got to be. Owned by the woman who owns the town with her three grandsons." She shook her head as she gawked.

"I would love to see the inside of that place."

Then she glanced over at him. "Looks like you aren't the biggest bank account in town."

He'd never thought or assumed he was. "Good to know. I guess." He wasn't sure what he was supposed to take away from that.

He changed the subject. Talking about his money never seemed useful anyway. "What kind of food does this place have?"

She shrugged. "You know, the standard stuff. Bar food. Burgers. Sandwiches. Salads. That kind of fare."

"I like all of that."

She smiled. "I know you do. Although you're supposed to be eating healthier."

"I'm trying."

Nina, on the other hand, was more than a little picky about what she ate, so he could already imagine how lunch was going to go. She'd end up with a salad, lettuce and vegetables only, no cheese, no croutons, no dressing, with plain grilled chicken. Or possibly plain grilled shrimp, if they had it.

They'd been together long enough for him to know the drill. That was her go-to meal when they went out to eat anywhere she considered questionable.

He'd be lying if he said it didn't bother him. What was the point of trying new places if she was just going to order her version of a safety blanket?

Maybe today would be different. This place was her idea, after all. But then again, Nina liked what she liked and not much else.

As he got into town, she gave him directions.

He listened, nodding, but looked around at the same time. "This place is really interesting. It's like a Halloween vibe, right?"

"Right. They celebrate it every day. That's the town's shtick. And why so many of the little kids are dressed up in costumes. And some of the adults. I guess a lot of the stores hand out candy if you're trick-or-treating."

"We should walk around after we eat lunch."

She laughed. "Why? You want some free candy?"

"No." He chuckled. "Just to see more of the place."

She nodded. "Sure, that would be great."

"Yeah?" He looked over at her.

She nodded. "Yes. I want you to like it here."

"I do like it here."

"No, you don't. Not really. You miss the city. I can tell."

He found a spot near the restaurant and parked. "Yes, I do. I won't lie. But this change of pace will be good for me. It'll give me a chance to be more focused on the work that matters."

"And more focused on *us*," she said. "And to get healthy."

"That too." He hadn't had an episode in about a month. He liked to think maybe they were behind him.

They got out and walked into the restaurant. It was busy, which he took as a very good sign. An empty restaurant at lunchtime didn't inspire much confidence.

The hostess smiled brightly at them. "Two for lunch?"

"Yes, please," Nina said.

"Just a moment." The young woman looked at the chart in front of her, marked a table with grease pencil, then picked up two menus. "Right this way."

She took them to a table near the right side of the floor. "Here you go. Billy will be your server. Enjoy your lunch."

"Thanks." He pulled out Nina's chair for her, then took his own seat. "This is an interesting place. Seems a little more biker bar than I would have imagined, but it works."

Nina looked like she wasn't sure if they should leave now or suck it up and hope for the best. But she'd chosen it, and she hated to admit defeat. "I think it's campy."

He picked up his menu. "I don't care what it is so long as the food is good."

Their server, a young man with a little bit of blue in his otherwise black hair, approached their table with two glasses of water. "Welcome to Howler's. I'm Billy, and I'll be taking care of y'all. Today's special is meatloaf, but we also have a special appetizer today. Cheddar-stuffed onion rings. They are so good. But first, what can I get you guys to drink?"

Nina didn't even look up. "Bottled water with lime."

"And for you, sir?"

Ethan smiled at the young man. "Iced tea?"

"Sure thing. Sweet or unsweet or peach?"

"Peach." Why not, he figured. "And let's try an order of those cheddar-stuffed onion rings to start with, and then I think we'll need a few minutes to decide on the rest."

"You got it." Billy tucked his notepad away as he left.

Ethan already knew he was getting the meatloaf, so while Nina focused on the menu, he looked around a little more.

His looking came to a stop on a booth on the other side of the restaurant. All because of the woman sitting in it.

He smiled.

Undrea.

7

"Incoming," Aaron said.

"What?" Undrea looked up from her fries. She loved fries with meatloaf so long as she got a side of gravy to dip them in. Along with her anchovies, which Aaron had also ordered. Because he understood.

He tipped his head toward the main part of the restaurant as if gesturing towards something. Or someone.

She looked over. And straight into Ethan's face. Uh-oh. He was in the restaurant and headed her way. Almost at her table now. So much for not seeing him.

He smiled at her as they made eye contact. "Hi there. I figured it wouldn't be neighborly to see you and not say hi. Now that we're neighbors."

How did he know where she lived? Or was he just speaking generally? That had to be it. Aaron nudged her under the table with his foot, bringing her back to the moment. She smiled. "Oh, right, hi. Great spot for lunch, isn't it?"

"I don't know. I've never eaten here before, but Nina thought we should try it, so here we are. Judging by the crowd, it must be good."

"It is." She looked past him to see the back of Nina at a table on the other side of the restaurant. Undrea brought her attention back to him.

"Do you eat here a lot?" Ethan asked.

"Almost every day. Well, here or Mummy's. And sometimes Salvatore's." It was hard not to look at him. Ethan was just as handsome in public as he was in his house. But then, had she expected that to be different somehow?

That stupid, love-inducing kiss was making her googly-eyed and airheaded over him. Mattie had better be researching extra hard. Of course he looked the same. A person's environment didn't change their looks.

"Salvatore's?" Ethan asked.

"Best pizza in town," Aaron said. He stuck his hand out. "Aaron Rigby."

"Nice to meet you, Aaron. I'm Ethan. You must be Undrea's…"

"Engineer," Aaron filled in.

Undrea nodded as she realized she'd zoned out and failed to make the introduction. "Aaron is my engineer and my right-hand man. He designs and oversees the building of our custom tanks. He's also the one who will be making sure your builder signs off on your floor." She looked at Aaron. "Ethan's house was where I was this morning. He's our new client. Potential new client."

She didn't want to assume anything.

"Probable new client," Ethan said with a smile.

Aaron nodded. "I look forward to building your tank."

"Thanks." Ethan stuck his hands in his pockets. "Well, I don't want to interrupt your lunch any more than I already have. Just wanted to say hi." He pointed at Undrea's plate. "Is that the meatloaf? I'm getting that too."

She nodded. "One of my favorites."

He squinted. "Is that a side of anchovies? That doesn't come with the meatloaf, does it?"

Undrea laughed. "Nope, special order." She changed the subject quickly. "Get the peach cobbler, too. It's amazing, which is why they're known for it. You won't be sorry."

"Yeah? Okay, we will. Thanks." He held her gaze for a long moment. "I'll talk to you soon."

She couldn't bring herself to look away. "Enjoy your lunch."

"Thanks." Finally, still smiling, he slowly turned and went back to his table.

After a few beats, Aaron leaned in, voice low. "You seriously weren't going to tell me our new client is Ethan Edmonds?"

She blinked and got her focus back on her own personal area. "I don't know his last name. His fiancée, Nina Hascoe, is the one who set everything up."

Aaron stared at her, open-mouthed. "You really don't know, do you?"

"Know what?"

Aaron lowered his voice to a whisper. "Who Ethan Edmonds is?"

"He's got money, I know that."

"No kidding." Aaron rolled his eyes. "Undrea, he's like one of the richest people in the country. He just sold his software company, Blnk, for about two and a half billion dollars."

She stared at Aaron. "Are you sure? How do you know all this?"

"For one thing, Google is your friend. For another, I don't know, maybe look at social media every once in a while?"

"I hate social media. You know that. It's part of why I hired Whitney. So she can run all that stuff."

"Yes, I know how you feel about all that." He shook his head as he picked up the second half of his sandwich. "Ethan Edmonds. How about that. I don't think the floor is going to be a problem. I'd say whatever he wants, he can afford."

She glanced over at Ethan's table and caught him looking at her. He smiled, but she glanced away quickly. "Yeah, I'm sure you're right."

Aaron swallowed his food before saying anything else. "You said that woman is his fiancée?"

"That's how she introduced herself."

"Funny, I feel like him getting engaged would be big news, and I don't remember anything about that. But I mean, she's clearly sitting there."

"And living with him."

"Big ring, huh?"

Undrea thought about that. "I...don't actually

remember." She thought some more. "I didn't notice, to be honest."

"I find that hard to believe." He gestured with a fry. "Not on your part, but because I'd imagine he'd get her a rock big enough not to be missed."

Undrea nodded. "I agree with you but mostly because she seems like the type that would want a rock like that. Unmissable."

"Funny, though."

"What is?"

Aaron took a sip of his Coke. "That an engaged man would flirt that hard. But then again, I suppose a guy like Ethan Edmonds is used to having whatever woman he wants. Kind of weird to think the one he's currently after is also my boss."

"Whoa now," Undrea said. "It's not like that at all."

"Right."

"It's not."

"Which is why he came all the way over here to say hi? Because he couldn't just wave?"

"He was just being friendly."

Aaron nodded. "Sure, let's go with that and not that it has anything to do with how sweet and pretty you are."

"Aaron." She dunked a fry in gravy and grinned. "I am pretty sweet, though."

His gaze narrowed. "Just watch yourself, Undrea. I'd hate to see you get your heart broken."

"Not going to happen, but I appreciate your concern."

He shrugged and went back to his sandwich. She tried to focus on her meatloaf, but knowing Ethan was so close made it tough. She wanted to look at him and had to actively fight the urge to turn her head.

Mattie had warned her about this, but Undrea couldn't exactly get up and walk out. She had to pay the bill, for one thing. For another, Ethan was a potential client. She didn't want to do anything weird that might sour him on using her services.

Her business needed this job.

She exhaled and tried to get her mind on something else. "What's on your agenda this afternoon?"

"Stock maintenance, coral rotations, supply inventory and I guess starting the sketches on the Edmonds job so we can begin estimating. How about you?"

"I'm going on a couple maintenance runs."

"Roxy?"

She nodded. "Then the library." They'd installed a tank there recently as part of a community project, and while the Ellinghams had paid for the equipment and supplies, Tanks A Lot donated the fish and the maintenance visits.

"I take it that means you approve my preliminary sketches."

"For?"

He made a face at her. "The Parker job. They were on your desk."

"Oh, right. Yes." So much for not thinking about Ethan. "That drawing you did is perfect to start with."

"You want me to work up some stock plans for Ethan, too?"

"Sure, if you want to. He wants everything. Fish, coral, inverts, you name it."

"Live rock, then."

"Definitely."

"Okay. I'll put three plans together for you to look over. And I think I'll do a really high-end, one-of-a-kind plan too. Just in case he wants stuff no one else has."

"Good. Although he doesn't strike me as being that kind of guy."

"No?"

"No." Undrea glanced over at Ethan's table. Nina seemed to be sending something back. "But the fiancée? Definitely. She's used to a life of privilege, I can tell. You know the type. Always had money, doesn't know how to function without it."

He nodded. "Yeah, I know the kind. I doubt Ethan would be like that though, because he didn't grow up that way."

"How do you know? Is this a social media thing again?"

Aaron laughed. "I read the interview *Money* magazine did with him. He grew up in a single-parent home, his mom worked three jobs to make sure he went to a STEM school, and he worked every summer himself."

"Really?"

Aaron nodded. "First thing he did when he made some money, which was at seventeen, by the way, was pay off his mom's house and buy her a new car. Said it was the first new one she ever had. When he hit it big, he immediately donated enough money to build a new science and technology wing on his old high school."

Undrea glanced over at him again. "Interesting." Amazing how a little bit of information about someone could make them even more attractive than they already were.

"I shouldn't have said anything. You're already picturing him as the father of your children, aren't you?"

She snorted and then threw a French fry at Aaron. "I am not. Stop that."

"I just know you're going to get all gooey over him."

"Zip it, Rigby."

He wiped his mouth with his napkin, then tossed it on the table. "You know what you need?"

"I'm afraid to answer that question."

"A good swim."

"Had one this morning, thank you."

"Then you need a night out with the girls. A little time in the VIP room at Insomnia."

"The VIP room only happens when Greyson's paying, and he's pretty busy these days."

"You don't need Greyson. Just go and have fun. You're a very attractive woman. Guys will be all over you. You'll forget about Ethan in a heartbeat. You'll see."

"Thanks for the vote of confidence." She grinned.

"For your information, we're working on a girls' night out already."

"Good. Go."

"You're just worried that me liking him is going to screw things up for this deal."

"It could. And getting a job like this would be pretty major for us." He shifted forward again. "You know his house could end up in a magazine. And any magazine that comes to take pictures of his place would be all over a big aquarium. They love stuff like that. Which means we'd get a mention in connection with Ethan Edmonds."

She hadn't thought about that. "You think so?"

"Yes." He let out a low whistle. "You know what that would do for business? You'd have to hire a second crew, for one thing."

She put her hands up. "I think you're getting a little ahead of yourself. That's a lot of what-ifs."

"Yeah, you're right. It is. But I can't help thinking about it."

She understood. She glanced down at her plate but cut her eyes at Ethan again. She couldn't stop thinking about *him*.

8

Ethan had no right to feel relieved that Aaron was just an employee of Undrea's. No right and no reason.

And yet, he *was* relieved. When he'd seen them in the booth on the other side of the restaurant, he'd immediately assumed that the man across from her was her boyfriend. That simple thought had gotten him up out of his seat and moving toward them before he'd even thought about what he was going to say.

Thankfully, he hadn't made a fool of himself, but the truth remained that Undrea continued to be firmly stuck in his head. The mental real estate she occupied seemed to be getting larger, too.

He didn't know what to do about that, either. For that matter, he wasn't sure he *wanted* to do anything about it.

"How's your meatloaf?" Nina asked.

"It's really good." He looked at her dish, feeling a little short-tempered because he'd predicted what she was going to order. "I'd ask how your dry salad with dry chicken is, but I can pretty much guess."

"It's not dry," she said. She dipped the first two centimeters of her fork in the vinaigrette she'd asked for on the side. "I'm having dressing."

"Are you though?"

She stared at him. "Are you bothered by how I'm eating all of a sudden?"

He took a moment, not really sure he wanted to open this can of worms. But then he kind of did. What was the point of letting something fester until it blew up? Better to tackle it in the early stages, right? "I'm not sure why you wanted to come here if you weren't actually going to eat anything that was on the menu."

"What are you talking about?" She laughed like he was being silly. "Where do you think this food came from?"

"That's your standard special order. A garden salad with no cheese and no croutons with plain grilled chicken and dressing on the side. That's not on any restaurant's menu."

"Maybe it should be. Then it wouldn't be a special order."

He sighed, already regretting the conversation. "You're missing the point."

"No, I'm not. You're mad at what I ordered for some reason, despite the fact that I've been ordering this same meal for at least the last two years that we've been together. Why now, Ethan? Hmm?"

"Because..." He thought a moment, picking his

words carefully. "It's not living life. Not in an enjoyable way."

"You think that plate of brown glop in front of you is living life?" She smiled sweetly in an attempt, he imagined, to soften her words. "Ethan, my love, you're a guy. When it comes to weight, you can get away with that kind of meal. I can't. To look the way I look, I have to watch what I put into my body. I have to be aware of the carbs and the calories and the sugar content. And that doesn't even touch on all of the other things I have to do to maintain how I look."

He knew all about that: the time she spent at the hair salon, getting her nails done, facials, the yoga and Pilates and all the other stuff that he wasn't sure he wanted to know about.

She gave him a look. "Not to mention you should be eating healthier anyway."

He shook his head. "Maybe. My episodes have yet to be tied to diet. And I don't eat like this all the time. I'm just saying, would it really be the worst thing in the world to let go once in a while? I know you're very conscious of what you eat. But does it have to be twenty-four seven? What kind of fun is that?"

She narrowed her eyes. "Why is all of this coming out now?"

"You're the one who wanted to eat here. I thought maybe just this once, you'd actually do that. Eat. Instead, you got your standard boring salad. Again."

She stared at him for a long moment with a sweet, patient smile fixed in place. Then she calmly reached over, picked up one of the cheddar-stuffed onion rings that were left and took a bite.

She took a second bite, and then a third, finally finishing the entire thing. After which, she took a sip of her water, then wiped her hands on her napkin. "Do you feel better now?"

He laughed. Nina was nothing if not capable of placating him. "Do you?"

"I feel great."

He wasn't so sure about that. At the very least, she was probably calculating how many extra steps she'd have to take on the elliptical to burn off that fried monstrosity, but he didn't care. He knew she'd done it to appease him. And somehow, it had worked.

It wasn't her fault that she was a picky eater. If her eating habits bothered him, that was his issue to deal with.

She'd pretty much just underlined that.

"Sorry," he said. "You can eat what you want."

"Thanks."

"You know, though, you don't have to be that skinny. I'd be perfectly fine if you were a bigger size or whatever."

"Sure," she said. "You have a long history of dating plus-size women."

"I…" He thought about that. "I've just dated the women who've crossed my path. I never intentionally set out to date only thin ones." Had he? Suddenly he wasn't sure.

He looked past Nina to Undrea's table. They were

getting up to leave. Undrea was definitely not as skinny as Nina. She was curvier. A lot curvier.

And he certainly found her attractive. Then he had another thought. Had Nina made that comment because of Undrea? Was she testing him in some way?

He sat back. "I dated Cindi Morgan in high school, and she was probably what you'd call plus-size." She'd been pinup-model gorgeous, too. "And you want to know something else?"

She smiled like she'd won something. "Sure."

"You're like supermodel skinny. Which is great if you're a supermodel, but in real life, it's very thin. Not that you asked. But since you brought it up, there you go. You almost look frail sometimes. Makes me worry about you honestly."

Her smile disappeared. "I am not too skinny. Or frail."

"I'm just saying I wouldn't be upset about having a little more to hold on to. But also if you're doing this because of some sort of ideal you think I have, that's not true. The outside matters less to me than the inside."

She was glaring now.

Honestly, he didn't understand women. What was wrong with what he'd said? He'd have thought she'd be happy about being able to loosen the reins a bit. "Would you rather I not tell you the truth?"

That seemed to take the edge off of her irritation a little. "No. I want us always to be honest with each other." She poked at her lettuce, then put the fork down. "You really think I need to gain weight?"

"Need to? No. But again if you're staying this thin because you think it's what I want, it's not. That's all I'm trying to say. Don't do this for me. Make yourself happy. And if that means eating dessert or fries or having a beer now and then, do it. Who cares what social media says?"

She seemed to take all that in. "Okay. But you realize it will be all over Twitter if I gain weight. Not to mention the camera adds ten pounds. And we get photographed a lot."

She wasn't wrong. He shook his head. "I wish that wasn't true."

She smiled again, but it was tight and thin. "I don't think I'll be having a beer anytime soon, but thank you for telling me all of that."

Billy came by. "I hope you folks left room for dessert. Our peach cobbler is pretty well known as our specialty, but we also have a mud pie and a raspberry cheesecake." He smiled. "So what can I bring you?"

Ethan had told Undrea he'd try the peach cobbler, and he was going to, regardless of the conversation he and Nina had just had. "We'll have the cobbler."

"Great choice." Billy reached for their dirty plates. "Can I get these out of your way?"

"Sure," Ethan said.

Nina held her hands up. "I'm done, too, thank you."

Billy took their plates. "I'll be right back with your cobbler."

Ethan drew his finger through the condensation on his glass of iced tea. "You don't have to eat any if you don't want to. Seriously. Whatever you want to do is fine with me."

"I can't wait to try it. If they're known for it, I'm sure it's outstanding."

She was just humoring him. He knew that. But he'd also realized something else. Nina was a good person, a stunning woman, and would absolutely make a fantastic wife.

For some other guy. She just wasn't the woman for him.

In the last two years, he hadn't given marriage a lot of thought. There was no reason to. Nina had filled the role of companion perfectly. She was great at parties, beautiful to look at, and exactly who everyone thought he should be with. Not only that, she'd nursed him through each one of his episodes with great patience.

She was the easy choice. The no-brainer.

But none of that was good enough anymore. None of that spoke to the need in his soul for a mate that understood him inside and out. Someone who shared his love of life. And his love of living it a certain way.

He wasn't going to pretend that Undrea was that person. He didn't know her well enough to make that call, but she had definitely awakened something in him that wanted to find out who else was out there.

For that, he was grateful.

But untangling his life from Nina's was going to be miserable. Was that really what he wanted to do?

Life with Nina wasn't that bad, was it? No, it wasn't. But they were just coasting, really. And he already knew Nina wanted more out of their relationship than he did. She hinted at it all the time. About their future and making things more permanent and, of course, the ring.

He couldn't commit to that with her. He studied her as she got her phone out, checked the screen, then set it aside. She really was perfect. Just not perfect for him.

He was about to make her hate him. He knew that. And already felt terrible. Was there a way to let her down easy? To part and remain as friends? Or at least not enemies?

He wasn't sure. He didn't have a lot of experience with breaking up. Plenty with being dumped. He hadn't really gotten successful with women until he'd started making money.

He didn't love that part, honestly. It made him question the motives of every woman who came into his life. That had been a factor in deciding to date Nina. She had her own money, but he also knew that she liked money. His or her family's. She'd never pretended otherwise.

He figured there was something to be said for that kind of honesty.

Billy returned with their peach cobbler. It looked amazing. Brown and crumbly with peaches and juice poking through the crust, while a big scoop of vanilla ice cream melted over the top of it.

"Don't touch it," Nina said, picking up her phone. "I need to Instagram this."

She'd gotten quite a following since they'd started dating. He held his hands up. "Go for it."

He wondered if she'd try to destroy him on social media when they split. He hoped she'd rise above that, but Nina definitely had a mean streak.

She took a few pictures, holding the phone at different angles and heights. "Okay, I got a good one."

While she worked on posting that, he picked up a spoon. "I can dig in now?"

"You can eat every last bite," she said. She looked up from her phone, smiled quickly and added, "Just save one for me."

"I'll be sure to." He dug in, making sure to get a bite with peaches, topping, and ice cream.

He ate it and instantly understood why Undrea had recommended it. "Wow," he mumbled around a mouthful of the warm, cinnamon-laced dessert. "This is amazing."

"Hmm?" Nina put her phone away. "Good?"

"The best thing ever."

She took a dainty bite. "Mmm, very peachy."

He laughed. That was one way to look at it. He ended up eating most of it, which didn't surprise him. After Nina had eaten the onion ring, he didn't imagine she'd eat much more.

He paid the check, and they got up to leave.

"You still want to walk around a bit?" Nina said. "I'd love to do a little window-shopping. See what there is to see in town. Get a feel for the place."

"Sure, that sounds great." It would also delay the talk they needed to have, which he was all right with. Might as well have one last enjoyable day together.

So they walked and looked in windows and went in a few places. The jewelry store, for one, which didn't surprise him.

He sensed several times that he'd been recognized, which he'd come to expect, but thankfully, those people left him alone.

But by the time they got home, he was oddly worn out. Maybe it was the thought of the conversation that needed to take place, which he was no longer ready to have, or maybe it was all the endless looking and talking and walking and inspecting things they had no intention of buying.

Or maybe it was pretending that things were fine. Which they clearly were not.

He went straight upstairs to his office, settled into his anti-gravity desk chair, hit the controls to rotate the chair into the anti-gravity position, then fired up his laptop to get some work done. Or at least attempt it.

At the sound of the chair's motor, Bowie looked up from his window perch and chirped at Ethan.

"Hey, boy. Yes, I'm finally home. And I promised you some play time, didn't I?"

Bowie jumped down and ran over to Ethan. He hopped up onto his lap and started making biscuits on his chest.

Ethan grinned. "You know I can't see the screen when you do that."

Biscuit-making continued.

As he scratched Bowie's neck, Ethan had a thought. Maybe work wasn't what he was supposed to be doing.

9

"The tank is really looking good, don't you think?" Roxy stood nearby watching while Undrea finished cleaning it.

"I agree," Undrea said. "It's matured beautifully. Those wrasses sure have made a home for themselves, haven't they?" She finished putting the last of her tools into her five-gallon bucket, then grabbed the shop towel she'd brought in with her and wiped up any water drips she'd left behind, giving the tank's acrylic a final polish as she went. No one wanted to look at their fish and see water spots.

"I love them. They're so colorful." Roxy's gaze was fixed on the wall-to-wall aquarium that Undrea had installed in her office several years ago, her smile a sign of her obvious delight. "It's hard not to love the clownfish too. Who doesn't love Nemo?"

Undrea laughed. "They are definitely the most requested addition for saltwater tanks." She straightened. "You're doing a really good job of taking care of this tank, too."

"Thanks. But you're the one who takes care of it." She laughed.

"You're still happy with it?" Undrea never wanted a client, especially one who was also a friend, to be unhappy.

"I still love it as much today as the day you installed it," Roxy said. "Probably more. Honestly, it is the most relaxing thing. And when I'm stuck in a scene or I don't know what happens next, I just turn my chair around and stare into that underwater world and kind of lose myself. A couple minutes of that, and the ideas just start to flow again. It's amazing."

Roxy was an author who wrote the most delicious paranormal romances. Undrea nodded. "Lots of great creative vibes to be had with water. Anything that relaxes you increases your dopamine production, which helps with creativity. The distraction of the tank can increase creativity. Anyone who's creative should have one."

"You should use that as a selling point. This town is filled with creative types."

"True." Undrea's brows lifted slightly. "Including my possible new client."

"Oh?" Roxy immediately looked interested. "Do tell."

"Do you know who Ethan Edmonds is?"

Roxy's eyes went big. "Are you serious? Who doesn't know who Ethan Edmonds is?"

"Well, I didn't."

Roxy laughed. "Okay, I'm sure there are people who don't. What does he have to do with this? Does your new client work for him?"

"My new maybe client *is* him."

Roxy's mouth came open. "Are you serious? Which house are you putting a tank in? His New York penthouse? Is he flying you somewhere? This is so exciting. You know, I've been thinking about basing a hero on him for a long time. There's something about a super smart guy in glasses."

Undrea didn't need convincing. "I'm not flying anywhere. He has a house here in Nocturne Falls."

"This just keeps getting better." She pulled out her desk chair and sat as she pointed to the chair against the wall. "Sit. I need to be comfortable for the rest of this story."

Undrea put her bucket of cleaning supplies down and took the chair.

Then Roxy opened the small fridge she kept beside her desk. "You want something to drink?"

"Sure."

Roxy tossed her a can of Diet Pepsi and got one out for herself. She popped the top. "Okay, tell me everything."

Undrea opened her can too. "He's got a house up in the hills. A big one. They must have had it remodeled because it looks very modern and fresh inside, but you can tell some of the original features were kept, like the big stone fireplace."

"Pandora would know the details on that, probably. She might have even sold him the house. Wait. You said they. Who's they?"

"Ethan and his fiancée, Nina."

Roxy wrinkled her nose. "He has a fiancée? That's bothersome."

Undrea bit her lip. "Well, here's the thing about that..." She hesitated. This was more than she could just jump into. "I really need to back up and start at the beginning."

Roxy kicked her feet up on her desk and leaned back, taking a sip of her Pepsi. "I am always here for a good story. And my word count is almost done for the day, so I have all kinds of time. Shoot."

Undrea went back to their first meeting at the lake and told Roxy everything the same way she'd told Mattie. She included the issues with the kiss, too, and how she probably was going to have no choice but to fall in love with him because of mermaid magic and how those things worked. That was as much as she shared about that.

But she figured it was worth doing because Roxy knew a lot about relationships, seeing as how they were sort of her bread and butter. Especially those that involved non-humans.

Roxy listened with rapt fascination. "Okay, I have to say, that is the best meet-cute I have ever heard. Did you really call him a creep?"

"I did. Heat of the moment and all that." Undrea made a face. "I did apologize for that."

Roxy laughed. "No wonder he's in love with you."

"He's not in love with—oh no." Undrea paused as a new thought came to her. "Could the magic work both ways?" Why hadn't that occurred to her before? Was it possible? "Do you think the kiss could be causing him to fall for me?"

Before Roxy could answer, Undrea pressed her fingers to her temples. "I can't believe I'm about to become a homewrecker."

"All right, hold up. If that does happen, you are not to blame. Magic causing someone to fall in love with you does not make you a homewrecker. Have you ever heard of a human kissing a mermaid to cause the human to fall in love as well?

"I've never heard of an issue with it, no. But then I'm a little removed from the merfolk community." And again, she also hadn't told Roxy the whole truth, about her genuine self and what that meant for Ethan. Mattie knew, but Mattie was working on a spell that might fix the whole thing.

Undrea just didn't see any benefit to outing herself to more people than necessary. Especially with the repercussions it might have.

"I know you don't want to ask your parents, but don't you think—"

"No. Absolutely not. Can't happen. My mother will flip. And my father will react in a way that only overprotective fathers can. They'll probably try to make me move home, too."

"Okay, parents are out. I get it."

"Aaron doesn't know about how we actually met or the kiss, but he thinks Ethan is flirting with me just because he's used to having any woman he wants and that's what guys like that do."

Roxy seemed to think on that a moment. "I don't know. Ethan Edmonds doesn't really have a rep as a player. At least not that I've read about. If he has a fiancée and he's flirting, I think it's the magic at work."

Undrea raised her brows. "If you had written this as a story, what would you have had the magic do?"

Roxy grinned. "Oh, he would definitely be under the spell of the beautiful mermaid, unable to think of another woman, besieged by thoughts of the mermaid's grace and charm, all of his waking and dreaming moments spent wondering where she was and if she was thinking of him. He would be completely besotted. I mean *gone*."

Undrea let out a long low groan. "I am so screwed."

Roxy's smirk didn't help. "You're actively avoiding this guy, right? At least until Mattie has some time to figure things out on your end?"

"Right. I still ran into him at lunch, but that wasn't intentional."

"Okay, but what if that's the wrong approach? Are you sure about the whole forty-eight hours thing? I mean, maybe this is one of those absence makes the heart grow fonder kind of magics? What if being together and quickly figuring out you're not compatible would make it all go poof?"

"I don't know." Especially because Undrea was suddenly questioning everything. "Maybe it would. But I think we are compatible. So..." She held her hands up.

Roxy rolled her eyes. "Based on what? A ten-minute visit to his house in which you were actively trying to win his business and a thirty-second conversation at Howler's where you suggested he try the cobbler? Really?"

"Hmm. When you put it that way, I guess we haven't spent that much time together. Not quality time, anyway."

Roxy shrugged. "Just a thought. I realize I'm just the romance novelist turned panther shifter in this equation, but it's something to think about."

"No, those are valid ideas. And you are certainly proof that magic doesn't always follow the rules."

"There is that."

"So you think I should spend some time with him?"

Roxy took a drink of Pepsi, then set the can on her desk and put her feet back on the floor. "What can it hurt? Mattie's either going to come up with something to help you or she's not. Whatever magic is in play is still going to be in play regardless of whether or not you see Ethan, so why not see him? You might figure out there's nothing about him to like and make Mattie's help irrelevant. And if that dislike is strong enough, why couldn't it overcome the magic?"

Undrea hadn't thought about it that way. "I guess so. Or this could be a terrible idea. I mean, what if I find out I really do like him?"

Roxy smiled. "And he finds out he really likes you?"

"He's got a fiancée!"

"And yet, he's flirting with you. So either that fiancée isn't what his heart wants or he's a scummy guy out to get some. You either end up with a great new boyfriend or a reason to never speak to him again. Seems like a win-win to me."

"When you put it like that..." Undrea couldn't argue with Roxy's logic. Except... "You know I'm trying to book a job with this guy."

"Well, if he ends up your boyfriend, you're definitely getting the job. And if he's scummy, just don't ice him out until he's signed the contract."

"You're so mercenary."

Roxy laughed. "Just a realist."

"I guess I need to come up with an excuse to see him."

"That shouldn't be too hard," Roxy said. "You just said yourself you're trying to do business with him." Then she tapped her chin in thought. "Did he seem excited about the tank?"

"He did. He asked a lot of questions."

"Good. Then you should have no trouble getting some more time with him. In fact..." She leaned forward. "You should try to see him outside of his house. At your shop. Can you come up with a reason for him to come visit you?"

"Sure, that shouldn't be a problem. Why do you think I shouldn't see him at his house?"

Roxy's eyes twinkled with all kinds of intentions. "Because I think you need to see him away from the fiancée. That'll really tell you what he's up to."

10

Ethan stared at Undrea's card as he dialed. The company logo was a smiling cartoon fish standing on its tail, giving a thumbs-up with one fin.

The phone rang once before being answered. "Thanks a lot for calling Tanks A Lot. Whitney speaking. How can I help you today?"

He grinned. The woman answering sounded young and eager and on the ball. He loved that kind of employee. He'd bet good money answering phones wasn't all she did. "Hi there. Is Undrea available?"

"She's in the warehouse, but I can page her. May I ask who's calling?"

"Absolutely. Please tell her it's Ethan."

"Just a moment, Ethan, and I'll see if she's available or needs to call you back."

"Thank you."

She put him on hold to the sound of bubbling water. It made him think of music. That thought intrigued him. Was there a musical parallel to the sound of water? His mind started working as he tucked Undrea's card back in his pocket and returned to scratching Bowie, who was still planted on his lap.

"Hello, this is Undrea."

What was it about the sound of Undrea's voice that made him so happy? All thoughts of water as music got pushed to the back burner. "Hey, it's Ethan. I'd like to come by your shop and have a look at how you do things."

"S-sure." She seemed surprised by that but not upset. That was a good sign. "I'd be happy to give you a tour of our facilities."

"Great." Checking out the inner workings of the businesses he dealt with was something he liked to do. Especially when he was going to spend a large sum of money with them. It was mostly for curiosity's sake, but in Undrea's case, he really didn't have any doubts about how she ran her operation. He could already tell she was completely hands-on and fully involved. "I just like to know how things get done. If that makes sense. I just can't turn off the part of me that's an engineer."

"It makes perfect sense. If you choose us to build this tank for you, then you should know how it's being done. This isn't a small undertaking either. I can see why you'd want to know what it entails. And how your money is being spent. Frankly, I'm surprised more people don't take the initiative. Generally, I'm the one who has to do the inviting."

"Oh. Good." That was a relief. Then he thought about what she'd just said. "Does that mean you were going to invite me?"

"Yes, actually. In fact, I almost asked if you were psychic because I literally have you on my list of people to call. I was going to see when you were available."

Fortune favored the bold. He grinned. "How about right now?"

That was another test. Those with something to hide generally wanted time to prepare. Granted, they could also be busy, too, but their response to his impending visit usually gave him a little more insight into their company.

"Oh. That's soon. But great. I mean, there's not a build going on in the shop right now. We're prepping for one, but there's nothing really to see on it. Even so, I can still show you how we do things. You can see the new stock that came in earlier, too. I'm here until five. When do you want to come by?"

"How about twenty minutes from now?"

"That works. I'll see you then. Do you know how to get here?"

"I have your card. I'll just plug the address into my GPS."

"Right. Okay. See you shortly."

He hung up and smiled at Bowie, who was giving him a disapproving look. "I'm just going to see how things operate. I'm about to spend a lot of money with her company. That's not a weird thing to do. I do it all the time."

Bowie continued to squint in that way he had, which to Ethan felt like he was questioning everything.

"Well, I *have* done it before. And I ended up investing heavily in two of those businesses." Ethan scratched at one of the cat's neck wrinkles, something Bowie really seemed to enjoy. "I know, it's partially an excuse to see Undrea. And a way of procrastinating having the talk with Nina."

He frowned. That was a lot of it. The procrastination part. But so was wanting to see Undrea. That was the biggest part. He had to find out if this chemistry between them was real or imagined.

Maybe he wasn't really interested in her. Maybe it was just the newness of someone like her. A beautiful woman with brains. He shook his head. "That's not it, Bowie, my man. That's selling her short."

He picked up a little mouse toy and tossed it. Bowie took off after it. There was so much more to Undrea than being smart and beautiful. One of the things Ethan liked most was how comfortable she seemed to be in her own skin. She was easygoing in a way that made it seem like she wasn't trying to be anything but herself.

Undrea was just who she was with nothing to hide. Unlike someone else. Bowie came trotting back with the mouse in his mouth.

Ethan took the mouse and tossed it again as he glanced toward the first floor of his house, his mind shifting toward Nina.

She wasn't really trying to hide anything, but she did put a lot of effort into the face she showed the world. It wasn't her fault she was who she was. Nina Hascoe was the child of old money and the result of a distinct set of values given to her by parents who were also children of old money.

People who grew up in that world were bound to look at things differently than those who'd scrapped and climbed and scrounged for everything they'd earned.

Nina was just someone with a wall up. A wall built of platinum bricks.

He didn't fault her for it. She hadn't asked to be born into that stratosphere any more than he'd asked to be the child of a single mother struggling to keep her head above water.

Their experiences growing up were as different as chalk and cheese, an expression he'd picked up from Trevor, a British buddy of Ethan's from his college days at MIT.

Trevor had also told him Nina wasn't the woman for him.

Turns out, he was right. Ethan would have to call Trevor soon and tell him the news. Bowie had curled up on the floor with the mouse and was chewing its tail off.

It wasn't just the difference in Ethan's and Nina's childhoods that made it seem like they weren't meant for the long haul. He needed a partner who wasn't interested in what others wanted them to be. He'd much rather someone interested in what they could become that would make themselves happy. Someone content in their own skin.

Undrea seemed like she was already there. She genuinely seemed happy with who she was.

And he wanted to know more about that. About *her*.

He shifted the anti-gravity desk back to a seated position and reached down to give Bowie one more scratch. "I won't be long, bud, I promise."

Then Ethan got up, grabbed his wallet and keys and headed downstairs. He'd just about reached the door when Nina called out.

"Ethan, is that you?"

"Yep. Headed out for a bit. Won't be long."

Dressed in cropped leggings and a strappy tank top, she appeared from the room they'd set up as a yoga studio. Her hair was twisted up in a messy bun that still looked good, her face aglow with the sheen of sweat. "Where are you going?"

He wasn't going to lie, but he put on his sternest business face. "I'm going to inspect that aquarium company. I want to see what their setup is like. How they run things. That tank isn't going to be cheap. I need to have faith in them."

She smiled oddly. "All right. Have fun. Could you stop by the grocery store on the way back? We're almost out of almond milk, and I don't think there will be enough for smoothies tomorrow. I can have it delivered, but that's really all we need."

He nodded, relieved she hadn't asked to go. And instantly felt guilty about it. They *had* to talk when he got back. "Sure. Almond milk. Got it."

"Thanks, honey."

"You're welcome." He slipped out. She was acting odd. She never called him honey. She hated pet names. What was going on? Did she still think he liked Undrea in a more romantic way?

He exhaled hard as he got into his SUV. What did it matter? Very soon, Nina was going to be his past.

And right now, all he wanted to think about was his future.

Undrea stared at her office phone for a moment before hanging it up. How had Ethan called at the exact moment she'd been about to call him?

She didn't want to say or think or *breathe* the word, but in the light of everything else going on, there was only one answer that made sense.

Magic.

He had to be under the influence. Just like she was.

Their only hope was to not like each other, because Undrea was not going to give in to her magically induced feelings and break up his relationship. That wasn't who she was. Or ever wanted to be.

Although not liking each other wasn't really their only hope. Mattie would figure something out. Which made Undrea wonder why hadn't she called yet? Was it really that hard to research merfolk lore?

Undrea dialed Mattie's number.

She answered with, "If I had found anything, I would have called."

Undrea braced herself for Mattie's response. "He's coming over."

"What? I told you to avoid him."

"I know, but listen. What if we really aren't meant to be? Spending some time together, more than five minutes, I mean, could cure us pretty quickly if we're not compatible. And there's every reason to think we aren't. After all, he's a big-city guy who likes technology, and I'm a small-town, underwater girl who hates social media. We aren't alike at all."

"You've been talking to Roxy, haven't you?"

"Maybe." Undrea grinned. "And if we do like each other, then we're no worse off than we were before. I'll just avoid him until you can come up with something. Which you will, eventually. I'll just let him think I've gotten really busy. He has no idea what's actually going on."

"And his fiancée?"

"She won't be a problem. She barely acknowledged my presence when I was at the house, and she didn't look at me during lunch."

"You had lunch with her?"

"No, she and Ethan were at Howler's when Aaron and I were there eating. Ethan came over to say hi."

"So that's what started all this. Then you went to see Roxy—"

"I had to. Today was her tank maintenance day."

"I see. Well, you've seen him, talked to him and are about to spend time with him. I guess you're right. The damage is done. You'd better hope I can find some magic that will reverse what's already in place or you're going to have a big mess on your hands. Especially when your *other* magic kicks in."

Undrea stopped smiling. "Yeah. I know. But by then, you'll have found a way to counteract it, I'm sure. Besides, I can't very well cancel his visit. I'm trying to earn the man's business."

"Just bear in mind that the more time you spend together and the more he hears your voice, the stronger this magic is going to get."

"But what if we realize we aren't compatible?"

"Sure. That'll happen. Because men find mermaids so off-putting."

"He doesn't know what I am."

"No, but has that ever stopped a mermaid's magic from working before?" Mattie asked. "Call me after he leaves and tell me how bad it is."

"I will. Sorry for making your job harder."

"You're not, I promise. It was already hard." Mattie laughed. "Talk to you later."

"Later." Undrea hung up and frowned. Why had she thought this visit was a good idea? Because of Roxy's thoughts. But Roxy could be right. Ethan could be totally wrong for her. And she could be totally wrong for him.

No doubt she was. His fiancée was proof of the kind of woman he liked. Sleek, sexy, and polished to a high shine. And Undrea was nothing like that.

She was just going to have to make him see that in the most obvious ways possible.

But how? She slipped into the employee bathroom to check her appearance. She looked the same as she had earlier. Light makeup, hair down and mostly air-dried, which had left her natural curls a little on the wild side. Minimal jewelry.

Tanks A Lot polo shirt and tan work pants with her favorite slip-on sneakers.

There wasn't much more she could do to be the anti-Nina. At least not appearance-wise. And from a manners and attitude point of view, Undrea felt like she was pretty different too.

She frowned at herself in the mirror. Maybe that was what he liked. How different she was.

But that implied he was only interested in her because she was the new and different thing.

That was good, right? After all, the new and different thing eventually became old and typical, didn't it?

She was confusing herself. She needed help. Or at least a collaborator. She went back out to the warehouse where Aaron was.

He looked up as she came out. "Hey, we had a stowaway in those new red crypts that came in."

That happened with freshwater aquarium plants. It was almost inevitable. "Let me guess. Snails?"

Freshwater aquarium snails were almost equally inevitable.

"Nope, come look. I put her in a quarantine tank."

"Her?" She followed Aaron over to the first small tank on the top shelf. Because it was a quarantine tank, there wasn't much in it.

He pointed. "Right there. Middle of the tank, left side."

Undrea peered in. Then gasped. "Oh, wow. A green jade? I knew that distributor had shrimp, but I didn't know they had jades. And she's berried, too."

The tiny green shrimp's undercarriage was loaded with minuscule eggs. Shrimplets in the making.

He nodded. "Yep. What do you want to do with her?"

Undrea grinned. "Feed her and set her up in a maternity ward."

Aaron laughed. "Are we going into the green jade business now?"

"Maybe. We'll see how she does. At the very least, I'll call APW and tell them we owe them for a green."

"I don't mind buying her off you. I could always set up another tank at home."

"Because the eight you have now aren't enough?"

"Nine. But who's counting?"

She laughed. "Listen, Ethan's on his way over for a tour. I think you might be right about him flirting with me. I'm going to make an excuse to leave for a few minutes during the tour. While I'm gone, I want you to suss him out. Man to man. You know what I mean?"

"Sure, see what I can find out about where his head is at with you."

"Exactly. Can you do that for me?"

"Absolutely."

"Don't punch him, though."

Aaron's brows lifted. "I don't punch people."

"Not regularly, no. But I know you can be a little protective of me."

"Come on."

She crossed her arms and gave him a knowing look. "The one night we invited you to Insomnia with us?"

He smiled. "Yeah, all right. I won't punch him."

11

Undrea's office was at the front of a warehouse in a more industrial part of the town. Ethan liked that. It made him feel like she was more focused on what the business needed to run properly than how the business looked. Which didn't mean the office would look bad. He was sure it would be just fine. It just didn't have a fancy exterior or the kind of high-rent address that a lot of businesses thought made them look successful.

Seemed very fitting to him. She was that way herself. More about what was really important and practical than about appearances or what anyone else thought. Hard not to appreciate that kind of approach to life.

He parked, walked to the office door, and went inside. The office was tastefully but simply done. A large aquarium filled with fish and greenery featured prominently against the wall of the small waiting area. Across from that was a reception desk.

The young woman sitting there smiled up at him instantly. "Good afternoon and welcome to Tanks A Lot and you're Ethan Edmonds." Her words came out in a rush, and her smile went slack as she recognized him.

He laughed. "Yes, I am. You must be Whitney."

"You know my name." She sucked in a breath. "How do you— Never mind. We talked earlier. When you called. But Undrea didn't say you were *the* Ethan Edmonds. Wow." She stood up and stuck her hand out. "I am such a fan."

He shook her hand. "Thank you. I'm a fan of yours too. High energy, pleasant manners, quick to respond. Undrea certainly knew what she was doing when she hired you."

Whitney's expression had gone from earnest fan-girl to slightly dazed. "Thank you. I handle the social media too."

"I had a feeling there was more to you than phones." He smiled. "Undrea is expecting me."

"I'll let her know you're here." She scooted around the desk and went through a metal door at the back of the small reception area.

He stayed where he was, hands in his pockets, gazing at the fish tank and all the activity within. He didn't wait long.

Undrea came through the door a few moments later with Whitney behind her. "Hi, Ethan."

"Hi." He shook her offered hand. "Nice to see you again."

"You too."

Whitney went back behind her desk but continued to gaze at him adoringly.

Undrea pushed the door open and motioned for him to come through. "Come on, I'll give you the grand tour and the not so grand tour."

He laughed. "I can't wait."

They walked into the warehouse space, and he was immediately struck by how neat and organized it was. And clean. It even smelled nice. Like the sea.

Then he realized that was Undrea.

She chuckled softly. "You made quite an impression on Whitney. I've never seen her flustered. Not once. That girl is about as cool and collected as they come. At least until you showed up."

"Sorry about that."

Undrea glanced at him. "It's not your fault my admin is a fan. A big fan."

"Well, I like her too. I generally consider myself a pretty good judge of character, especially when it comes to employees. She strikes me as someone with the drive and ability to go places."

Undrea nodded as they came to a stop. "I hope so because that's what I think, too. I hired her right out of college because I needed someone to take care of the general admin stuff, but then as soon as she found out how much I hated social media, she offered to take that over for me, and she's done a fantastic job."

His brows lifted in amusement. "You hate social media?"

"Yes. The world would be a better place without it. Sorry, I know that's kind of your thing, but—"

"No need to apologize. I understand. Besides, I sold Blnk. I take it you're not one of its millions of users then?"

"Nope."

"If you're not on social media, you probably wouldn't need it anyway."

She smiled. "I'm not. Whitney does all of that." She turned a little and gestured toward the space before them. "As you can see, this is our warehouse space. It's divided into two main areas. The fish rooms where we keep our stock of the most popular fish used in our setups and also any special-order fish that we get in for clients."

She pointed to another door marked Workshop. "Through there is my engineer's office. Aaron Rigby. You met him at lunch."

"I remember."

"And out here is where we do the actual tank builds and the building of all the equipment that goes into those tanks to run them and process the water."

She took a step backwards, toward the rooms on the side. "Let's go see the fish rooms first."

"Okay."

She took him into the first one. The lighting was low, except for what was used to illuminate the tanks. "This is our freshwater room."

He stopped almost immediately. "Why don't the tanks on this first wall have any decorations in them?"

"Great question. Those are quarantine tanks. Our hospital tanks look the same way. A bare tank makes it easier to assess a fish's health but also makes it easy to net them for moving to a different tank. An empty tank is also a snap to clean because it's so much less work to strip down."

"Oh, right. Makes sense." He pointed to the tanks. "So all the fish in here are in quarantine?"

"Yep. Once we know they're fine, they'll go into gen pop."

He laughed. "You make it sound like prison."

She shook her head, clearly amused. "I promise you, it's not. Our fish are very well taken care of, and all of our freshwater tanks are planted, giving the fish the most natural environment possible."

"Like the tank in the front office?"

"Exactly like that. Live aquatic plants produce their own oxygen and use the fish waste as food. A planted tank basically becomes a closed ecosystem. It's very possible to run one without a filter."

"Interesting. I like that idea a lot. Maybe I should do a freshwater planted tank instead of saltwater."

"Really?" Her brows lifted. "You certainly could. A nine-hundred-gallon planted tank could really be amazing."

"Yeah?"

"Absolutely. You could do several large groups of schooling fish, a few bigger show fish, some amazing bottom dwellers. And the scape you could do would be phenomenal. Think anything from mangrove-style roots to a fully grassed floor. We'd want to go longer versus taller, but it would really be something."

He couldn't stop smiling. He loved how excited

she got talking about something she loved, which was obviously fish. "That sounds pretty cool."

"It is. And you can still do shrimp. The varieties of freshwater shrimp would probably surprise you. Actually, look at this."

She led him to one of the bare tanks. "See that shrimp in there?"

He peered in, letting his gaze travel until he located the little guy. "Hey, it's green."

"Yep. A green jade. That's her trade name. She's pregnant, too. See the cluster of white eggs under her abdomen?"

He nodded. "That is really cool. Is she in quarantine?"

"Yes. But mostly because she was a stowaway. She came in from one of our suppliers hidden in some plants. It happens. But because she's one of the rarer colors and pregnant, we're going to take special care of her. We're going to get her set up with some moss and floating plants to make her feel safe. Probably a little piece of wood too."

"I like the idea of the shrimp. I'm liking the whole freshwater tank idea, really. I never even considered it. I guess I thought it was mostly goldfish."

"Nope. There is so much more. I'd be happy to show you some examples. It would be a cheaper tank, too. Not that you probably care about that, but freshwater doesn't carry the same price tag saltwater does. Not in the setup, the stocking, or the maintenance."

"I'd definitely like to see some examples." It was

rare someone tried to sell him something that cost less. He liked her more and more.

"All right, I'll send you some links this afternoon. Give you some ideas of what can be accomplished." She moved toward the door. "Let's go look at the saltwater room anyway, though, because when it comes to showy color, you can't beat saltwater."

She took him through that room, pointing out some of the fish that he could do in his tank, then they went out to the warehouse.

It was a very different space. Bright, with tall ceilings and a lot of wide-open space. Equipment lined the walls, as did lengths of lumber, enormous sheets plywood and more sheets of thick, clear acrylic coated in paper to keep it pristine.

"This is where we build the custom tanks and the housings that will hold their equipment."

Aaron walked toward them. Seeing him when he wasn't sitting at a booth made Ethan realize the guy was built like a football player, although the short hair and tattoos peeking out from his shirtsleeves made him look more like former military. Aaron stuck his hand out. "Nice to see you again, Ethan."

"You too, Aaron. So this is your department out here, huh?"

"More or less." Aaron stuck his hands on his hips. "How'd you like that peach cobbler?"

"Man, that was so good."

"You can't go wrong with Howler's cobbler." With a grin, Aaron pivoted toward the open space behind him. "We don't have a tank being built at the moment, but I'm happy to walk you through the process."

"Great."

Undrea held her hand up. "If you could excuse me for a moment? I just remembered something I need to check on. Be right back, Ethan. You're in good hands."

"No problem," Ethan said. He got the sense this was preplanned, but he was okay with that.

As Undrea left, Aaron walked him to where the big sheets of acrylic were. "These are what we build our custom tanks from. Acrylic is lot lighter than glass and allows us great flexibility in our designs."

"My tank will be acrylic?"

"Most likely. That's a pretty big tank you're talking about. Going with glass would really increase the weight load. The downside with acrylic is that it does scratch, but that's just something you have to be aware of. If we're doing your maintenance and cleaning, it's not something you have to worry that much about."

"Good to know."

Aaron paused for a moment, a little smile bending his mouth. "You like Undrea, don't you?"

Ethan smiled. This was why she'd left them. He was sure of it. "I do."

Aaron's gaze narrowed, and Ethan prepared himself for some sort of big brother speech. "Don't you have a fiancée?"

Ethan frowned. "A fiancée? No."

Aaron's brows popped up. "Really? Because that's

how your girlfriend introduced herself to Undrea when she called. Ethan Edmond's fiancée."

Ethan grimaced. "That sounds like Nina. She'd like to be my fiancée, but I'm not there yet. Girlfriend is as far as I'd go." And soon that wouldn't be true either.

"But you live together. And yet you're flirting with my boss."

"Okay, let's back up a step. You're clearly protective of her, which I appreciate very much. And yes, I like her. A lot." He took a breath. "So much so that it's made me rethink some things. Well, one thing anyway. Nina."

Aaron frowned. "What does that mean?"

He was about to confess something very personal to this man. That wasn't something he ever did. But he didn't want Aaron to think he had nefarious intentions toward Undrea. "It means that I have come to the realization that Nina is not my future."

Aaron blinked. "That's heavy."

Ethan nodded. "I didn't get to where I am by being afraid of taking risks, and I take a lot of them. But attaching myself to a woman who doesn't feel like the right choice isn't the kind of risk I like to take. I plan on talking to Nina this afternoon when I get home. I'm going to lay it all out."

He didn't relish that, but it had to be done. "Part of the reason I came here today was to see your operation. The other part was to see if the chemistry I felt between myself and Undrea was real or imagined."

"And?" Aaron asked.

Ethan smiled again. "I really do like her. Enough that I want to get to know her better."

Aaron seemed to take that in but said nothing.

"You want to weigh in on that?" Ethan asked.

"You're both adults. You can make your own choices."

"But?" Ethan waited.

Aaron stared like he was trying to see into Ethan's soul. "But if you hurt her, I will kick your—"

The warehouse door opened and Undrea walked out. "How's it going?"

Aaron gave her a big smile, which Ethan took as a positive sign. "Going great, boss."

Ethan nodded and wondered if he'd just passed some kind of test. He asked some questions during the rest of the tour, but his mind was working overtime. Not enough to keep him from having a very enjoyable time and learning a little more about Undrea, but two things became very clear.

Not only did he need to talk to Nina, but he needed to talk to Undrea as well.

As his visit came to a close, he made his move. "Would you walk out to my car with me?"

She looked surprised but nodded. "Sure."

He said goodbye to Aaron and Whitney, then he and Undrea went outside. He didn't waste any time. He stopped by his car and turned toward her. "I understand you think Nina is my fiancée. Because she introduced herself to you that way."

"That's right. She did. And I do."

He put a hand on the trunk. "She's not. We aren't engaged. Never have been. We've been together for two years, and as much as she hints at an engagement, it's never happened. Nor will it, despite the fact that we're living together. Which basically came about because she kind of gradually moved herself in with me. And I was too caught up in the sale of Blnk to pay close attention."

"Okay. Can I ask why you're telling me this?"

"Because I like you. And I didn't want you to get the wrong impression of me. That I was involved but also looking for something else." He frowned. "That's just shady and underhanded and not my style. At all."

"That's good to know." She crossed her arms. "But that doesn't change the fact that you're still living with her."

"I am. At least for a little while longer." He exhaled. "When I get home, I'm going to tell her how I really feel. I'm going to break it off. I'm also going to let her know I expect her to move out immediately."

"Wow." Her eyes widened. "I did not see that coming. And I do not envy you that conversation."

"Thanks. I'm not looking forward to it either, but you've made me realize that I want a different kind of woman in my life. I *need* a different kind of woman. One...more like you."

Her eyes went even wider. "Ethan, I don't know what to say."

"You don't have to say anything because I know

this is a lot to take in. I like you. I think you like me. If you don't, that's fine. But I wouldn't mind knowing that this chemistry I'm feeling isn't one-sided."

"And if it is? Are you going to stay with Nina?"

He shook his head. "No. That relationship is over regardless."

"It's not. One-sided. The chemistry, I mean. I like you too."

He smiled. "Great. Once I'm unencumbered, why don't we go out to dinner and see how that goes? Take it slow. Get to know each other. I'm in no rush."

"That sounds good. We can definitely do that. You have my number."

"I do?"

She nodded. "It's on my business card."

He reached into his pocket, pulled out the card, and took a look. "So I do. How about that. Pretty bold move putting your personal cell on your business card."

She shrugged. "When you're dealing with aquariums and fish, there can be emergencies. The last thing I need is someone freaking out because they have a leak at 3 a.m. and can't reach me. So I put my number on there. So far, no one's actually called me at 3 a.m., but I suppose there's always a first time."

"I won't be that person, I promise." With a little laugh, he took out his phone and texted her. "There. Now you have my number too."

"Thanks."

He nodded as he stuck his phone back in his pocket and reached for his car door. "Don't go selling that on eBay to the highest bidder now."

She laughed. "I'll do my best." Then her expression went serious again. "Good luck with Nina."

He sighed. "Thanks. I'm going to need it."

12

Ethan went straight home, buoyed by his conversation with Undrea and, although not looking forward to the talk with Nina, eager to get it over with.

As soon as he walked in, he found her in the living room on her laptop looking at furniture. He sat down across from her and laid it all out, speaking from the heart with as much kindness and honesty as possible. She listened without reaction until he was done.

Her eyes narrowed in contemplation, and she stared at him for a moment without answering. Then she shook her head. "No."

Ethan frowned. "What do you mean no?"

"I mean we are *not* breaking up." She closed her laptop, set it aside, and crossed her arms. "You've had your head turned by some little piece of local action, and I am not about to ignore our last two years together because you think the fish girl is hot and available."

"Nina, that is not what I said. Not even remotely." He wanted to tell her to stop calling Undrea the fish girl, but Nina would latch onto that as proof of what she was saying.

She shook her head. "You're a man. Your head is always going to be turned by what's new. I'm not going to let you throw away what we have because your brains are all in your pants."

His teeth clamped together, and a soft growl gathered in his throat. "You aren't listening to me. This isn't about some new shiny, this is about us not being right for each other."

"Which you only think because of the new shiny." She got up, walked into the kitchen, and came back with her purse. "You need time to think about this, and I'm willing to give you that time. I have to go out anyway because you forgot the almond milk."

So he had. But then his mind had been on more important things. "Time isn't going to change anything."

"We'll see. I'll be back in a bit." She had her keys in her hand, but she stopped just before opening the door. "I want you to know I don't blame you for this. To be honest, I'm surprised it's just happening now. I understand you are a very desirable man and women are going to want you. But Ethan, those women aren't going to be able to handle the pressures of being your partner the way I do. You need a woman capable of dealing with all the stress and attention of being at your side. Not to mention a woman who can take care of you when you've had one of your spells. Think about that. You'll see I'm right."

She walked out, leaving him a little dumbstruck by her reaction.

He'd expected her to rant and rave. But to flat-out refuse to accept they were breaking up? He hadn't prepared for that.

Undrea went back into her office, a little stunned by the conversation she'd just had. Ethan was breaking up with Nina and all because of feelings Undrea had awakened in him. Or rather, her magic, but he didn't know that.

His news was a lot to take in. Her entire foot and ankle ached now. The one thing that made it easier to bear was that he'd said he was breaking up with Nina regardless of Undrea's feelings about him. That took a little of the weight off of her.

She kept walking until she was in the warehouse and next to Aaron, who was crouched down and rearranging the coral casts on the bottom shelf. "What did you say to him?"

He looked up. "I'm assuming you mean Ethan. I asked him why a man with a fiancée was sniffing around my boss."

She pressed her fingers to the middle of her forehead. "Please tell me you did not say sniffing around."

"Not in those exact words. But that was the gist of it. And then he explained that he wasn't really engaged and things with his girlfriend were about to change in a big way and that he was definitely interested in you. Then I threatened him a little if he hurt you and you came back in." Aaron shrugged. "That's about it."

"He told me all of the same stuff outside just now. Except for you threatening him." She sighed and shook her head but couldn't help but smile. "Aaron, you're awful and wonderful and thank you."

He grinned. "You're welcome. Us waterkin have to stick together."

"We do." She turned as she stood to lean against the shelving. "You think he's really going to do it?"

"Break up with her?"

"Yes."

"He has to now. Or he looks like a liar."

"True." She glanced at the time on the big warehouse clock. The day would be over shortly. "I guess we'll know soon enough, huh?"

Aaron nodded. "I imagine you will, anyway."

She didn't move. "What do you think of him?"

"As far as billionaires go?" Aaron laughed. "He seems like a genuinely nice guy. But that's based on a pretty short assessment period."

"I trust your judgment all the same. You either like people or you don't."

"That is true. Not sure that's a good quality."

"Right now, I'm going with it. Because my judgment can't be trusted."

He stood up, making a face. "Why not?"

She took a breath and realized she hadn't told him about her first meeting with Ethan at the lake. "Well..." She gave him the short version that didn't include her true identity.

His expression took on a look of amusement. "Undrea, you are in serious trouble."

She nodded. He had no idea. "I know. Do your kind have anything like that?"

"Magical kisses? Not that I know of. But we have our own weird lore." He brushed off his hands. "You have Mattie working on this, right?"

"I do. And I should probably call her and give her an update." She started for the office.

"Tell her I said hi."

Undrea smiled and decided to tease him a little. "You're not her type."

"Tell her anyway."

Back in her office, Undrea dialed Mattie right away. No answer, which could mean she was outside or elbow-deep in honey. Undrea left a quick voicemail to tell her she'd spoken to Ethan and things had changed for the better.

Then, on impulse, she called Roxy next. That call also went to voicemail, so Undrea left a very similar message.

A few minutes after she hung up, her phone rang. Mattie calling her back.

"Hey, did you listen to my voicemail?"

"No," Mattie said. "I just saw that I'd missed your call and wanted to get back to you right away. I was labeling a new batch of mead."

"I figured it was something like that." Undrea took a breath. "Ethan was just here."

"Mm-hmm. And how did that go?"

"His fiancée was never his fiancée—that was just her being overly enthusiastic—and brace yourself: He's breaking up with her and telling her she has to move out. Then he wants to take me to dinner."

Mattie was silent long enough to make Undrea wonder if she was still on the line. "I don't know how I feel about this. Is he breaking up with his girlfriend because he's under the spell of your magic? If so, what's going to happen when that spell is broken?"

Undrea stared at the small five-gallon tank on her desk that housed her beta fish. "I hadn't thought about that."

"Well, you might want to, because it sounds to me like this is all in motion and there's no stopping it. Whatever happens, you'd better be prepared to step up and deal with it."

"You mean because she's going to be mad at me?"

"That, but also because there's a good chance he's going to be following you around like a lovesick puppy dog. You know how your magic works."

"No, I don't. Not really. I've never seen it in action. I just know what I've been told."

"Even so, you'd best prepare yourself."

The ache in her foot spread up her shin. Undrea groaned softly. "I need to go home and soak in the tub."

"Probably a good idea. Call me if anything happens?"

"I will. Thanks. Hey, are we on for Friday?"

"Yes."

"Excellent. Talk to you soon." Undrea hung up, shut down her computer, turned off the lights in her office and went out to the warehouse. "Aaron?"

"Yeah, boss?"

"I'm going home for the day. Feel free to knock off early too if you want. Just don't leave Whitney here by herself."

"I won't. I'll finish what I'm doing, then she and I can both go. Organizing the rest of the molds can wait until tomorrow. I'll text Amanda and Curtis to finish up their maintenance appointments and call it a day as well. Have a good night."

"Thanks. You too." She went out the front and stopped at Whitney's desk. "I'm headed out now. Aaron's finishing up his work too, then you can both go, okay?"

Whitney looked up from her screen. "I was going to stay late and update the website. But I could do that at home too."

Undrea tilted her head. "Are you counting all that extra time? I don't want you working unpaid."

"I am. Promise. What about Amanda and Curtis?"

"Aaron's already texting them."

"All right. See you tomorrow."

"You too." Undrea went to her car and straight home. As soon as she got behind the wheel, she called and ordered her dinner from Thai Garden to be delivered. She was not in the mood to cook. And Thai Garden was exactly what she needed. She ordered crispy spring rolls, steamed shrimp dumplings, soup, seafood pad Thai, and tempura cheesecake with caramel drizzle, because why not?

There wouldn't be leftovers. And she was going to eat it in the tub in her mermaid form while watching reruns of *Fantasy Island.* Because it had been that kind of day.

She got home and went through her usual routine of turning on the outside lights, checking on the fish in her living-room aquarium, then doing a little straightening up. There was no point to getting in the tub until her dinner arrived, so she started a load of wash and folded the basket of towels she hadn't yet gotten to.

As she was putting those towels away, her doorbell rang. She smiled. That was fast. But Thai Garden usually was. She turned on the water to start filling the tub and went to answer the door.

But the woman standing on her porch wasn't the regular delivery person from Thai Garden. It was Nina.

"What are you doing at my house?" Undrea had about a thousand other questions, but that seemed like the most pertinent.

Nina glared at her. "Stay away from Ethan, do you understand? He's not for you."

"Or what?"

"Or else," Nina snarled.

Job or no job, Undrea wasn't about to be threatened like this. "You're trespassing. If you want to speak to me, you can call my office."

She started to close the door, but Nina stuck her hand out and stopped it. "I don't think you understand who you're dealing with."

"I understand perfectly." The jilted girlfriend. At least Undrea assumed Nina had been jilted. Of course, that also assumed Ethan had had the talk with her. But then why else would Nina be here?

"Do you?" Nina leaned in, and Undrea saw tiny sparks in her eyes. The kind that signaled magic lived within. "You're not human, fish girl. I know that. I know most people in this town aren't, either. That's why I wanted to move here. But make no mistake, whatever you are, I'm more powerful than you can imagine. And I will not allow Ethan to be taken from me. Do I make myself clear?"

Undrea held back the curse dancing on her tongue. "I knew you weren't exactly human either." Actually, she hadn't had a clue. Merfolk were lousy at detecting other supernaturals. "So what are you?"

Nina's gaze narrowed, and her chin lifted. "I am a rare witch. Cross me, and you will pay the price."

Undrea had no idea what a rare witch was. But again, she wasn't especially versed in all the kinds of supernaturals that existed. "I haven't crossed you, and I haven't made any kind of play for Ethan. You need to understand that."

Nina glared a second longer and looked like she was about to say something else when a car pulled into Undrea's drive. Her Thai food had arrived. Nina took a step back. "Just stay away and you won't force my hand."

With that, she took off, jumping into her car and pulling away before the Thai Garden guy made it onto the front porch.

Undrea watched her go, furious in a way she couldn't accurately describe. She'd bet good money that Ethan had no idea Nina was a witch or that she'd come to Undrea's house.

"Evening, ma'am. That'll be thirty-two eighty-seven."

"Just a second," Undrea said, still staring after Nina. "I need to get my money. And turn the water off in my tub. I'll be right back."

She ran to the bathroom, turned the water off, then grabbed her wallet and paid the guy, making sure to include a good tip. She took the food as he handed it over. "Thanks. Have a good evening."

She locked the door, still miffed by Nina's appearance. What utter nerve. And to threaten Undrea like that... Nina clearly thought a lot of herself.

But what was a rare witch? Undrea put the bag of food, which smelled amazing, on the kitchen table then sat for a few minutes, thinking it over and replaying the conversation in her head. She didn't have a clue about the whole rare witch thing. But she knew someone who did. She grabbed her phone.

Pandora answered on the third ring. "Hey, Undrea, what's up?"

"Hi, Pandora. I won't keep you long, but I have a quick, random question for you."

"Shoot."

"What's a rare witch?"

"You mean like the rarest kind of witch? I'm not sure. I'd have to ask my mom. Or Alice Bishop. Although she might qualify as a rare witch, all things considered."

"No, I don't mean the rarest kind. I mean like if it were the same thing as a green witch or a Celtic witch or a fire witch. What's a rare witch?"

"That's…not a thing."

"Listen, someone just told me they were a rare witch. It has to be a thing."

"Hmm. You should ask my mom. I can give you her number."

"I don't want to bother her."

"She won't care. In fact, I'll text her and let her know you're going to call."

"You're sure?"

"Positive. If she doesn't know, she can ask around. Maybe even ask Alice Bishop. Although besides them, I'm not sure who else could answer this one for you. Mattie isn't as tied in as the rest of us."

"Which is why I called you. I thought you'd have a better shot at answering this one." Mattie hadn't joined the coven. She said Celtic witches were solitary creatures and the bees were all the coven she needed. "Okay, I'll call your mom."

"Great. I'll text her, then send you her number."

"Thanks. Oh, hey, are you going Friday night?"

"Insomnia? You know it."

"Awesome." Undrea smiled. Pandora was married to Cole, one of the professors at the local academy, but she still liked to get out with her friends when she could. "See you then."

They hung up, and Pandora's text came in shortly after.

Undrea dialed Corette Williams's number, feeling a little nervous. Corette ran the bridal shop in town, but she was also the secretary of the Nocturne Falls coven, which made her a pretty important and powerful witch.

But then, that was why she was a likely candidate to answer Undrea's question.

Corette answered right away. "Good evening. Is this Undrea?"

"Yes, ma'am. Pandora said I should call you."

"I'm happy to help. What can I do for you?"

"Someone just told me that they were a rare witch, and I was wondering what that means?"

Corette laughed softly. "I haven't heard that a while. Let me see…how to best explain. A rare witch is often what very weak witches call themselves. The only thing rare about them is usually how little power they wield. It sounds impressive to the uninformed, but it protects the witch from claiming powers she doesn't have."

"So a witch could get in trouble for that?"

"If someone really wanted to make an issue of it and bring it up to the council, the witch could find themselves in a little bit of trouble. Censured, perhaps."

"That's interesting. So you think this woman is a witch but not a very strong one?"

"Yes, that's right. Most *rare* witches have a very thin bloodline of magic. So thin that at best they might be able to light a candle with their magic or stir a cup of tea."

"Or find where someone lived?"

"Yes, something like that." Corette paused. "Did this person know you were a mermaid?"

"No, but she knew I wasn't human."

"That might be the extent of her powers then. Being able to tell you're a supernatural but not what kind."

"Huh. Would another witch be able to tell how powerful she is? Or isn't, as the case may be?"

"Possibly. But weak magic is hard to detect. There are plenty of humans with a tiny strain of power in them, and it amounts to no more than knowing when the phone is about to ring or having a strong hunch that comes true. That kind of thin magic often manifests as a weighted feeling or premonition. All of those people could just as easily call themselves rare witches too."

"So I have nothing to worry about from her?"

"I would say no. Just a moment, now. Did this woman threaten you?"

"You could say that."

"That's another matter altogether. You could absolutely file a complaint with the council, if you so desired."

"I don't. I really don't think this is going to turn into anything. She's just mad about something she can't control. But, for the sake of curiosity, what would I have to do to file a complaint?"

"You'd have to appear before three members of the local coven, explain your case, the threat that was made, name the woman, and swear on your own supernatural abilities that you're telling the truth. It's actually a very simple procedure. It might not be a bad thing to do, either. It would establish your case now. And if she were to approach you again, you'd already have things underway."

Undrea nodded, but she already knew this wasn't something she could do. Not if swearing on her own supernatural abilities meant revealing what she was truly capable of. It wasn't a chance she wanted to take. "I'll think about it. Thank you so much for all of this information. I feel a lot better now."

"You're very welcome. Let me know if there's anything else I can do to help."

"I will. Have a good night."

"You, too, Undrea."

She hung up and thought about what Corette had told her. Getting the complaint underway wasn't a bad idea, but not if it meant admitting the truth about what she was. That wasn't something she was about to do.

Not for Nina, the weaksauce witch.

13

Ethan wasn't quite sure what to do. Nina couldn't just refuse to break up with him. Could she?

He understood her point. Whoever went out with him had to be prepared for a certain amount of pressure and scrutiny because she would eventually become a news article and because of that, a minor celebrity. She'd be scrutinized and criticized. That was just the way of things in his life.

But was that such a big deal? He lived under the same magnifying glass and he'd learned to ignore it.

As for his blacking-out issues, was it so difficult to care for him on those rare occasions? He didn't think Nina had ever done more than get him to a safe place to lie down. Not that he could remember anything that happened when those episodes took place.

In his opinion, those things weren't enough reason for Nina to act like she was his only option for a partner. That was ridiculous. And the longer he thought about it, the angrier he got. He waited for her to return, which she finally did after what seemed like an awfully long time to get almond milk.

"Nina, it's over between us."

"I already told you that it's not." She walked past him and into the kitchen.

He followed her. "Saying that means nothing. Just like your refusal to accept what's happening changes nothing. Refusing to believe the sky is blue doesn't make it green."

She took the almond milk out of the bag, stuck it in the refrigerator, then turned to look at him. "Ethan, you are a brilliant man in many ways. Knowing what's best for yourself on a personal level isn't one of them. Look at the state of your love life when I met you."

He frowned. She wasn't wrong. He was dating a well-meaning young woman who couldn't make a decision to save her life, which had left him feeling exhausted and like he was the only one putting any effort into the relationship.

Nina's decisiveness had been a breath of fresh air and one of the things he'd loved about her right away.

The bloom was off that rose, however.

"I'm not the same person I was then."

She smiled. "Neither of us are. Thankfully. Now I promise all you need is a good night's sleep, and in the morning, you'll see things much more clearly. This infatuation with the fish girl is just a…blip on the radar of life. A passing fancy. You'll see."

"You're wrong."

"Am I?" Her smile had a coy undertone. "I bet you'll find she's cooled off toward you tomorrow. Because after a night of thinking of it over, she's going to realize just how much work it is being involved with a man like you. How much sacrifice it requires." Nina shook her head slowly. "Not a lot of women are up for that kind of effort. Or being scrutinized by social media."

Was that true? He backed away, suddenly giving serious thought to what she'd said. He didn't believe her. But she'd still managed to open a crack of doubt in his confidence. He needed to get away from her. Really away.

Out of the house.

She poured herself a glass of wine. "I'm going upstairs to take a bath, and then I'm going to bed to read."

She didn't wait for him to respond, just took her wine and left.

As soon as she was gone and he heard the bedroom door shut, he grabbed his keys and went out the front door. He started driving without knowing where he was going, but he ended up heading toward town. He wasn't sure that was where he wanted to be, but where else was he going to go?

He parked, pulled on a ball cap, and walked, drifting through the crowds of tourists, who paid no attention to him. The dark gave him a little cover, as did the hat.

Several minutes in and he found himself at a park in the center of town. It had a big gargoyle fountain.

People were throwing coins in and making wishes and asking the gargoyle questions, which the creature answered.

Ethan smiled. That was pretty clever. The animatronics looked remarkably lifelike. And the answers never repeated either. Whoever was behind this bit of entertainment had done an outstanding job.

He sat for a while, watching people, but the number of couples that went by made it impossible for his thoughts not to return to Nina.

How dare she tell him they weren't breaking up? That wasn't for her to decide. It was over, and she needed to move out. And on. Granted, they'd just moved into that house. He'd have to give her some time to find a new place. That wasn't an issue. He'd be happy to do that.

He had more money than she did, so he'd move out while she looked for a place. In fact, maybe he'd do that tomorrow. Provided he could find a place that would take Bowie.

He couldn't go back to the New York apartment because it was being painted. And the place in L.A. no longer held much appeal. Maybe he'd buy something else.

But then, why should he be the one to leave this town? He suddenly felt the need to stay in Nocturne Falls. And why not? After all, Undrea was here.

He smiled. Then the smile vanished. He'd have to tell Undrea what was going on. Bring her up to speed. For one thing, now was not the time to be installing an enormous fish tank.

He looked at the time. It wasn't that late. After all, he'd promised not to be that needy customer at 3 a.m. He took his phone out and sent her a quick text. *Sorry for this, but I need to put the fish tank on hold for now.*

He set his phone on the bench beside him and went back to watching the gargoyle. The smell of caramel corn drifted past, making him realize he hadn't eaten any dinner. Well, there were a lot of places to choose from. He tried to remember the two other restaurants Undrea and Aaron had mentioned.

His phone vibrated with an incoming message. He picked it up and read Undrea's response. *I'm sorry to hear that but I understand. Is this because of the talk with Nina?*

A moment later, another text from her arrived. *Ignore that. Not my business.*

He smiled. *Yes, it is because of that.* He hit send, then started typing again. *Any chance you could meet me for dinner? Or a drink? Or coffee?*

I could definitely meet you for dinner. Where?

I'm sitting in the park. Where the gargoyle is. What's close?

Mummy's Diner. I can be there in fifteen minutes or so. You need directions?

I'll find it. He couldn't stop smiling. *See you there.*

Undrea drained the tub. She'd been searching the term rare witch on her laptop and the water had cooled off anyway. She'd soak later. Her food had cooled too, so she put the entire bag from Thai Garden into the fridge for tomorrow's dinner. Or breakfast. Whatever, it would get eaten.

But after Nina's surprise visit, there was no way Undrea was missing a chance to see Ethan. It was like she was morally obligated to go just to prove to Nina how unafraid of her rare witch self she was.

Rare witch. Undrea snorted. Witch, please.

She changed into skinny jeans, a gray striped V-neck sweater, some dangly earrings, and silver flats. Then she added some extra makeup. Nothing crazy, just a swoop of eyeliner, another coat of mascara and some plum lip gloss. She finger-combed her hair and scrunched it a little with wet hands to revive the curls, which was all her hair ever really needed, then grabbed her purse and jumped in her car.

It took her a couple of minutes longer than expected to get to Mummy's because town was busy. She wasn't sure why. Just tourists, she supposed. But then she didn't often come to town in the evenings, so maybe it was always like this?

Parking took another minute, and by the time she was headed into Mummy's, she was five minutes late. She didn't like that, but it couldn't be helped.

Ethan already had a booth. He waved at her, smiling.

She joined him, sliding into the empty side. "Hiya."

"Hiya yourself. You look nice."

"Thanks. Sorry I'm late. I didn't realize there'd be so much traffic."

"No problem. I had to wait a few minutes for the booth anyway. I just got seated." He glanced at his menu. "You've eaten here, right?"

"Many times. It's all pretty good."

"Great, because I'm starving."

She smiled. "So am I. To be honest, I was just about to eat when you called, but your offer was better."

He looked up. "Yeah? I feel honored."

She shrugged. "I had to come." Should she tell him about Nina? She kind of had to, didn't she?

"You had to?" He pushed his glasses back. "Because I canceled the tank and you want to talk me out of that?"

"What?" She laughed and shook her head. "No. Because Nina showed up at my house tonight, and you should probably know what kind of crazy you're getting rid of."

All humor left his face. "She what?"

Undrea nodded. "Not sure how she found my house, but then it's probably not that hard to do with Google and whatnot. But yeah. She basically told me to stay away from you or else, and I don't take well to those sorts of threats, so how could I not show up? To be honest, I still hate social media, but I've never wanted to post a selfie with you so bad as I do right now."

He was still staring. "I am so sorry. That's inexcusable."

Undrea shrugged. "Eh. I mean, it's all over with now, right?"

"Not...exactly." He blew out a breath. "I told her we were done, and she said no, we weren't."

Undrea tipped her head. "She said you weren't?"

"Yep. She refused to accept it."

"Can she do that?"

"Yes and no. I'm powerless to make her accept it, but I'm certainly not going to wait around with my life on hold until she does. In fact, the reason I texted you about canceling the tank is I've come to the decision that I need to move out."

"You just bought that house."

"I'm not moving out permanently. Just until she's gone. And my leaving will show her just how serious I am."

"I think that's a good idea."

He smiled again, finally. "Do you know any place that will take pets? I can't leave Bowie there."

She shrugged. "I could take Bowie."

Still smiling, he shook his head. "That's really sweet of you, but we're a package deal."

The image of Nina's scowl remained firmly planted in Undrea's head. "Then I guess I'll have to take both of you."

He blinked. "What?"

"I have a guest room. It's not the Ritz or anything but—"

"I really appreciate that, but I can afford a place. I promise."

"But how fast can you find one? Town looks pretty busy to me. And you need a place that will take a cat. I'm not saying you have to move in with me for the rest of your life. I'm just saying if you want out tonight, my guest room is yours." She smiled. "And Bowie's."

He didn't say anything for a moment, so she continued. "Look, none of this would be happening if you hadn't met me. That makes me partially responsible."

His eyes narrowed slightly. "Maybe that's a little true. But are you also doing this because Nina showed up at your house?"

Undrea gave him a stern look. He really was a smart guy. "Let's just say I don't take kindly to threats. And she needs to know what sort of woman she's dealing with. Also, I have a pretty serious crush on Bowie, so this is my opportunity to get closer to him."

Ethan snorted. "You're something else, Undrea."

He had no idea. "Does that mean you're taking me up on my offer?"

He hesitated. Then nodded. "Yes. But only because I want out of there tonight and only on a temporary basis. I'm sure I'll find something tomorrow."

"Good. You're buying dinner."

His smile widened. "I wouldn't have it any other way."

They both ordered cheeseburgers. She got hers with cheddar, extra pickles, and a side of onion rings. She left the anchovies off, for his sake. He got his with pepper jack and jalapeños and a side of fries with cheese. He also ordered a vanilla milkshake, while she got a cherry Coke.

She nodded as the server went off to put their orders in. "You eat like a frat boy, I see."

He laughed. "I'm comfort eating, I suppose."

"Do guys do that?"

He nodded. "I guess we do." He gave her a more serious look. "You sure you're okay with me staying with you?"

"I wouldn't have invited you if I wasn't. Look, I realize I don't know you very well, but you're a pretty well-known guy. I feel fairly certain you're not a celebrity tech guy *and* a serial killer." Besides, she could overpower him pretty easily if she wanted to. In more ways than one. If anything, he was the one that ought to be scared.

Well, not scared exactly. But wary. Then again, he had no idea whose home he was about to be a guest in.

He held his hands up. "I promise, I'm not a serial killer."

"Good," she said. "I promise I'm not either. As far as you know."

That made him laugh, and when their food was delivered, they attacked it.

Undrea was so hungry that she chowed down with the kind of gusto usually reserved for home. She took a breath and reminded herself that not only was she in public, but she was sitting across from a guy she found attractive. She didn't want him to think she was uncouth.

Then again, he was moving in with her. He was about to find out she wasn't the most ladylike of ladies.

She wiped Mummy's burger sauce off the corner of her mouth and looked up to find him watching her. It was too late, apparently, to pretend like she was refined and dainty. "I know. I eat like a linebacker, right?"

He shook his head, amusement in his gaze. "You eat like someone who actually likes food. I didn't mean to stare. I just haven't seen that in a while, that's all."

Undrea grinned. "How's your burger?"

"Really good. This is another great place. You're two for two so far."

"You'll have to try Salvatore's pizza then, and it can be three for three."

"All right. Tomorrow night then. It's a date."

"Oh," she said, shaking her head. "I can't. I have a girls' night out thing."

"That sounds fun."

"Actually, we could go early. Right when I get off from work. What do you think? Then I'd have time to get ready and meet my friends. Or is that too soon for you to eat dinner?"

He leaned in. "What if we do lunch instead? Then you won't be rushed."

"I love that idea. Okay, lunch it is."

And just like that, she and Ethan had plans for a second date.

14

Ethan couldn't stop looking at Undrea. He admired her more than he could say. A lot of women found Nina intimidating. He'd seen it with his own eyes. The way they deferred to her like she was some kind of alpha wolf. Like they were afraid she might take their heads off.

He understood that Nina's relationship with him gave her some of that power. It validated her in the eyes of other women, like an announcement that she had something about her potent enough to attract and keep a man of his status.

Such nonsense.

Thankfully, Undrea hadn't given in to it. Not even after Nina had purposefully tried to intimidate her with that surprise visit. Something Ethan was still livid about.

Dinner with her at the diner was so far the most low-key evening out he'd had in a long time, and it was wonderful. He smiled across the table at her.

No one had bothered him either. Maybe because they'd recognized he was out with someone special.

Because that's what Undrea was. Someone special. In every sense of the word. She'd offered him and Bowie a place to stay, something he'd never expected.

Sure, he knew part of that offer was Undrea rubbing it in Nina's face, but he was fine with that. Nina wasn't the only one allowed to play games.

And she'd started the game, so what was Undrea supposed to do? Forfeit? No. Instead, she'd made her move. And it was a big one. He applauded her for her boldness.

Nina wouldn't like him staying with Undrea. He knew that. He didn't care what she thought about it. But he wasn't sure how she'd react. She wasn't used to someone not backing down.

Maybe she'd finally understand just how done they were?

He paid the bill for his and Undrea's meal, and as much as he wanted to go back to the house, grab Bowie and his stuff, he wasn't ready to end the evening just yet. "Do you want to walk for a bit? Or something?"

Undrea smiled at him, the most beautiful smile. "Sure. Or we could just sit in the park where you were before and people-watch. I kind of like doing that."

"So do I. Okay, let's walk over there."

They left Mummy's, and as they hit the sidewalk, he slipped his hand in hers.

She gave him a curious glance, then a hesitant

smile as she took hold. They walked the rest of the way to the park like that. He hadn't held hands with Nina in forever. He'd forgotten just how wonderful such contact was.

They found an empty bench on one side and claimed it for themselves.

He put his arm along the back of the bench. Sort of around Undrea's shoulders. But not exactly.

Undrea leaned back. She had to feel his arm behind her. She didn't say anything as she glanced up at him. "Staying at my place will be a good test of how Bowie behaves around a fish tank."

"It will be." He nodded. Even in this low light, she was stunning. "Hey, is that the dream tank you mentioned but wouldn't tell me about?"

She smiled. "You're a good listener. Yes, it is."

"Then I'll get to see it. I can't wait."

"It might not be what you think."

"I'm sure it'll be great, whatever it is."

She leaned into him. Just a few inches, but enough that her side now touched his side. Feeling the warmth of her against him was remarkably comforting. There was something very centering about being this close to someone else. Like a reminder that he wasn't alone in the world.

He hadn't sat this close to Nina in ages.

Hadn't held hands, hadn't sat close, hadn't been out to a simple meal where she actually seemed to enjoy herself.

Why was that? They lived in the same house, attended the same functions, and yet…they were rarely close. Rarely in sync, either.

But then no one ever sat that close at the events they went to. It just wasn't done. Or couldn't be done because of seating arrangements. But those excuses didn't exist at the house. When they watched a movie, which was a rare occurrence these days, she usually lay on the loveseat while he took up the couch.

They'd just settled into a sort of distant, separate way of living.

He realized now how much he hated that. It was fine to have time to yourself and do your own thing. He certainly did that often enough. But to lose that need to touch each other…that seemed like dangerous territory.

He slipped his arm off the back of the bench and properly around Undrea's shoulders. She reached up and twined her fingers with his.

They sat in comfortable silence, watching people and listening to the gargoyle interact with those who stopped by.

He shook his head. "The animatronics are amazing. There must be a camera, right? And someone hidden away giving those responses? Because they never repeat."

She nodded slowly. "It's something like that. From what I understand."

"It's so well done."

She smiled but said nothing else.

After another twenty minutes or so, he spoke. "I could sit here all night, but at some point, I have to get Bowie and my stuff."

She leaned forward like she was about to get up. "I could sit here too, but I do have work tomorrow. I kind of have to set a good example, being the boss and all."

He nodded. "You're right. Plus putting it off won't help."

As he stood, she got to her feet as well. "I'll text you my address, then you can come over when you've got your stuff." She pulled out her phone. "And if you don't show up, it's okay."

"Why wouldn't I show up?"

She shrugged. "I'm sure Nina can be very persuasive. Which way is your car?"

"Over there." He pointed. "You think she'll do something to keep me from leaving?"

"I'm parked that way too." They started walking, and she shook her head. "I'm just saying I won't hold it against you if you change your mind. Tonight was fun, but you have history with her, and I'd understand if you changed your mind."

"I won't. That's not how I operate. When I say I'm done, I mean I'm done. There's nothing she could do that would change my mind. In fact, if I had been wavering, her showing up at your house would have pushed me over the edge."

"Okay." But there was no faith in her tone.

He understood. She didn't know him. So why should she trust him? "If I don't show up in twenty minutes, feel free to call the cops because then she probably did do something. Like she's got me at gunpoint."

Undrea's eyes went wide. "You think she'd do that?"

"No, I'm just saying that's what it would take to keep me there. Twenty minutes. You'll see."

"This is me." She stopped alongside the same truck she'd driven to his house and leaned against the driver's door.

"Twenty minutes. Possibly twenty-five if Bowie is hiding." He wanted to kiss her. Right there, with all kinds of people milling by, and he didn't care.

She smiled. "Like I said, if you can't—"

He pressed his mouth to hers, hoping to erase her doubts. In the process, he turned them both a little so that his body shielded them from most of the people going by.

Her lips were as soft as he'd remembered from that first time in the lake. Warmer now. He took his time, in no rush to do anything else.

Her hands rested lightly on his chest, her touch easy and comfortable. The softest sound drifted out of her, a lyrical little sigh, and for a moment, he felt as though he'd been entranced. As if he were hers to command.

Suddenly, she pushed back, sucked in a breath, and stared up at him, a little wide-eyed and seemingly happy, but with a little anxiousness mixed in. She patted his chest. "Yep, you'd better go get your cat."

He laughed. "Okay. See you soon."

She nodded and climbed into her truck.

He went back onto the sidewalk and waited for her to pull out, then headed to his own vehicle.

He barely noticed the drive home. He went inside, glad Nina was already in bed reading. Except she wasn't. She was watching television in the living room. A cooking show. In French. With subtitles.

Was he going to have trouble with her? Was that why she was in the living room? To wait up for him? To confront him?

Whatever. He chose to ignore her and focus on getting out.

With a shake of his head, he went upstairs to pack some clothes and toiletries. Enough for a few days. Then he went to his office and grabbed his main laptop and his idea notebook. Those both went into a backpack. He shut everything else down and closed his office door.

Bags in hand, he went downstairs. Bowie's soft carrier was in the coat closet. He got that out and found Bowie in the kitchen, lying on the table. He wasn't supposed to be up there, but Ethan knew he liked being able to look out the window.

Nina had yet to say a word to Ethan. He wasn't sure she even realized he'd come home.

He packed a small shopping bag with Bowie's food, then put Bowie in the carrier and took him, the shopping bag, the backpack, and the clothing out to the car.

He returned for Bowie's downstairs litter box, which thankfully had a handle on the locked-on top, the scooper, and the jug of litter. He found Bowie's favorite crinkle ball on his walk toward the door.

He stuffed that in his pocket, the sound like a candy bar being unwrapped.

Nina finally stretched her neck to see what he was doing. She frowned at the sight of the litter box in his hand. "Where are you going with that?"

"I'm moving out until you find a place to go. I just think this separating thing will work better if we have our own space."

Her lips parted, but no sound came out for several seconds as she stared at him. "You can't be serious."

"I told you I was." He decided not to say anything about her visit to Undrea's. He didn't want to tip his hand that he'd seen Undrea, mostly for Undrea's sake. But there was a lot to gain from keeping your cards close as well. "If you could be out in a week, that would be great."

She stood up. "A week? We just moved in."

"I apologize for the inconvenience of it all, but life doesn't always work the way we'd like it to." He smiled to soften his words. "It's been a good couple of years, Nina. It really has been. But it's better we figure this all out now, don't you think? Before things really get complicated."

Her lower lip actually protruded like she might cry. That would be a first. He'd never seen her shed a tear in the time they'd been together. "You're making a mistake."

"I'm not. But even if I was, it's my mistake to make." He sighed. "You have my number. One week. Please." He headed for the door. Time was ticking, and he wasn't sure where he was on the twenty-minute countdown, but not disappointing Undrea felt very important.

"Where are you going?"

He didn't answer. It wasn't her business. Nothing about him was anymore. He shut the door behind him, got in the car, and drove.

Once he was away from the house enough that Nina could no longer see his car, he pulled over and plugged Undrea's address into his GPS. She was another seven minutes away.

That twenty minutes was going to be just about up when he arrived, but he was going to make it.

With a smile on his face, he pulled onto the road again and glanced over at Bowie. "We're going to stay somewhere else for a while, bud. I hope you're okay with that."

Bowie meowed, pawing at the mesh front of the carrier.

"I know, you hate being in that thing. But it won't be for long. And you like Undrea. Remember her? The pretty woman who came to the house about the aquarium?"

Bowie lay down.

"Speaking of, don't do anything to embarrass me, okay? Like don't try to eat the fish in her tank and don't drink out of it and don't fall into it and don't break anything in her house or pee where you're not supposed to or scratch stuff up or poop in her shoes or any of that. I realize that's a tall order. It's like asking you not to be a cat, but try, okay?"

Bowie just stared at him, his blue-gold gaze both uninterested and somehow judgmental at the same time.

"At least you look handsome." He was in his yellow and black striped bumblebee sweater.

Which was what made Ethan realize he hadn't grabbed any of Bowie's other sweaters. He sighed. "I guess you're wearing that one for a few days."

It would warm up soon. But Bowie got cold easily. Ethan would have to go back to the house at some point anyway for more clothes for himself. He'd just have to remember to get some for Bowie, too. He could always order some things online, he supposed.

He shook his head, chuckling as he thought about loading up a cart with cat sweaters. Taking care of Bowie felt like having a kid sometimes.

Which would be nice. Having kids, that was.

Hmm. How did Undrea feel about children? It was too soon to have that discussion, he knew that. She'd go running for the hills. Or call the cops to have him removed from her house.

But the truth was, Ethan thought she'd be a great mom.

And he'd never thought that about another woman in his life.

15

Undrea stared at the fish in her tank. "Listen. There's a cat coming. Fair warning, because I have no idea how he's going to act around you guys."

The fish hovered near the glass, listening.

"I'm not saying there's going to be trouble. Just don't get too near the surface if he jumps on top of the tank or at least not near any of the holes in the lid, and you'll be fine. I don't want to lose anyone. Got it?"

They stared at her for a moment longer, then swam off.

That was about as close to listening as they got. Tetras were notorious for being a little rebellious.

And giving them a warning was easier than thinking about what she'd almost done to Ethan during that kiss. She knew the sound she'd involuntarily made had affected him. How could she think otherwise?

He was human and she was…not.

That couldn't happen again.

She turned to look out the living-room windows, eager to focus on something else. From here she could see some of the twinkling lights of the town proper. It was beautiful at night and not a view she'd realized she'd had until the first night she'd been in the house.

Now it was one of her favorite things about the place. She imagined Ethan had an even better view of town since he was a couple of miles over in the right direction.

She looked at her watch. The twenty minutes were almost up. She didn't know if he was coming or not, truth be told.

He seemed sincere, but what guy didn't when they had their arm around you? And Nina didn't strike Undrea as the kind of woman who took no for an answer. Or reacted well when that *was* the answer.

She looked at her watch again. Two minutes to go. Or seven, if Bowie was hiding.

Smiling, she shook her head and went to make a cup of hot chocolate. Maybe he'd show. Maybe he wouldn't. She wasn't going to freak out either way. She checked her phone. No text message.

The guest room was ready. He'd have to use the bathroom down the hall, but this was a house, not a hotel.

She added milk to a saucepan to heat for the hot chocolate. Mattie had given her a container of drinking chocolate for Christmas, and it was about the best thing Undrea had ever had out of a cup. It deserved to be made the right way, not dumped into a mug and hot water stirred into it.

Besides, she was in the mood for a little indulgence now that it seemed like Ethan might not be coming.

Maybe she'd finally get to take that bath and shift. The ache was all the way up to her knee and had begun in the toes of her right foot now, too. She could use a shift. Get herself back to center again.

Inviting him to stay had been a little spur of the moment decision, partially motivated by Nina's visit. Undrea would happily admit that Nina's threat had made her angry. And made her want to do something in return.

Putting Ethan up seemed about the most she could do without actually confronting Nina in person.

She got the tin of chocolate down, measured a scoop of the dark powder, then added it to the simmering milk. She gave the mix a little stir with the small wire whisk that had come in the set.

Her doorbell rang.

Could that be him? She looked at her watch. The twenty minutes was up.

She turned the burner down, set the whisk aside, and went to answer the door.

Ethan stood on her front porch, loaded down with bags and a carrier that Bowie peered out of. "You didn't think I was coming, did you?"

She shook her head. "Nope. I didn't."

"Have you changed your mind? Want to rescind the offer?"

"Nope. I don't." She stepped out of the way. Bowie meowed at her. She smiled at him. "Hiya, kit-cat. Nice to see you too." And it was really nice to see

Ethan. So nice, her right ankle started to ache.

Ethan stepped inside. "He hates being in the carrier."

"Poor guy. Let him out then."

"You're sure?"

She laughed. "Well, you can't keep him in there forever."

"I just thought because I didn't have his litter box set up—I'll go get that right now." He put the carrier down with the rest of his bags and unzipped the top. Bowie hopped out. "There you go, bud."

He looked at Undrea. "Be right back."

"Okay." She wiggled her fingers at the cat, who was now standing in her foyer. "Hi, little dude. How are you? You look very handsome in your sweater. Like a kitty-bee. My friend Mattie would love it."

Bowie was looking around, paying no attention to her. She figured that was how it would go. He'd need to get the lay of the land and sniff everything at least once before he felt comfortable.

"It's cool," she said. "Have an explore. See what there is to see. I don't mind. I do have to go check on the hot chocolate, though, so don't get into trouble while I'm gone, okay?"

He'd wandered into the living room and was sticking his head under the couch. Maybe he was going to crawl under there? She knew cats liked to hide. "Um…maybe don't go under there, though?"

She could only imagine how much dust he'd end up covered in. She couldn't remember the last time she'd cleaned under there. That would make a great impression on Ethan, wouldn't it? Turning his handsome Sphynx cat into a common household dust bunny?

With a sigh, she went into the kitchen, turned off the burner completely, and set the pan aside.

The front door opened, and the sounds of Ethan returning filtered in. She went back out to see what she could help with.

He had the litter box, a jug of litter, and another bag with him. He looked around the foyer. "Where's Bowie?"

"Living room. He might have gone under the couch. Come on, I'll show you."

Ethan rolled his eyes. "That cat." He followed her in, then stopped and stared. "That has to be the tank."

Undrea smiled. "It is."

"It's…amazing." He put the litter box, litter jug, and the other bag down. "Explain it. What am I looking at?"

Her grin widened. "It's an Amazon-style naturally planted and scaped six-hundred-and-fifty-gallon tank with ember tetras, green neon tetras, albino Corydoras, a pair of dwarf gouramis, and blue velvet shrimp. Those are just like the green jade you saw at my shop. Only blue. There are a couple varieties of snails in there too."

He took a step closer, his eyes never leaving the tank. "That's a lot of fish."

She nodded. "Two hundred and fifty in each tetra school, twenty-five of the cory cats and who knows how many shrimp. They breed like rabbits."

His smile was a little lopsided. Hitched up higher on one end. "I feel like I'm looking through a window into some underwater jungle scene."

He got it, which made her all kinds of happy. "That's pretty much the idea of an Amazon-style tank."

He glanced at her. "This is modeled after the Amazon river?"

"That's the general idea." She went over to the light switch and turned off the room lights, leaving the tank as the only illumination.

"Wow," he breathed. "How do you do anything but watch this tank all day?"

"Why do you think that chair is there?" She pointed to the Eames-style recliner that sat across from the tank. "Go on, sit. I have to finish the cup of hot chocolate I was making. Do you want one?"

He shook his head. "No, I'm good. Thanks." He took a seat.

She returned to the kitchen and got her cup, adding a swirl of whipped cream to the chocolate after she poured it in.

When she came back to the living room, Bowie was sitting in Ethan's lap. Thankfully neither he nor his sweater were covered in dust, either. "I see someone showed up."

"He did." Ethan glanced over, smiling. "I think he's as enthralled by this tank as I am. I want one of these. This Amazon-style tank. When I get my house back. The saltwater is great, but this is..." He shook his head. "I want this."

"You can have more than one tank, you know."

He laughed. "I'm starting to get a feel for your business model."

"Fish are addictive. Just saying." With a grin, she pulled the small ottoman over and sat beside him.

He watched her. "I took your seat."

"Because I offered it to you. It's fine." She crossed her legs and drank her chocolate while looking at the tank. It was something to behold, for sure.

"Why did you call those albino fish cory cats?"

"Corydoras are a type of catfish. Cories or cory cats is shorthand for them."

"I think one went up for air." He frowned. "Is that possible? It's not sick, is it?"

She nodded. "Nope, not sick. They do that occasionally. They can also move their eyes independently, which makes it look like they're blinking at you. They're really entertaining. And there are lots of varieties, so you don't have to go with the albinos."

"They're really cool." He went back to just watching.

Bowie stood with his back feet on Ethan's lap and his front feet on the arm of the chair and looked at Undrea.

She smiled at him and gave his cheek a scratch. "What's up, little man?"

He leaned into her hand, then made a little chirp and pawed at her.

She laughed. "What do you want?"

Ethan snorted softly. "He wants to sit in your lap."

"Really?" She put her cup down and patted her leg. "Come on."

Bowie climbed over and curled up in the crook of her legs.

She stared down at him, petting his velvety head. "Look at that. He nestled right in."

Ethan slanted his eyes at the cat. "Boy oh boy, didn't take him long to make himself at home. He really likes you. The only other person he likes as much as me is my mom. You're in rare company."

"Well, I like him right back." She smiled at the charming, purring beast in her lap. "He's just the sweetest thing."

As if he understood her, Bowie turned his head upside down and somehow made himself cuter.

"Show-off," Ethan said, laughing.

After scratching Bowie a little more, she glanced over at Ethan. "Did you tell Nina you knew about her coming over here?"

"No." He shook his head and looked pleased with himself. "Didn't tell her I was staying here, either. Wasn't her business."

"And if she finds out?"

"I'll deal with her. If that becomes necessary. Which I don't think it will."

"Good."

"You know, moving out was the right thing for me to do. She's finally taking this seriously. At least I hope she is. She seemed surprised that I was really doing it."

"Do you have a history of talking about things but not following through?"

He snorted. "Pretty much the opposite. If I say I'm going to do something, I do it."

"You did show up here."

"See?" He smiled and turned his gaze back to the tank. "No, I'm sure Nina just thought I'd gone along with the status quo for so long that I wasn't really going to change it. Now she knows better."

Undrea wondered what was going on in Nina's mind. And how soon it would be before she made whatever move she was going to make. Because there was no way Nina was just going to let Ethan go that easily.

Undrea wouldn't, if she was in Nina's place. She smiled down at the now sleeping cat in her lap. "I hate to move Bowie, but I should show you the guest room."

"Just pick him up. He'll probably stay asleep. He loves to be carried like a baby. He won't mind."

Undrea scooped him into her arms, holding him just like Ethan had said as she stood up. The little cat snuggled against her. "Okay, I might actually be in love with your cat."

Ethan's gaze narrowed as he got to his feet. "Give it some time. Wait until he digs all the socks out of your drawer to make a spot to sleep. Or flings litter all over in an attempt to cover his business. Or lays across your face in the middle of the night so you wake up thinking you're being suffocated."

She gave Ethan a look. "Don't bad-mouth my boyfriend."

He laughed. "I see how this is going to go."

So did she. And the answer was very well.

Too well, maybe. Because she no longer cared if Mattie found a cure for that kiss. Just a cure for the effect of her powers on him. Then all she had to worry about was keeping Ethan from discovering her true self and she'd be fine.

How hard could that be?

16

Ethan stood in the guest room staring at the bed he'd be sleeping in tonight. His thoughts weren't on sleeping, however. They were on Undrea.

He knew it was too early to be in love with her. But he was definitely in *like* with her. Serious like. The kind of like that would very soon turn into love with the way things were going.

But didn't love happen that way sometimes? Fast and hard and without warning? Wasn't love at first sight a thing? It was, according to his mom. She loved to tell him the story about how she'd seen his father across the gymnasium at a high school dance. She'd known who he was. Jimmy Edmonds was one class ahead of her. As handsome as any movie star. Already destined for the Army.

And that night in the gym, she'd figured out he was the one. The first dance, she liked to say, confirmed it. The first kiss reinforced it.

Jimmy Edmonds *had* been the one, too. At least

until he'd been killed in a motorcycle accident eight months after Ethan was born, leaving Cathy Edmonds to raise her infant son alone.

Ethan often wondered what his father would think of the life Ethan had made for himself. From his mom's stories, he knew his dad had been a simple guy. After a stint in the Army, he'd gotten out and become a mechanic at a garage, moving up to manager pretty quickly thanks to the skills he'd learned in the service.

In that way, Ethan was like his late father. He loved to work with his hands. To build things. To fix things.

But no amount of fixing was ever going to bring his dad back. Didn't stop Ethan from wishing it was possible. Or wishing he could talk to his dad sometimes. Like now. Now would be great.

Because falling for a woman so soon after untangling himself from another one seemed crazy, but Ethan was powerless to stop what he was feeling.

He unpacked his bag, taking out the clothes he'd brought. Thankfully, he'd remembered pajama pants.

What was the point of trying to stop those feelings? His head and heart didn't want him to. They liked Undrea. It was his sense of propriety that was fouling things up.

Did that matter? Who cared if it was improper to like Undrea so soon after Nina? Social media would. They'd have a field day with it.

He shook his head. Maybe a hot shower would help. Or even better, a talk with his mom. Because as much as she believed in love at first sight, she was also fond of telling him there were plenty of fish in the sea. He was pretty sure that was in reference to Nina, however.

Before he could get his phone out, a soft knock sounded on his door.

"Ethan? I just wanted to let you know I was going to take a bath and go to bed, so if you plan on taking a shower, maybe wait a few minutes?"

He opened the door. "I was going to take a shower. I was thinking about it anyway. Are you psychic?"

"Yes, I am. I forgot to mention that. Sorry."

"So you're a forgetful psychic."

She nodded. "Which is why I can't make a living at it."

He laughed. "Have you seen my cat? I put the litter box in the guest bathroom, by the way. I hope that's all right."

"That's perfect. And no, I haven't seen him."

"Maybe he's still looking at your tank."

She shook her head. "I doubt it. I turned the light off. It's a lot harder to watch now."

"Hmm. Well, I'm sure he's around. If he bothers you, let me know. Because there's a good chance he will."

She snorted. "I doubt that. I don't even care if he wants to sleep with me."

"Give it time. Trust me. He's quite the accomplished butthead. But a lovable one."

She grinned. "I'll take your word for it, but I think

you're just trying to make sure I don't kidnap him and keep him when you leave."

"Now that you mention it..." He laughed. "Seriously, though. If he's being a pest, just tell me, and I'll come get him."

"Okay, will do. Have a good night. I'll see you in the morning. Oh, I make coffee every morning, but I don't really cook, so breakfast is usually cereal or Pop-Tarts or—"

"Did you say Pop-Tarts?"

She gave him a guarded look. "Why? Are you on some kind of macrobiotic organic whole grains and yogurt kind of thing? Because based on what you ate at the diner..."

He shook his head. It was interesting to see the kinds of ideas she had about him. "No, but Nina makes us a low-carb, high-protein super foods shake every morning. I haven't had Pop-Tarts since I was kid. Nina would never allow anything like that in the house. She wouldn't like what I ate at the diner, either."

Undrea's eyes narrowed. "You're like...a billionaire, right?"

"Something like that."

"And you don't eat what you want for breakfast?"

He knew what she was implying. He wasn't going to argue, either. Nina was a little controlling. He nodded. "Point taken."

She held her hands up. "Sorry, it's not my place to judge."

"No worries. You're right. But does that mean

you're going to share your Pop-Tarts with me?"

"Sure. You did buy dinner." With a smile, she headed to her room. "See you in the morning."

"Sleep well."

He waited until her door was shut before he shut his. The thought of her in the bath just a few rooms away was tantalizing. And not an image he could easily shake.

A call to his mom would help that. He dialed and lay down on the bed to talk to her.

"Hi, honey."

He smiled. "Hi, Mom. How are you?"

"I'm doing great. I love that meal delivery service you sent me. Sarah Jane comes over once a week and we cook together."

"That's nice." Sarah Jane was his mom's neighbor, another older but very active woman. They walked almost every day and went to the gym together three times a week. They did a lot of things together. "How's she doing?"

"Pretty good. Her arthritis is bothering her a bit, but what can you do?"

"Not much. What else is new? How's Molly?"

"Oh, that dog is going to get me kicked out of the neighborhood. She chased Mr. Murphy's cat again. I told him if he doesn't keep that cat out of my yard, there isn't anything I can do."

"Don't you keep Molly on a leash?"

"Yes, but she rips it out of my hand. She's crazy about that cat."

Ethan grinned. Molly was a black lab. And Mr.

Murphy was a grump who also happened to be the president of the HOA. "Please don't get kicked out. You'll be miserable if you have to move."

"Speaking of moving, how's your new town?"

His first thought was of Undrea. "It's good. Really good. And that's kind of why I'm calling."

"Oh?"

"Nina and I broke up."

"You did? Is this a temporary thing or permanent?" The amount of hope in her voice surprised him.

"Permanent. She's not the right one for me, Mom."

"No, she's not."

He almost stared at the phone in disbelief. "I thought you liked Nina?"

"I liked her for your sake, but she never seemed like a good fit. You're not an uptight guy, Ethan. You never were as a kid, either. You're like your father in that respect. Easygoing, roll-with-the-punches kind of guy. Nina is too regimented. Too concerned with appearances. That's the old money in her."

He nodded. "You're right about that."

"Plus I was a little concerned she was a gold digger. I know she has her own money, but your money makes hers look like green stamps. Not that you know what those are."

"*Mom*." He laughed.

"Well, honey, it's a real consideration. You're a very wealthy man. Money makes women do stupid things."

"I love you so much."

She laughed. "That's very good to know. So. What's her name?"

He sat up. "Who?"

"You could have left Nina last year. But now that you've moved into a new house in a new town, you make that decision? People don't do hard things that quickly without meaningful incentive. So what's her name?"

He swallowed. "Undrea. And she's really something."

"She must be to get you out of a two-year relationship. Tell me everything."

And so he did, from their first meeting in the lake to the fact that he was lying on Undrea's guest-room bed. All the in-between stuff, too. About how Bowie loved her and how she knew all about fish and had her own business and ate Pop-Tarts for breakfast.

When he was done, he waited for his mom's response.

"She sounds wonderful. Just the kind of girl my boy should be with. I'd like to meet her."

"I'd like that too. How about you fly down here as soon as Nina's out of the house?"

"That might take longer than you think."

"Maybe. But I don't know." He shrugged. "I hope not."

"Tell her I'm coming. That'll speed her up."

"Why? Nina likes you."

His mom snorted. "Oh, sweetheart. Men can be so oblivious. She liked me enough to make you think she liked me."

"Really?"

"Really."

What surprised him about his mother's response was that she hadn't said anything about the timing of it all. "So, Mom, about Undrea. You don't think I'm rushing into this? That it's all happening too fast?"

"What's fast about it? This is how love works. Sometimes it's slow, sometimes it's fast, but it's rarely when you want it or expect it. Don't worry about that. I can tell by your voice that you're happy. And you never sounded that way with Nina."

"I didn't?"

"Not even once." She sighed. "I love you, son. I don't like that you're still too far away, but I'm glad you're out of the city. I never liked you living there."

"I think you'd love this place. Hey, I have an idea. Why don't you and Sarah Jane both come? Make a little vacation out of it?"

"Oh, that would be wonderful. I'll talk to her tomorrow about it. But I'm not sure she can afford it right now."

"Mom, just use the credit card I gave you. For both of you. The trip is on me."

"Honey, that's too much."

"Whatever it costs, I'd pay triple to see you."

She laughed. "You're my favorite child, you know that?"

He grinned. "I'm your only child. And I love you too. Thanks for talking to me."

"Anytime. Night or day."

He smiled at her standard answer. "Talk to you soon."

"You know it. Night."

They hung up, and he let the phone drop to the bed beside him. He stared up at the ceiling. He felt like his mom had just given him her blessing to be in love.

There was nothing standing in his way now.

Nothing but Nina in his house. He frowned. He had to get her out of there. And he had a thought about how to make that happen.

17

Undrea stripped down while the water was still running. She couldn't wait to get in the tub. She needed to shift more than ever, especially with Ethan being so close. The ache in her legs would only get worse if she didn't, and at a certain stage, it would become unbearable.

She never let it get to the point of pain. There was no reason to. Why would anyone want to feel like they were walking on razors if they didn't have to?

As the water level rose, she wound her hair up on top of her head in a messy bun and secured it with a wide elastic. She put a hydrating face mask on too. One of those sheet masks that had been positioned as an impulse buy near the drugstore register.

Might as well use it, she figured. No point in not taking advantage of her time in the tub. The steam always seemed to make the masks work even better.

The water was almost where she wanted it, so she set her phone nearby, then climbed into her big rolltop, footed tub and sank into the water, shifting instantly. She flopped her tail out over the end. The relief that came from shifting was immediate and very welcome.

With a satisfied exhale, she rested her head against the inflatable bath pillow suctioned to the end of the tub. This tub had absolutely been a deciding factor in buying this house. It was modeled after one of those old-fashioned claw-foot types, except this modern interpretation was larger, deeper, and had the faucet in the middle, meaning none of the fixtures got in the way of relaxing.

Having a faucet and handles at one end might be okay if you had feet, but when you had a tail you needed space for, not having them there was much more comfortable.

The tub was full enough, so she reached over and turned off the water, then sank a little lower.

She let out a happy sigh with the perfection of it all. She closed her eyes and drifted deeper still. Just as she was really floating and mellowing out, her phone rang. Naturally.

With a sigh, she reached down for it and looked at the screen. Mattie. She answered with a smile. "Hey, girl. What's up?"

"I have some good news and some bad news."

"Yeah?" Undrea didn't really care about the bad news that much. She no longer felt any pressing need to rid herself of Ethan. In fact, keeping him around had gotten much higher on her priority list. She would have to find a way to protect him, but that had to be doable. "What's the bad news?"

"I can't find a way to break the kissing spell."

"That's all right."

"It is?"

"Yep." Undrea laughed and lowered her voice, even though there was no way Ethan could hear her.

"Okay, what's going on that you haven't told me yet?"

Mattie was so intuitive. "Ethan left Nina."

"And?"

"And…he's currently staying with me."

"What?" Mattie almost shouted into the phone. That was very unlike her. She was pretty laid-back. Actually, she was about the chillest person Undrea knew.

Undrea quickly explained everything that had transpired. "And so he needed a place to stay right away that would also accept pets. Plus I felt a little responsible. And a little like I wanted Nina to know she doesn't scare me."

"Hmm," Mattie said. "I can understand that, but I don't like the whole rare witch thing."

"How do you know she's a rare witch?"

"Pandora called me."

"Oh, that's cool. Anyway, Corette said it's nothing to worry about."

"I trust her on that. She's a lot more dialed in to all that general witch stuff, but there's just something about Nina. She comes off as the type eager to make trouble."

"Maybe. Nothing yet. Not saying I disagree with you, but she might not want to make a big thing out of this. After all, she just got dumped. What woman would want to draw attention to that?"

"I suppose that's true. But this isn't just any guy we're talking about. Ethan is a man of means. He's got fame and fortune. A lot of women would fight tooth and nail to keep a guy like that." She paused. "He's been in your house, what? An hour? Two? It's early still."

"I know. But I think she might have gotten the idea that he really meant things were over when he moved out."

"Sure." Mattie snorted. "Let's hope that's really how she feels."

"I guess we'll see soon enough."

"Hey, you're not backing out of going to Insomnia tomorrow, are you? Now that he's staying with you?"

"No way. In fact, I'm doing a mask right now while I'm in the tub. Just so I can look my best."

"That honey mask I made?"

"No, just one of those cheapie sheet masks I picked up at the drugstore. I should snap you because I look crazy."

Mattie laughed. "Do it. I could use a laugh. Blueberry got into my craft supplies, and there are currently about three thousand seed beads scattered throughout my cottage. I told him he doesn't get another cookie until they're all picked up, but it's going to take days with the production he's making out of it."

"Oh my. You really do need a laugh. Hang on." Undrea opened up her camera.

And saw a cat face staring back at her on the

screen. She shrieked, realizing a second later it was Bowie, but not in time to stop from dropping her phone.

She grabbed for it in a desperate attempt to save it from going under, but her hands were damp, and the phone slipped through them like a bar of soap.

It fell into the water and sank like a stone.

She scooped it out, scowling at Bowie, who had his front paws on the edge of the tub and was staring over the rim with great interest. "How did you get in here?"

He meowed at her.

"You're cute, but that was a rotten trick. But then I guess your father warned me about how naughty you can be." She shook the phone in the hopes of getting any excess water out, but she had a pretty good idea it was dead. Water and electronics didn't mix. With a sigh, she shifted back into her human form, climbed out of the tub and dried off to see if there was any way to salvage her phone.

Bowie looked into the water like there might be something in there for him.

"Go ahead," Undrea said. "Jump in. See how you like it."

He didn't.

She got dressed and took her dripping phone out to the kitchen. Ethan was already there, getting a glass of water.

"Oh my," he said as he saw her.

"What?"

He circled his finger around his face. "That's, uh, quite a look."

She groaned. She still had the sheet mask on. She pulled it off and dropped it in the trash. "I forgot about that."

He leaned on the counter and took a long drink. "Short bath."

She frowned and held her phone up. "I dropped my phone in."

"Oh no, that sucks."

Bowie came sauntering in like he was completely innocent.

She glared at him, miffed despite still thinking he was very cute. "Yes, it does, doesn't it, you naughty little beast."

Ethan's brows bent. "Why am I sensing there's more to this story?"

"Somehow Bowie snuck into my bathroom and I didn't see him, and when I was on my phone he startled me and that's why I dropped it in the tub."

Ethan frowned at his cat. "Bowie, what did I tell you about behaving?" He shook his head as he looked at Undrea. "I am so sorry. I'll pay whatever it takes to make it right, but I might have a trick to save it."

"Let me guess. Stick it in rice?"

"Better. I'll be right back."

As he left, she took the case off her phone and wiped it dry with paper towels. She didn't hold out much hope that it could be saved.

Ethan returned with a big zip-top plastic bag half-filled with little milky-colored beads. "This is a next-gen desiccant I've created for situations just like this. May I?" He held his hand out.

She gave him her phone. "Sure." She had nothing to lose. Literally. The phone couldn't get worse.

He stuck the phone in the bag and pressed it between his hands. "The heat helps activate the beads."

"How long will it take? If it's going to work, that is."

"Fifteen, twenty minutes? If you want to go finish your bath, you can."

"I should at least drain the tub." Although the water was probably still hot. "Fifteen minutes?"

"At least."

"Okay. Maybe I will get back in for a bit." She gave him a wave and headed back to the bathroom.

This time she checked under the tub for Bowie. Then behind it. Either spot would have made a good hiding place. She stripped down again and got in, shaking her head. Ruining her phone was not in her budget, but what could she do?

Maybe Ethan's magic beads would work, but the phone had gotten good and truly soaked. There didn't seem like much chance anything could fix it.

She shifted and relaxed in the still-hot water until it began to cool. She retook her human form, got out, dried off again, and dressed. She went to look at her phone to see the time, remembering as she searched for it that it was in the kitchen.

Funny how ingrained some habits were.

She walked out and checked the time on the microwave. Ethan was sitting at the table, reading something on his phone. It had been seventeen minutes. She took a seat. "Do you think it's been long enough?"

He looked up from his phone. "How long was it in the water?"

"A second or two. Only as long as it took me to drop it, then get it out again."

Bowie hopped up on the chair between them, making Ethan shake his head. "You're a bad cat."

"He didn't mean it." She scratched his bald little head. "Did you?"

Bowie leaned into her caresses.

"I still feel awful. Nothing like opening your home to someone with a personal-property-destroying pet, huh?"

She smiled. "It's kind of hard to be mad at this face though. I mean, look at it."

Bowie's eyes were closed, and he looked completely blissed out by her attentions.

"Yeah, I know. He chewed through two of my guitar strings once. I was in the middle of telling him what a rotten thing that was to do when he rolled over and started making air biscuits. It's like he knows just what level of cute is necessary for forgiveness."

Undrea laughed.

Ethan grabbed the bag with her phone in it. "Let's see if my desiccant has done any good."

"Fingers crossed." Fins too.

He opened the bag and took the phone out. "Look at the beads."

She studied them. "They look bigger."

"They've absorbed water."

"Now you're just getting my hopes up."

He pressed the power button. For a moment, nothing happened. They both stared at the black screen.

Then the startup icon appeared.

She sucked in a breath as she glanced at him. "I can't believe it."

"We're not out of the woods yet. Just because it starts doesn't mean it's functional. Unfortunately." He looked at her. "You do have everything backed up to the cloud, right?"

"Um… I think so?"

He made a face. "I hope you do. If you lose all of your pictures and other stuff because of Bowie, I will feel even worse. I promise you, I'll help you get that all set up when you're back to having a working phone."

"Okay. Thanks."

He glanced down at the screen and frowned, then tipped his head. "Did you have the camera on?"

"I did. I was going to take a selfie in my face mask to send to my friend to make her laugh." She looked down at the phone in his hands.

And saw a slightly blurry but still very distinct picture on the screen. Her tail sticking out of the end of the tub.

18

Ethan stared harder at the image before him. "That looks like—"

Undrea snatched the phone out of his hands. "Seems like it's working. That's great. Thanks. I really appreciate the help. I should put it on the charger. Battery was pretty low. Wouldn't want it to go dead again."

And with that she disappeared down the hall in a flash of frantic energy.

Leaving him to wonder what that was all about. He knew what he'd seen. A large fish-like tail sticking out of the bathtub.

Sure, the picture had been crooked and slightly blurry, but not enough to make him question what the subject matter was. Tub, water, tail. It was about as straightforward as you could get.

In fact, a man with a more fanciful imagination might have even thought it was a mermaid tail. It was certainly big enough. And it had the kinds of colors and iridescence you'd imagine a mermaid tail would have.

He stared into space a little longer, his mind working overtime. Was that really what he'd seen? A mermaid tail? It had to be a filter, right? Although it looked so real. In what scenario would that happen? Was it possible Undrea had one that she put on to…imagine herself as a fish?

Would it be that strange for a woman who owned a custom aquarium business to have a fish fetish? Or that kind of rich, fantasy life?

He imagined not. After all, she'd told him she was also a free diver and working on being able to hold her breath for long periods of time. That fit with the mermaid tail, too. But if that was true, it would explain why she'd freaked out about him seeing that picture.

She clearly hadn't expected anyone to find out about what she did in private.

He looked at Bowie, who was still sitting on the chair. Keeping his voice down, he asked, "Did Undrea have a tail on in the tub? Is that what made you so curious?"

Bowie just blinked at him.

"Maybe it was just a filter. But it's too bad you can't talk. Then again…it's probably better that way." What was he going to do about Undrea? She was obviously embarrassed by what he'd seen.

He didn't want her to feel that way. What did it matter what she liked to do in the privacy of her own home?

He had to try to make things right. He felt bad that she felt bad. And a little like he'd invaded her space. She was probably regretting inviting him.

"Wish me luck, Bowie." He stood up and went down the hall. Her bedroom door was shut. He knocked gently so he didn't disturb her too much. "Undrea?"

A moment of silence passed before she answered. Her voice held a tentative note, like she wasn't sure what he could want to talk about. "Yes?"

"Whatever that picture was, I don't care. I really don't. What you do in the privacy of your own home is none of my business. But it's cool with me, too. I swear. I do a lot of things people would think are weird, so I get it."

After a moment, the door opened a crack. "Yeah?" There was no belief in her tone. "Like what?"

"Well, I don't snap pics of myself in the tub with a mermaid tail filter, or maybe that was an actual costume tail? Anyway, whenever I go to Japan, I sing karaoke. A lot of karaoke. Embarrassing amounts, actually. And to be perfectly honest, I can't carry a tune to save my life."

She peered through the door at him. "You thought that was a mermaid tail filter?"

He nodded. "I did. I mean, what else could it be, right? Unless it was part of a costume or something."

"Right." She exhaled. "Totally a filter."

"Don't freak out about it, though, please. I don't think it's strange at all."

"You don't?"

"You own a company that designs custom fish tanks. You're working at becoming a free diver. And you obviously love fish. Why wouldn't you want to imagine being one?"

She just looked at him. Maybe she wasn't convinced he really meant what he said.

He leaned against the door on his side of the hall. "You know, you should get a tail and take it out to the lake with you next time."

She snorted.

"I'm serious. Seems to me it would be a lot more fun than a filter in a bathtub."

"No, you're right. It totally would be." She opened the door a little wider. "Karaoke isn't really that weird. What else you got?"

He shook his head. "You don't really want to go down that road."

"Sure I do. Come on, impress me."

He wrinkled his nose like he was reluctant to tell on himself. "I have some obsessive-compulsive stuff going on when it comes to numbers, which is all kinds of fun when you're an engineer. Used to be worse, but I've done some work on it. I can actually have an odd number of vegetables on my plate now."

Her brows lifted slightly as if questioning what he'd just said.

He nodded. "I'm serious. You can ask my mom. She stopped serving peas for dinner because I had to count them before I could eat them and there had to be an even number of them. Same with carrots.

Any vegetable really. Or mac and cheese. I'd have to count the noodles."

"Spaghetti?"

"Nope. Not on the menu. It would take me hours."

"So what did you eat?"

"Usually four chicken nuggets and thirty French fries. For lunch, one sandwich with two slices of cheese and two slices of bologna. Although peanut butter and jelly was a good option because there was nothing to count. That is, after my mom figured out that chunky wasn't going to work because…all those chunks."

"Really?" Her mouth stayed open slightly.

"Yep."

The door opened wider without either of them touching it. They both looked down to see Bowie rubbing against it.

Ethan scooped him up. "I really am sorry about my incredibly bad cat and your phone."

"It's no big deal. It's fixed now anyway."

"Are you sure? Did you make sure it was all working?"

"I did. Seems fine. Your magic beads did the trick. Thank you for that."

"You're welcome. Is Bowie forgiven? I mean, if he's not, I totally understand. I'd be happy to ground him or take away his car keys. Whatever you think is appropriate."

She grinned. "I told you, I couldn't stay mad at that face."

"I can't either. Thank you for being so understanding. And again, for opening your home to us."

"You're welcome." She gestured over her shoulder. "I think I'm going to turn in. It's been a long day."

He nodded. "It has. See you in the morning."

"Night." She closed the door.

He took Bowie back to his room, but he wasn't really ready for bed. He didn't want to work either. He felt completely unsettled. And not because he wasn't in a place that felt like home.

Undrea's home was a very welcoming space. He just had a weird energy in him that made him want to do something without knowing what that something was.

Maybe if he watched a movie, he could settle down a bit and relax enough to sleep, but he knew this feeling. A long time ago, a therapist friend had said it was a sign of the highly creative, and that the best way to work it out was to try to determine what action would satisfy him the most in the moment.

To figure that out, he had to boil down what he was feeling.

So.

What was it?

The easiest way to figure that out was to start with Maslow's hierarchy of needs. It wasn't a basic need that he was feeling. It wasn't safety. It wasn't food or water or sleep. That left the higher levels of needs. The psychological needs. And the self-fulfillment needs. So was it one of those things?

Maybe. The self-fulfillment needs were things like achieving your potential and creative endeavors. And while there might be some of that in what he was feeling, he generally felt pretty accomplished in the creative potential department.

That left the psychological ones. It certainly wasn't anything to do with esteem or prestige. If anything, he had too much of that.

Which left one remaining tier. Belonging. And love. The needs that had to do with friendship and intimate relationships.

He glanced toward Undrea's room. Was that what he was feeling? The need to be closer to her? The desire to do something that would bring them closer? A yearning to build the trust between them?

He would like to do something for her. But what? Was there something she needed? He didn't know her well enough to determine that. He got up and paced, doing his best to be quiet. Her house was nice. Neat. Simple. Not overly fancy. He liked all of that, actually. He opened a door off the kitchen. It led to a basement, but he didn't go down.

He stopped again in front of the fish tank. The light was off now, but he could still see flashes as the fish swam past. That tank was truly amazing. He'd love to have something like that in his house.

Once Nina was gone, of course. And getting Undrea to build and install a tank like that for him would be good for her business. But that didn't really work in the immediate.

What could he do to thank her for taking him in? Flowers? Not every woman liked flowers. Sure, most did, but as he glanced around, the only plants he saw were in her aquarium.

Chocolates? She liked sweets. Maybe that was the way to go. He went into the kitchen, and although there was no light on except for the one under the microwave, he peeked through her cabinets to get a sense of what she liked. She wasn't kidding about the Pop-Tarts.

One shelf held four boxes, all different flavors. There were also sugary cereals, boxes of granola bars, bags of chips, a jar of honey-roasted peanuts, and some hot chocolate mix. And she'd accused him of eating like a frat boy.

He grinned. Something about that was so endearing. Maybe it wasn't the healthiest, but she was obviously an active person, and far be it from him to tell her what to eat. She seemed like she was doing just fine to him.

In fact, he gave her props for eating what she wanted. Once again, he couldn't help but compare her to Nina, who seemed to treat eating out like a personal affront. That was no way to live. Life was meant to be enjoyed.

He looked in her fridge too. All the usual stuff. Lunch meat and sliced cheese, condiments, some leftovers, creamer for coffee, a jug of iced tea, apples, some random veggies and a slice of chocolate cake in clear, supermarket packaging. There was a big bag of takeout food, too.

Her freezer was a little different. Although she did seem to have some typical things. Some burger patties, ice cream, some foil-wrapped mystery items. But she also had more than the standard amounts of frozen seafood. She had two big bags of shrimp and another one of scallops and a third of fish filets. There were also three boxes of coconut shrimp.

Was it strange that a woman who liked fish so much also enjoyed eating them? He wasn't sure. But he liked seafood too, so he wasn't going to make a big deal out of it. Especially if he was going to date her.

He'd much rather be able to take her out for a lobster dinner than not be able to enjoy a thing like that with her.

Hmm. That was a thought. Maybe he should send her a lobster dinner. He knew you could send lobster to people. He'd done it before. But was that weird? He knew he sometimes did things that seemed perfectly normal to him but weren't to anyone else.

Maybe he should just take her out for a lobster dinner. That was probably a better idea.

He went back to the living room and stood in the dark, looking at the tank, but his gaze was drawn to the view outside the window. The town sparkled in the distance.

He had this view from his own house, but he'd never really taken the time to enjoy it. Mostly because they'd just moved in but also because his time didn't always feel like his own when he was there.

He walked to the corner of the window to get the best view of the town and stood there, just taking it in. The longer he looked, the more his eyes adjusted and the more he saw. Including a dark shape at the edge of the property.

A dark shape he recognized.

Nina.

19

Undrea was tired, but it wasn't the kind of tired that meant she wanted to fall into bed and sleep, even though she was in her pajamas and her teeth were brushed. The tired she felt was more of an emotional and mental thing than a physical one.

She sat in bed, staring at some old *Law and Order* rerun without really seeing it. She couldn't concentrate on the drama when she had enough of her own to focus on.

Ethan thought her tail was essentially a camera trick. Which was fine, as assumptions went. It was better than him suspecting the truth, but what human man would jump to the conclusion that she was a real mermaid? That wasn't how the standard thought processes worked.

No one went straight for believing the thing that was least likely in their realm of perception.

For that, she was grateful. And he'd been exceptionally sweet and understanding about it. But it also made her realize that she was playing with fire. Inviting an upright into her house, one who was clueless about who she really was, was a bad idea. Obviously.

She'd acted based on feelings. And a little magic persuasion. Or maybe a lot of magic. Jury was still out on that one. Whatever the reason, she liked Ethan. He was handsome and smart and funny. He was good at conversation. And he didn't think fish were weird. That made him very easy to like. Their magic connection because of that stupid kiss only intensified all of those things.

And then she'd gone and kissed him *again*. Well, he'd kissed her. But she'd let it happen.

Stupid mermaid. She only had herself to blame for that. What had she been thinking? Ugh. She knew what she'd been thinking. Or rather, what she'd been thinking *with*. And it hadn't been her head.

She had to tell him to leave. That this wasn't working. And there was no way they could date. That would be even worse! What was she supposed to do, eventually confess that she'd lied to him about a few minor details? During what date was the right one to come clean about being a mermaid? The second date? The fourth?

The one right after they did more than kiss?

A noise broke her concentration. It sounded like a door opening and closing. The front door.

She grabbed her robe and pulled it on as she went to see what was happening. Bowie meowed at her when she reached the hall, making her glance back.

He was sitting on the guest room bed, but the lights were off and Ethan wasn't in the room.

She crept out to the living room. Ethan wasn't there either. She kept the lights off. Had he gone outside for something? To get something out of his car, maybe? That was probably it. She relaxed as she looked out the front windows and saw him walking across her driveway.

Yep, he'd just gone out to his—she tensed again. Nina was plainly visible at the edge of the property. And he was walking right toward her.

Undrea's eyes didn't need much light to see clearly, but hearing through closed doors and windows wasn't a skill she possessed. She couldn't read lips, either.

She went to the third and smallest bedroom, which faced the front of the house. She eased up the window just a crack. From here she could see and hear whatever was about to go down.

Ethan reached Nina and spoke first. "What are you doing here?"

"I should be asking you that question," Nina shot back. "Shacking up with the fish girl? Really?"

Fish girl. Undrea stuck her tongue out at Nina.

Ethan shook his head. "Stop calling her that."

Nina snorted. "That's cute. Defending your little townie fling. I didn't realize you felt the need to slum once in a while."

Slum? Undrea's teeth ground together. Nina had no idea who Undrea was. How dare she assume? What a snob.

Ethan's hands clenched in fists at his sides, but he didn't raise his voice. "Get out of here, Nina. Nothing you say is going to change anything except maybe for how I feel about you. And it won't be for the better. I'm also starting to understand that the only slumming I've done lately was with you."

Undrea nodded. Nice one.

"I'm not done with you, Ethan. I'm not done with us."

"There is no us. The sooner you understand that and move on with your life, the better for all of us."

All? Was he including Undrea in that?

But Nina refused to back down. "You really think she's what you need?"

"Yeah," he said. "I do. She's amazing in ways I never understood a woman could be. But there's no point in explaining all of that to you. Because the bottom line is...it's none of your business."

He'd called her amazing. Undrea smiled.

"You're wrong. It is my business. I've put too much time and effort into this relationship to let you throw it away." Nina lifted her chin in a defiant gesture. "You have no idea what's at stake."

"Nina, please. Just go. Before you force me to—"

She raised her hands and whispered something that sounded to Undrea very much like a spell. Latin, maybe? Spoken softly but with stern urgency.

He stopped speaking and stiffened as though a current had run through him. A second later, he collapsed to the ground. Nina started toward him.

Holy carp. Undrea jumped up and ran to the front

door, yanking it open and rushing out to do... something. "Get away from him!"

Nina was standing over him, one hand outstretched and reaching for him. But her head jerked in Undrea's direction, her eyes wide and mouth open in surprise. She snarled. Then she disappeared.

All that remained where Nina had been standing was a wisp of smoke and the smell of sulfur in the air. She'd used magic to transport herself. That didn't seem like the ability of a weak witch. But now was not the time to focus on Nina.

"Ethan?" Undrea dropped to her knees beside him, cradling his head on her lap. Panic and worry and a little fear whirled inside her. "Are you okay? Can you hear me? Ethan? Please, be okay."

After a moment, he moaned and blinked up at her. "What just happened?"

Exhaling in relief, Undrea shook her head. "I'm not really sure." Although she had a rough idea, she just wasn't sure how to tell him.

"Nina," he whispered.

"Yes, that's right. She was here. How do you feel?"

His eyes rolled back in his head for a moment, then he seemed to come to again. He took a breath before answering. "My head is killing me."

"I bet it is." There was no way she was going to tell him he had to leave now. Nina had just used witchcraft on him. "We need to get you inside. Do you think you can walk?"

He pushed up with his hands to a sitting position. "Yes. She was arguing about how we weren't done.

Then she said something, Latin maybe, and right after that…everything went black. What did she do?"

"I don't know for sure. Don't worry about it right now." He'd picked up on the Latin, which was no surprise because of how smart he was. And yet, he'd never figured out what Nina really was. Or she had him bespelled not to figure it out.

Either way, he deserved to understand exactly what and who he was dealing with. And that included Undrea coming clean, too. "We need to talk. But first, let's get you inside."

"Okay."

She helped him up and back into the house. She got him into the kitchen and made him sit at the kitchen table. She felt his forehead. He seemed warm. "Do you want something to drink? Or some aspirin or something?"

"Maybe some water."

She nodded and got him a glass, then came back and sat with him. This wasn't a conversation she ever imagined she'd have. Not with him. Not with any upright, actually. "I don't know where to start with this. In fact, I'm not sure there's a right place. So I'm just going to dive in."

He sipped his water and nodded. He kept blinking like he was having trouble focusing.

"Nina is a witch."

He put his glass down. "Yeah, she is. She's worse than that, if we're being real, but my mom hates when I use that word so—"

"No, Ethan. I'm not calling her a name. I mean she's an actual witch. Like a spellcasting, witchcraft using, coven-joining witch."

He stared at her. And didn't say a thing.

"She told me so herself. She told me she was a rare witch, and according to a friend of mine who knows about this kind of stuff, that's not supposed to be a very powerful type of witch, but obviously, Nina lied about that, because whatever spell she threw at you had real power in it."

He was still staring. And still quiet.

She put her hand on his. He was burning up. "Are you okay? I know this is hard to believe, but I promise it's completely true." She took a breath, gathering her courage. "I know because I'm a—"

"Undrea."

"Yes?" The word mermaid remained on the tip of her tongue, ready for speaking.

"I don't feel…so…" His eyes rolled back in his head, and he slumped down in the chair. She grabbed him just in time to keep him from hitting the floor.

"Ethan? *Ethan!*" But he was really out this time.

She bent and hooked her arms under his, clasping her hands together in front of his chest. With her grip secured around him, she dragged him down the hall and hoisted him halfway onto the guest bed. All thanks to her supernatural strength, because without that, she never would have managed it.

He wasn't a bodybuilder, but he was solid. He was taller than her, too, which didn't help in maneuvering him.

Bowie stood at the foot of the bed, meowing. Could he sense something was wrong?

Undrea lifted Ethan's legs onto the bed and straightened him out. "I don't know, Bowie. I have no idea what just happened. Let's hope Mattie does, though."

She grabbed her phone and dialed, speaking as soon as Mattie answered. "I need you. Right now. Witch emergency. *Major* witch emergency."

"Back up. What happened?"

"Nina was here. And she cast a spell on Ethan, and he just passed out for a second time. I've tried rousing him and no luck. Not even dragging him down the hall woke him."

"I'm on my way."

Undrea paced from the guest bedroom to the living-room windows and back again about three hundred times while waiting for Mattie to arrive. Ethan didn't move once. She checked that he was still breathing about a hundred times. He was. Thankfully.

But her impending sense of doom grew with each passing moment. What had Nina done to him?

Bowie never left Ethan's side, which Undrea found very sweet. She'd never thought of a cat as being loyal, but he certainly seemed to be concerned about Ethan's well-being.

By the time Mattie's car pulled into Undrea's drive, she was practically vibrating with worry. She opened the front door and stood there, waiting for Mattie to come in.

Mattie got out of her car and started for the house, then stopped, turned and lifted her face into the breeze. After a moment, she came inside.

"What were you doing?" Undrea asked.

Mattie shook her head, looking very solemn. "Investigating. She used serious magic. More serious than she should have been capable of, according to Corette."

Undrea nodded. "That's what I thought too. But how did you know?"

"The scent of sulfur. That's not a good sign. Did she vanish after she cast her spell on him?"

"Yep. She sure did. Right in front of me, too. She was standing over Ethan as I was running out of the house. She had her hand out like she was going to zap him again. I yelled at her and spooked her, I guess. She just vanished in a puff of smoke and rotten egg stench."

Mattie frowned. "We're going to have to tell Corette about this. I'm not a member of the coven for my own reasons, but those women are still my sisters in the craft. We can't have a witch with this kind of power loose in town and keep it a secret. Not when she's used her magic against a human."

"I agree. But first, please see if there's anything you can do for Ethan."

"Yes, of course. Let's go."

"Guest room." Undrea led her back. He hadn't budged.

Mattie sucked in air at the sight of him. "I have a bad feeling about this. Tell me again what happened."

"Nina said something, cast some kind of spell on him. He went stiff, like he'd been shocked, then he fell down. Like I said, she looked like she was going to spell him again but vanished as I was running toward him, leaving just the smoke in the air and the scent of sulfur, like you noticed."

Mattie nodded. "What happened after you reached him?"

"He came to as I was next to him, and then I helped him into the house. His forehead felt warm. I got him a glass of water, and we sat at the kitchen table, and I was explaining to him what had happened because he had no understanding of it. I was trying to tell him that Nina was an actual witch, and I was about to tell him I knew that because I was a mermaid, but he was just looking at me blankly. Then his eyes rolled back in his head and he passed out. He's been like this ever since."

Mattie took a deep breath, exhaling it slowly as she looked him over. She put her hand on his head. "Still warm." She dug into her purse, pulling out a small pot of something.

Honey and something else, Undrea realized as Mattie took the lid off. Her own concoction, no doubt.

Mattie scooped a little of the mix out on her finger and swiped it across Ethan's forehead. *"Verum monstrant,"* she whispered.

The streak of honey turned black.

Mattie's eyes gleamed with a cold light. "That's not a good sign. Whatever magic she used, it was something heavy. And since I don't know what she did to him, I don't know exactly how to help him."

Undrea swallowed, feeling sick to her stomach. "This is my fault. All of this has happened to him because of me. I have to do something."

Mattie tipped her head and gave Undrea a stern look. "This isn't your fault. It's Nina's. You didn't make this happen."

"Right, fine, but if he'd never met me, he wouldn't be lying here comatose on my bed. You can't argue that."

Mattie sighed. "We'll help him. I'm just not sure how. If we only knew what she did to him..." She glanced at Ethan, then back at Undrea. "You can't remember what she said?"

Undrea shook her head. "It sounded like Latin—Ethan even said that—but she spoke the words so softly, they were impossible to make out. I'm sorry. I wish I could remember."

Mattie gazed at her with a strange expression. "Ethan knew it was Latin?"

"He seemed to think that. He's a smart guy. That didn't seem weird to me."

"Me either. But it means he heard her." Mattie's brows lifted slightly. "You might be able to make him tell you."

"How would I—no." Undrea shook her head as she realized what Mattie was suggesting. "I'm not doing that."

"He won't know. He's out cold."

A chill swept down Undrea's spine. She'd turned

her back on that side of herself a long time ago. The dark side of herself. The deadly side.

Sure, Mattie was asking her to use it in a positive way, but that felt like opening a very dangerous door. How many times could she use it before something went wrong? Before her darker urges took over?

Because if the answer was only once, she'd be in all kinds of trouble.

Mattie put her hand on Undrea's arm. "I know what I'm asking. I know how much you want nothing to do with those abilities, but this might be your chance to use those powers for good."

Maybe. But it didn't feel that way to Undrea. "And it might unleash something in me I can't shut down. He's already at risk of my powers. This could make it worse." She shook her head. "I'm afraid of it taking over. And if it works, how do we explain knowing what curse Nina put him under?"

"I won't let the darker side of you take control." Mattie shrugged. "And we'll just say you heard her and told me and I figured it out."

"But that would be a lie."

"A white lie. And only you and I will know it." Mattie looked at Ethan again. "I don't know how else to help him without understanding what she did to him."

Undrea put her hand to her throat, torn with trying to decide what to do.

"It might not even work," Mattie said. "Nina might be more powerful than you. You might not be able to reach him through whatever spell he's under."

"I know what you're doing," Undrea said. "You're using psychology on me."

"Is it working?"

"A little." Undrea didn't know what else to do. She reached out and took Ethan's hand. "Forgive me."

20

Undrea couldn't believe she was about to do the one thing she'd vowed never to do in her life. Not knowingly anyway. Not with this kind of intention.

"What do you need me to do?" Mattie asked.

"Protect him from me. Afterwards, I'm going to want to feed. And if I get ahold of him..."

Mattie nodded. "I know. I won't let you. Is there something else in the house that will get rid of that craving?"

Undrea glanced toward the living room. "Yes, but don't let me near the aquarium. There's plenty of seafood in the freezer. If that doesn't seem like it's doing the trick, give me sugar. That can often balance out the urges."

"Okay, I'll make sure that's what you have."

Undrea chewed on her bottom lip. "I need to fill the tub too. I'll have to shift as soon as I can after I feed. It's the best way to reset myself—you know what I mean?"

"Yep."

"But you might have to force me into the water."

"I can do that," Mattie said.

"Whatever it takes. Use magic if you have to."

"I promise. I'll get you in there."

Undrea felt like crying. "I really don't want to do this."

"I know. But I don't see what other choice we have."

"Me, either." She glanced at Bowie. "Sorry about this, buddy, but I promise what you're about to see and hear is just to help your dad. I swear."

Bowie meowed and lifted one paw.

Mattie grinned. "He's a sweet cat. And I'm not just saying that because he's dressed like a bumblebee."

"He really is sweet. He hasn't left Ethan's side since I got him in here."

"Maybe he shouldn't be here during this. In case it freaks him out. The last thing we need is to worry about Ethan's pet."

"Yeah, that's a good point. I'll put him in the hall bath where his litter box is, then I'll start filling the tub." Undrea gave Bowie a little scratch on the head before picking him up. "Come on, little man. Just for a few minutes."

"I'll get the seafood out." Mattie followed her out of the room. She hung by the hall bath as Undrea took Bowie in. "Hey, um, this won't affect me, right?"

Undrea shook her head. "No. Only men." She held Bowie close, petting his velvety skin. "Please don't be afraid of me. I mean, it's okay to be afraid of me when

I'm not myself, but I don't want this to make you afraid of me beyond that. You're the best friend I have, Mattie. I don't want to lose you."

Mattie smiled. "You won't. I promise."

Undrea nodded. "Okay." But Mattie hadn't seen the dark side of her. No one had. She wasn't even fully sure what she was capable of. She just knew that darkness lived inside every one of her kind.

She closed the door on Bowie, then went into her bathroom and started filling the tub for the second time that night. Then she took a long, hard look at herself in the mirror. She could see the monster she was about to become. And if it didn't make Mattie afraid, then nothing probably would.

Steam began to fog the edges of the mirror.

She went back out and found Mattie in the kitchen, getting the bagged seafood out of the freezer.

Mattie turned toward Undrea. "Should I put this stuff in the microwave to defrost it? It's all rock-solid. Also, I sent Corette a text and gave her the details. She wanted to know Nina's full name. Do you know it?"

"Nina Hascoe."

Mattie pulled out her phone and started texting. Then she hit send. "Good. That will help with her research."

Undrea hoped something would. She gestured limply at the food. "Won't matter if the stuff is frozen. Not when I'm in that state."

"Good to know." Mattie put a bag of shrimp on the table. "Ready to go?"

She wasn't. But there was no reason to put it off.

She could already hear Bowie crying to be set free. "Might as well."

Mattie grabbed her hand. "Hey, it's going to be okay. Maybe it wouldn't be if you were alone, but you're not. And I'm not just anyone. I'm the most powerful Celtic witch in this town. We've got this."

Undrea nodded, then made herself smile. "Right."

"Well, that was super convincing."

Undrea laughed softly. "No, you're right. We can do this. We're going to do this. And it's going to be all right. We have to save Ethan. And there's no other way without understanding the magic he's under."

"That's it. That's exactly what you're doing. Helping him."

Undrea turned and went back toward the guest room, but she knew instantly something was wrong. She could see the bed from the hall. And Ethan was no longer on it.

She went into the room and checked on the other side of the bed to make sure he hadn't rolled off. He hadn't. She looked at her friend. "He's gone. How is that possible?"

Mattie's eyes narrowed. "Witchcraft, that's how. I don't know what kind of witch this Nina is, but this level of magic isn't beginner stuff."

"You think she magically transported him out of here?"

Mattie nodded. "Can't you smell the ozone?"

"Ozone? No. My sense of smell isn't any better than a human's, unless I'm underwater."

"Well, trust me, it's there."

Undrea's gaze shifted to the hall, and she ran out of the room and down to the bathroom to check on Bowie. She opened the door and found him curled up in the sink. She looked at Mattie, who'd followed her. "So Nina took Ethan but left his cat."

Mattie arched one brow. "I get the sense that Ethan is the only pet she wants."

"What am I going to do? I'm worried about him. About his safety. I can't let her have him. What if she puts another spell on him and forces him to marry her? He doesn't want to, you know."

Mattie nodded. "I agree, she can't be allowed to get away with this, but this is bigger than the two of us now. We have to get Corette involved. Maybe Alice. Maybe the whole coven. We need to figure out what kind of witch she is so we know how to deal with her."

"But you're not a member of the coven."

"No, but that won't keep them from helping us." She gestured at Bowie. "Is he going to be all right here by himself?"

Undrea nodded. "I'm sure he'll be fine. He's a good boy."

"All right then. Get dressed while I put the seafood away. We need to go talk to Corette."

"Shouldn't we go by Ethan's place and make sure he and Nina are there? Because if she left town with him, then what?"

"That's not a bad idea. I'd bet good honey that's where they are. She just used a *lot* of serious magic. Unless she's some kind of super witch, she's going to need some downtime."

Undrea put her hands on her hips. "Maybe we could steal him back."

Mattie tipped her head. "Neither one of us is James Bond, so dial it down. The last thing we need is a breaking and entering charge. Or for Nina to zap us."

"Can't you..." Undrea wiggled her fingers. "Magic him out of there?"

"No, I can't." Mattie frowned and stared off into space for a moment. "What kind of power does she have?"

Undrea knew that was a rhetorical question, but she shrugged anyway. "Beats me, but I need to know that Ethan is safe. At least for the time being."

Fifteen minutes later, they were in Mattie's car with Undrea driving. Undrea knew how to get to Ethan's house and Nina knew what her truck looked like, so it made more sense to go in Mattie's Nash Rambler.

Not that the 1959 butter-yellow sedan was exactly inconspicuous, but there was no other option.

"Are there security cameras?" Mattie asked.

"I don't know. I don't remember seeing any. But you'd think a guy like Ethan would have them. Then again, they just moved in. Maybe they weren't installed yet?"

Mattie shook her head. "I bet they were. Just because you didn't see them doesn't mean there aren't any. You probably weren't looking."

"I wasn't."

"You'd better park on the road then. We can't risk her knowing we're around."

Undrea looked over. "Afraid she'll zap us?"

Mattie frowned. "Yes. Aren't you?"

Undrea shook her head. "I was, but then she had the chance and didn't. In fact, she ran from me. Poof. Gone. Just like that."

"Hmm." Mattie was staring at Undrea but not really looking at her. "What kind of witch would be afraid of a mermaid?"

"I don't think she knows I'm a mermaid, but a better question is *why* would a witch be afraid of a mermaid?" Undrea slanted her eyes at her friend. "Why would you be afraid of me?"

Mattie hesitated, clearly thinking. "Well…you could drown me. Take me under and keep me there until I was done."

"Okay, but that would require a body of water. Something that isn't easily accessible at my house. I don't think Nina was afraid of me doing that."

"Maybe. But since Nina doesn't know what you are, it has to be something else." Mattie smiled suddenly. "All she knows is that whatever spell she's had Ethan under these last couple of years, you broke it. And now she thinks you're as powerful, or more powerful, than she is. She might even think you're a witch too."

Undrea's eyes narrowed as she thought. "That's interesting. But can't a witch tell another witch?"

"I don't think that's always true. Besides, we don't know what kind of witch she is yet. She might truly be something rare, which is why she's so powerful."

"I really hope Corette can help us." Undrea slowed

and pulled off onto the shoulder just before Ethan's driveway. "We're here."

Mattie rubbed her hands together. "Let's go see what she's up to. Phones on silent. I say we stay in the trees at the property line until we get close. And let's stay together, okay?"

Undrea nodded. "You don't have to ask me twice."

They got out of the Rambler and picked their way through the trees toward the house that lay up the hill. Only a few exterior lights illuminated the outside. And only a soft glow came from the inside, like there was a television show playing or a computer on. From a distance, it was impossible to tell if anyone was home.

And there were no cars in the driveway, but the house had a garage, so that meant nothing.

They went as fast as they could without making too much noise. The closer they got, the more Undrea's stomach knotted up. If Ethan was in there and Nina was doing something awful to him, what was Undrea supposed to do?

How was she supposed to keep Nina from harming him? Because that was exactly what she'd want to do. What woman didn't want to protect the man she was falling for?

Even if those feelings were all magic dust and moonbeams.

21

Ethan's head hadn't stopped spinning since he'd opened his eyes a few minutes ago. There wasn't much point in having his eyes open, actually. He couldn't focus on anything. Not with the room twirling like a carnival ride and him feeling like he'd eaten one corn dog too many.

He'd closed his eyes right away. Was he going to throw up? He hoped not. But he definitely wasn't feeling right. And he wasn't sure why. He'd had another episode, he knew that. But this wasn't like one of his usual spells. They never made him sick like this.

He thought back to the last thing he could remember clearly, hoping to focus on something that might help quell the nausea.

A beautiful tail in a bathtub. He smiled. He'd been at Undrea's house. Is that where he was now? It must be. He wasn't quite ready to risk opening his eyes and throwing up on her guest bed, however, so he kept them closed. She was probably wondering what was wrong with him. He should have told her about his episodes. "Undrea?"

Off in the distance and to the left of him came a hissing sound. Bowie?

"The fish girl isn't here."

Nina. At Undrea's? He had to look. He peered out between slitted lids. The spinning had tapered off enough for him to realize he was in his own bedroom. And he didn't need his glasses to make out Nina standing at the foot of the bed. Bowie was nowhere that Ethan could see.

He *had* been at Undrea's. "How did I get here?"

"I brought you home," Nina said. One arm was crossed against her body, supporting the other arm so that hand could rest on her chin. "You had an episode."

He knew he'd had one, but he didn't remember it happening. He never did when his body shut down like that. Even so, something felt wrong. The blank spot in his memory was even bigger than usual. He shook his head. Bad move. His stomach revolted instantly. He closed his eyes and willed the nausea to go away. "I don't remember."

"You never do." She let out a little half-sob suddenly. "Oh, Ethan, you were so ill. I was afraid you'd hit your head when you passed out."

He risked another look. "And you came to my rescue?"

She seemed to realize his eyes were open again. She clasped her hands in front of her and walked around to sit on the side of the bed. "I did." She smiled sweetly. "Don't I always?"

"Yes," he whispered. What was he not remembering? Why was the blank space so big this time, so hard to navigate around? "How did you know where I was?"

"Andrea called me. Asked me to come get you."

"Undrea," he corrected. Was that possible? Had Undrea done that? Why couldn't he remember? But then, why should this time be any different than any of the others? "Where's Bowie?"

"Downstairs, eating." She put her hand on his arm. "Rest now. You'll feel better in the morning."

"Okay." But he didn't want to sleep. He wanted to figure this out. And he wanted these wretched blackouts to end.

But no doctor, not even the specialists Nina had found for him, had discovered the cause of his troubles. Proof that there were things money couldn't buy, he supposed.

"Do you want anything before I go? Something to drink? Something to eat?"

The mention of food made his stomach roil. "No," he whispered as his mouth watered with another onslaught of nausea. "Nothing."

"All right. I'll close the door so you can sleep. I'll sleep in the guest room tonight, too. I don't want to disturb you, sweetheart. You rest now."

A few seconds later, he felt her get up, then the door closed.

He lay there, feeling miserable. And a little sorry

for himself. And a lot angry. What was going on with him? He was perfectly healthy otherwise. Okay, maybe his diet wasn't the best, but he'd had more tests than he'd thought possible, and not a single one had indicated that his food choices were definitively to blame.

Didn't stop Nina from trying to feed him healthy things all the time.

He sighed. Maybe he was too hard on her. She wasn't perfect, but she wasn't as bad as all that. After all, she really did seem to be looking out for him.

And she was right that she'd always been there for him when he needed her. These attacks had started not long after they'd met.

Stress, the first doctor had said. And many doctors after that. But stress had become the fallback answer because there was nothing else to pin them to.

His frustration grew. Not just because of the episodes but because there seemed to be no cure. And no way to find one. If the problem couldn't be accurately diagnosed, how could it be solved?

He wasn't used to things like that. Problems, yes. But he'd yet to run into one that couldn't be solved. Even his ion membrane would eventually be worked out. He knew it. Time and effort. That's all it took.

Except when it came to his health and figuring out what was wrong with him.

He exhaled and tried to calm his racing mind. All of that angry thinking was probably just making things worse. He needed to focus on something calming. Something that wouldn't raise his stress levels any higher.

Instantly, his mind went to Undrea.

He smiled. Now that was a happy thought. But after a moment, a new worry crept in. How had things gone between her and Nina?

Nina said Undrea had called when he'd had his episode. That seemed…odd. She would have had Nina's number from the fish tank business, but why hadn't Undrea called 911? She was a practical woman. And that seemed like the practical thing to do.

He also questioned Undrea calling Nina because of the tension between them. After all, Nina had shown up at Undrea's house for the sole purpose of telling Undrea to back off.

Or something like that. But whatever it had been, that incident seemed like it might keep Undrea from reaching out to Nina. He wouldn't blame her for that either.

A little twinge at the back of his brain felt like a memory trying to come through. What had triggered that? Thinking about Undrea? Thinking about Nina going to see Undrea?

He tried to remember, tried to narrow down his thoughts to the fragment trying to slip through.

But as the seconds ticked by, the fragment evaporated, leaving him even more frustrated.

He opened his eyes and stared into the darkness. A little moonlight came through the window, enough that his eyes adjusted and he could see shapes. The spinning had almost completely stopped.

He wished Bowie was with him. The cat was a great distraction and a wonderful comfort. Ethan felt like that's what he needed right now. Something to take his mind off what had just happened to him, but he didn't want to read or be on the computer or his phone. He wanted the connection of another living being.

One who wasn't Nina.

He sat up slowly. What a terrible thought to have after she'd done so much for him, but he couldn't help what he felt.

He didn't want her. He wanted Bowie. Or Undrea.

Sitting felt all right, so he felt around the nightstand for his glasses, put them on, then took hold of the headboard and tried standing. He wobbled for a moment, then that last bit of instability seemed to pass. Maybe fresh air would help. He went to the French doors that led out to the second-floor balcony and opened them.

A gust of cold night air greeted him. He grabbed his robe off the footboard and tugged it on, then slipped outside.

It was cool, but with his robe on, it was bearable. He settled onto one of the two chaise lounges and lay back to watch the stars. The sky was beautiful here in Nocturne Falls.

So crisp and clear and filled with more stars than seemed possible. The night sky in the city reflected too much light to see anything but the very brightest of stars and the moon.

The sky here was like something out of a sci-fi movie. He took a deep breath of clean air. Maybe he *should* change his diet. Nina would love that.

He frowned. Why did it matter what Nina

thought? They weren't getting back together. That hadn't changed just because he'd passed out again.

Did she think otherwise? Knowing Nina as he did, she was probably already making plans for their engagement party.

The muscles in his jaw tightened. The woman was relentless, he'd give her that much.

But nothing had changed. If anything, he was more determined to get on with his life.

He squinted in thought. What if Nina was the cause of his stress? He laughed softly. Wouldn't that be something?

He stared up at the sky, a strange, melancholy feeling coming over him. It was almost a feeling of grief, but there was no reason for that. Things might not be great right now, but they would improve.

They had to. Believing otherwise led down a dark road. And he didn't like to dwell on what was wrong. He lived too grand a life filled with too many privileges to feel sorry for himself.

He glanced into the bedroom. What he needed was to get back to work. To sink into a project that would totally absorb his thoughts.

The ion membrane called to him. He got up and went back inside.

22

Undrea led the way with Mattie close behind. They walked through the trees along the property line, deep in the shadows, until they were just below the big windows that looked out toward town.

"Can you see anything?" Undrea asked.

"Not really. Just a few shapes, really. Doesn't look like anyone's home. Or at least they're not downstairs."

"Where else would they be?" Undrea inched closer, trying to get a better look. "Maybe we should go up the hill and see what's around back."

"We're here. Might as well go all the way around."

A light came on inside, flooding the first floor with a brightness that made Undrea blink.

"Okay," Undrea said. "Someone's home, and I'm guessing it's Nina."

Seconds later and Nina walked down the stairs and went into the kitchen.

Mattie straightened a little, lifting up on her toes

like she was trying to get a better look. "Doesn't look like much of a witch to me. Looks like she could use a burger and a day off from the gym."

Undrea snorted. "Well, she might not look like one, but we know what she's capable of."

"He has to be in there somewhere, don't you think?"

Undrea nodded. "She's not about to let him out of her sight again. If she can help it." Then she thought a moment. "I'm pretty sure the master bedroom is upstairs. We should walk around and see if there are any lights on up there."

"Okay, let's go."

They trekked farther up the hillside. They were about a third of the way from the top when Mattie grabbed Undrea's arm and yanked her down.

"What?" Undrea whispered.

"Nina was coming toward the side window. I thought she was going to look out."

"You think she can see us in the dark?"

Mattie shrugged. "We don't know what she's capable of."

"Good point."

They stayed that way for a little bit longer, watching Nina through the windows as best they could. She disappeared again, then came back with a mug in her hand. She stood in front of the sunken living room, the spot where the tank would go, and stared up as she sipped whatever was in that mug.

The look on her face seemed like a mix of triumph and anger. But she also looked tired.

"He's up there," Undrea said. "She might have him bound and gagged for all we know."

"You think she'd go that far? He might still be passed out."

Undrea shook her head. "Something is telling me she'd do whatever it takes to keep him from leaving her again. If we don't stop her…"

"What?"

Undrea exhaled. "I think she's going to bewitch him into marrying her. And then keep him bewitched to prevent him from leaving. Maybe she's drugging him with some kind of home brew that numbs him. Makes him think everything is all right."

Mattie's eyes narrowed.

Undrea made a face. "You think I'm wrong?"

"No. That's what bothers me. I think you could absolutely be right. What bothers me is I don't know exactly what kind of witch we're up against, so I don't know how to fight her. And we're getting into a gray area here. He doesn't know she's a witch."

"I tried to tell him."

"Do you think he remembers?"

"No idea. Maybe."

Mattie looked at the house. "It could be worse for him if he does. Especially if he says something to Nina about being a witch. Then she'll know you told him."

"You think she'll come after me?" Undrea hadn't considered that.

Mattie frowned. "She might. You do still have his cat."

"A hundred bucks says she tells him Bowie ran away. Or something like that. I don't think she likes the cat very much. Actually, I don't think Bowie's that fond of her, either. Despite that whole witches and cats thing."

Mattie frowned. "You mean the archetype of the cat as the witch's familiar?"

"Yes, that."

"Hmm." Mattie peered at the house.

"What?"

"Just thinking. That's an archetype for a reason."

"Well, think while we move. I need to know that Ethan's in that house and that he's all right."

"Lead on."

They got to the back of the house, but there were no lights on upstairs that they could see. And Undrea didn't know where the master bedroom was. They continued around until they were back at the front of the house. The light was off again, but the television was definitely on. Probably Nina in the sunken living room watching something.

Undrea grunted in frustration. "We still have no proof he's in there."

"Maybe he's still unconscious and sleeping?" Mattie offered.

"Maybe. But I want to know."

"There's only one other thing I can think of that will help us." Mattie stuck her hand down the front of her sweatshirt, then pulled it out again and uncurled her fingers. Blueberry lay on her palm, fast asleep.

"You had Blueberry in your bra?"

She shrugged. "He gets cold. And after the incident with the seed beads, I was not leaving him home alone." She gave him a little nudge with her finger. "Psst. Blueberry, wake up."

He rolled over and rounded into a ball.

She leaned in. "Hey, I need you. I'll give you a cookie."

He sat up.

She turned her hand so that he faced the house. "I need you to do a little fly-by and see if there's a man in that house. Dark hair, glasses, tallish. Can you do that?"

Blueberry stood up and nodded, giving her a sharky little grin with all his pointed teeth showing. He fluttered his wings for good measure.

"Good. Thank you."

He hovered over her palm for a moment, then zipped off, leaving a thin trail of blue shimmer behind him that disappeared like sparks going out.

Undrea leaned against a tree. "You sure Nina won't notice him? All that imp magic flitting around her house?"

Mattie grinned. "She might be a powerful witch, but Blueberry's an imp. He's not a human with magic; he's all magic. He trumps her. You get what I'm saying?"

Undrea nodded, hooking her thumbs in the belt loops of her jeans. "Yes. And good. Because I'm tired of feeling like she's one-upping me."

"I hear you."

Less than a minute later, Blueberry came flying

back to them. Mattie held out her hand, and he landed. "So?" she asked. "Did you see the man?"

Before he could answer, the lights blazed to life again in the house, and the muted sound of a loud voice filtered through the evening air.

In full view of them, Ethan came down the stairs, brows bent, jawline tight. "Nina, answer me."

She stood up from the area of the sunken living room, turned, and answered him. Her voice was too quiet for them to hear.

"Blueberry," Mattie whispered. "Amplify."

He lifted off her palm again, hovering about a foot above their heads. When he spoke, it was with Nina's voice. "Ethan, you're not well. You need to be in bed."

Ethan's scowl showed how well Nina's answer went over. "Where is my backpack? It has my laptop and my notebook in it. And my phone."

She put her hands on her hips. Blueberry became her voice again. "My only concern was you, not your things. They must still be at the fish girl's house. I'll get them for you in the morning. Unless you're concerned that she'd steal your ideas."

Ethan frowned. "That's not what I'm saying." He looked around. "Bowie. Here, boy."

Undrea leaned toward Mattie. "Bowie's the cat."

"Right." She nodded.

Ethan glared at Nina. "Where's Bowie?"

From the rise and fall of her chest, it was easy to see Nina sigh. Blueberry continued to speak her words. "He's still at the fish girl's, too. He wouldn't come to me. I'll get him in the morning, too. I told you he was here because I didn't want you to worry. Now, please. Go back to bed. You're only going to work yourself up and—"

Ethan came down the last few steps. "I'm going back to Undrea's."

Undrea sucked in a breath and grabbed Mattie's arm.

"Ethan." Nina's voice came through loud and clear on its own that time. It held a stern warning. Or maybe threat was a better word.

"No, Nina. I'm done. I told you that. I'm not staying here."

"Yes, Ethan. You are." She raised her hand toward him. "*Egin eta ahaztu.*"

He froze in place. Then collapsed, out of sight. Nina ran toward him.

"That's not Latin," Mattie said. "I don't know what that is, but it sounds old. And vaguely European."

"Man dead?" Blueberry asked.

"He'd better not be," Undrea answered, her heart in her throat. "Or the lady's going to wish she never stepped foot in my town." She looked at Mattie. "We have to do something. Nina just knocked him out again."

Mattie nodded. "It's time to visit Corette. I'm not sure Nina isn't something more than just a witch."

Undrea frowned. "Like what?"

Mattie stared at the house. "I don't know. I'm hoping Corette can help us figure that out."

"Are you sure it's safe to leave Ethan here?"

"We don't have much choice. Besides, if she wanted to hurt him, he'd already be hurt. They've been together for two years, after all. I'm pretty sure she needs him alive."

"I hope so."

Mattie offered a thin smile, meant to comfort, Undrea thought. "All she's doing is incapacitating him. Keeping him from leaving. Until we know what we're dealing with, we could end up incapacitated too."

"But we're not human. Well, I'm not."

"No, you're not. But your gifts don't affect women, so you're less powerful than I am in this situation."

Undrea did not want to leave Ethan there, but she had no choice. She pushed away from the tree she'd been leaning on. "You drive. I'll call Pandora and get her to meet us at her mom's."

"Okay." Mattie held her hand out. "Blueberry, let's go."

He landed on her palm. "Cookies now?"

"No, nap now. Cookies when we get home." She tucked him back into her bra.

Undrea started through the woods back to the car. Her friend was transporting an imp in her brassiere, but even that wasn't enough to get her mind off Ethan.

What did Nina want with him? Was it his money? Undrea knew that could be a powerful draw for some women, but her gut said there was more to it than that.

She just didn't know what. And she wasn't sure how to find out.

If Corette couldn't help them, Undrea would have to find another way to rescue Ethan. She was in too deep now. She couldn't just let Nina have her witchy ways with him.

But what could Undrea do? Her skills weren't designed for use on land. Her heart sank, and she trudged back to the car, unable to feel anything but defeated.

23

Corette looked over the rim of her elegant porcelain teacup at Undrea, Mattie, and Pandora. They were all sitting in her lovely living room. Stanhill, her husband, had prepared tea and a generous plate of cookies for them, although he'd disappeared after bringing the refreshments out. "You're sure that's what she said? Those were her exact words?"

Mattie nodded and repeated the phrase they'd heard Nina use.

Pandora made a face. "Do you know what it means, Mom?"

Corette didn't respond immediately. Instead, her delicate brows bent, and she seemed lost in thought for a moment, her gaze on her teacup. "I don't. And the language seems…not exactly archaic but definitely old."

Finally, she looked up at Undrea. "I apologize, but I haven't had a chance to research her properly. I got as far as running her name through the American Council of Witches database when a bride texted me in the middle of a panic attack about her dress."

Undrea tipped her head. "What kind of panic attack happens over a dress?"

"All sorts. In this case, being unable to decide between crystal white or candlelight." Corette smiled. "That's all handled now. But back to Nina. She didn't come up in the database, but her family name did. The Hascoes are an old line and go back nearly to the 1800s. That much I can tell you."

"How about that," Pandora said. "Then she's definitely more than a rare witch. That's too long of a family history not to have some serious power."

"Like we saw," Mattie said.

Corette nodded. "I agree. Her rare witch comment was clearly meant to fool Undrea into underestimating her."

"It worked, too." Undrea shook her head. "But what do we do about it? Every minute Ethan's with her could be his last. We have no idea what she intends to do with him, despite the fact that she hasn't harmed him yet. I just don't trust her."

"I don't either," Mattie said. "Especially now that I know what she's capable of."

Corette set her teacup on the gleaming wood coffee table. "I need to finish my research on the family and see if I can find anything about her that might be useful." She glanced at her daughter. "We could also reach out to Alice."

Undrea shook her head. "I'd rather hold off on

that until it's a last resort kind of thing." Getting Alice Bishop involved seemed like taking one step closer to having her secret revealed. "How long will it take you to finish your research?"

"Depends on how deep the Hascoe records go and if there's any mention of Nina in particular. There should be, considering the family's lineage. So it could be a few minutes, but more likely it will be much longer. I'll get started immediately."

Undrea nodded. "Thank you. What else can we do?"

Pandora inched forward on her seat. "Mom, what about casting a protection spell around the house? Something to keep Nina from using any witchcraft that might cause Ethan harm?"

"Can you do that?" Undrea asked. "Because that would be great."

Corette shook her head with reluctance. "It's a wonderful idea, but it would end up protecting Nina as well. And that might not be something we'd want to do."

Mattie pulled open the neck of her sweatshirt and whispered, "Shh, later," to her chest. Then she smiled apologetically. "Sorry. Blueberry smells the cookies."

"Let him come out," Corette said. "He won't bother anything."

"You don't know what he's capable of," Mattie said. But she pulled the neck of her sweatshirt open again. "Come on."

The imp flew out of her shirt and hovered near the plate of cookies. Mattie quickly grabbed one, broke it into quarters and gave him the smallest piece. "Here. No more fussing now."

He took it and flew off, perching on a nearby lampshade to eat. Crumbs fell like raindrops.

With the soft clearing of his throat, Stanhill reentered the room. "Ladies, I don't mean to intrude, but couldn't the spell be cast so that it only protected the young man in danger?"

Corette smiled knowingly. "Were you eaves-dropping?"

"Me? Hardly." He winked at her. "I was just coming in to see if you needed anything else."

"I see," she said. "As for your question, it could be. But we'd need something of Ethan's. Something personal enough that the magic would respond to it. A few strands of his hair, a fingernail, some tears..." She looked at Undrea. "Any chance you have any of that?"

"He did leave his things at my house. There might be a strand of hair in his comb." Undrea straightened. "Wait. I do have his cat. And Ethan loves Bowie dearly. I don't think there's much that could be more personal than that. Outside of that other stuff you mentioned. Could you use Bowie?"

Corette's smile turned sly. "His cat, hmm? I believe there's definitely something we can do with him." She took a breath. "Ladies, we have work to do."

Pandora smiled. "Do you want me to call Marigold and Charisma?"

"No need," Corette said. "We have three already."

She glanced at Mattie. "That's assuming you're willing to help us create this spell and cast it?"

"Absolutely." Mattie hitched one shoulder up. "Thanks. Considering I'm not in the coven."

"You should be," Corette said with a motherly tone. "But I know we all have our reasons for doing what we do."

She stood. "Undrea, we'll need you to go get Ethan's cat and bring him back here."

Undrea got to her feet. "No problem."

Mattie held out her keys. "Here you go."

Undrea grabbed them and started for the door. "I'll be back as soon as I can. Provided he lets me put him in the carrier."

"I'm sure you'll find a way to persuade him. And while you do that, we'll prepare. The sooner we can do this, the sooner I can go back to the database to complete my research. Ladies, if you'll follow me to my practice downstairs, we'll begin."

Undrea drove straight back to her house. She parked but took a good look around before getting out. Just to be sure Nina wasn't there. She even rolled the window down a crack and sniffed for sulfur. Nothing.

She got out and made a run for the door just in case Nina was lying in wait. But apparently, she wasn't, because Undrea got into the house without incident.

She locked the door behind her and turned on all the lights just for good measure. That earned her a meow as Bowie trotted over. She put Mattie's keys on the little table in the foyer and crouched down.

"Hey, baby. How are you doing? Missing your dad?" She felt sorry for him. Did he have any idea what was going on?

He sat a few feet away and meowed at her again.

"I know. I miss him too. And I'm worried about him, just like you are. But I promise, we're doing something about it. We being me and my friends. I hope you're cool to get in the carrier and come with me, because we need your help."

He just stared, his bicolor gaze peering into her.

The carrier was still in the foyer where Ethan had left it. She pulled it closer and unzipped the opening. Bowie stood, like he knew what was coming.

"Please don't run and hide," Undrea said in her sweetest voice. She straightened, still smiling at him. "We just need to go for a visit."

Bowie backed up a step.

That seemed like a warning sign that he was about to bolt, so she abandoned the carrier for the moment and tried something else. "Bowie, you want a treat?"

Ethan had left the bag with Bowie's food in the kitchen. He'd set up a food and water bowl against the wall where the table was, too, making certain the cat had everything he needed. Which was why she was sure she'd seen a packet of treats in that bag.

She headed for the kitchen. "Come on, Bowie boy. Treat time. Come on. Here, kitty kitty."

Whether he was just curious or knew the word treats, she wasn't sure, but he followed. Thankfully. She found the container, pried off the top, and took a few out.

The first one was just to whet his appetite. She tossed it to him. He watched it arc through the air and gobbled it down a second after it touched the ground.

"Good boy! Do you want another one?" Undrea backed out of the kitchen, holding the treat out. When she was about halfway to the carrier, she tossed it to Bowie.

He snarfed it down and kept following.

She stayed where she was but turned toward the carrier and tossed a treat at it. The little chicken-flavored snack landed a couple of inches away. Bowie went after it and made it disappear. "Good boy," she cooed at him again.

She went over and sat beside the carrier, putting a treat directly in front of her crossed legs.

Bowie ate it, then rubbed his face on her knee.

She leaned down and scratched his head. "Are you going to get into that carrier and let me zip it up? Because this is important. And I really like you, but if I have to drag you out from under a bed, things could get awkward between us, you know?"

He leaned into her hand.

She stopped scratching him to grab a few more treats and toss them into the carrier.

Bowie looked at them. Then hopped in.

"Good boy!" While he was occupied with the treats, she zipped the top closed, then exhaled in relief. "Thank you, Bowie. I appreciate your willingness to be hornswoggled by food. I think that might make you my spirit animal, because I'm pretty sure I could be captured that way myself."

She snatched her keys, then hitched the carrier's long strap over her shoulder. "All right, handsome, let's go do some magic."

24

Ethan woke in the same dark room with the same spinning head and sick stomach. Or at least it felt like the same one. Had he been here before? Or was the strange sense of déjà vu just some awful new twist to these stupid episodes?

He honestly wasn't sure.

He kept his eyes closed and tried to think back to the previous episodes. Had he ever felt déjà vu with them before? He didn't think so. But then his ability to remember the aftermath of those episodes was weak.

That was part of what the spells did to him. They erased portions of his memory. Always the bit right before he blacked out. He had yet to remember having a single one of them.

When he woke up from them, he was left groggy, dizzy, occasionally forgetful, and this time...angry.

That was a new feeling. But not that surprising. Having unexplainable blackouts was enough to tick anyone off, he imagined.

He'd tried numerous doctors. A list of medications and therapies longer than his arm. Nothing had worked. The last thing that remained was changing his diet, something Nina had been pushing him to do. He'd been reluctant to do that, however, because he'd eaten the same way all his life. Why now would it be the cause of something that had only just started happening to him?

But it was time to clean up his food choices and see if that made a difference. There was nothing left to try. Nina would be happy about that decision.

He'd have to tell her just as soon as he was well enough. Tell her. Something about that caused a fragment of memory to come back. The idea of wanting to—no, *needing* to talk to Nina. Was that what it was about? His diet? He couldn't remember. Must have been. Although, maybe not...he couldn't remember.

He sighed out a soft curse and pushed his face into the pillow, balling his fists in frustration.

Even that small amount of movement exhausted him. He was too tired and too drained to think about anything except sleep. He closed his eyes and let the blackness take him.

By the time Undrea got back to Corette's, Bowie had finally stopped yowling. She didn't know if it was the carrier or the car ride, but he'd been pretty vocal about his displeasure at one of them. Nothing she'd said or done had calmed him down, either. Maybe it was both.

"I'm sorry you were so miserable, but we're here now." She picked up the carrier and went to the front door. He was still making small, grumpy noises.

Stanhill opened it before she could knock. "They're waiting for you in Corette's practice."

Undrea frowned. "Her practice?"

"Her craft room, if you will."

"Ah." She understood he meant crafts of the witchy variety, not the bedazzling kind.

Bowie let out a little growl.

Stanhill shifted his gaze to the carrier. "Hello there, young man."

Bowie let out a slightly miffed meow.

"He's not happy about being in the carrier."

Stanhill nodded. "Poor fellow needs his freedom, don't you? Although he might like a piece of chicken, too. He's one of those hairless ones, I see." He laughed. "About as different from Captain Underpants as you can get."

Captain Underpants was Delaney's enormous black and white Maine Coon cat, an animal Stanhill knew well because he was Delaney's husband's rook. Hugh was a vampire, and Stanhill was sort of a half-turned butler. He had some heightened abilities but none of the sensitivity to the sun, enabling him to take care of any daytime things Hugh couldn't.

Not that Hugh and Delaney really needed that kind of help. All of the Ellinghams had some special gift that allowed them to be out during the day, so Stanhill was really more of a regular butler. And since he and Corette had married, he only worked at the Ellinghams' during the day anyway, or evenings if he was needed for a dinner party or something.

"Follow me," he said. "I'll show you through."

"Great." She followed him into the house and to a door off the kitchen. Bowie made one small meep but then settled down. Maybe the new surroundings were more to his liking.

He opened the door, and she could hear female voices. "Just down those steps."

"Thanks." She started down. Stanhill shut the door behind her. She put her hand on the side of the carrier to steady it and called out, "I'm back, and I've got Ethan's cat."

"Perfect timing," Pandora said as Undrea joined them. "We're ready for him."

Undrea lifted the carrier. "This is Bowie. I think he's a little freaked out."

Corette's basement practice looked pretty much like what Undrea thought it would: cream plastered walls, bronze lighting fixtures with Edison bulbs, a wide-planked dark wood floor, and a crackling fire in the fireplace on the rear wall. Beside that was a large, whitewashed worktable. On one end, a delicate crystal vase held ivory roses and greenery. On the other sat a collection of beeswax candles in mercury glass holders.

Shelves spanned the adjacent wall, each one filled with the books, jars, boxes, bags, and containers that made up her accumulated supplies—years of gathering, Undrea imagined. A beautiful rug of woven jewel tones had been rolled out of the way, and now a salt circle took its place.

The scents of woodsmoke, beeswax, and roses perfumed the air. It was a gorgeous, refined space.

Corette came over, speaking in hushed tones to Bowie. "Welcome to my home, sweet cat. We know your father is in trouble, and we want to protect him, but we need you to be a part of that. Will you help us?" She held her hand in front of the mesh opening at the carrier's end.

Bowie sniffed her, then pushed his head against her fingers through the mesh.

Corette smiled. "What a good boy." She nodded at Undrea. "Bring him into the center of the circle. You can leave him in the carrier. There's no need to stress him any further by taking him out of it."

"Okay." She carefully stepped over the salt line and set the carrier in the middle, then turned to go.

"No, Undrea," Pandora said. "Stay in there with him."

Undrea frowned at her. "You want me in here too?"

Mattie nodded. Blueberry was sitting on her shoulder, braiding a strand of her hair. "We figured we'd better protect you too. Just for good measure."

"Okay." She'd never had any witchcraft directed at her. That she was aware of. She went back to the middle and picked the carrier up, hugging it to her body. Being spelled, even for her own protection, was...weird.

After all, she had her own magic. She shouldn't need— "Hold on."

Corette was about to light a candle. "Yes?"

"I think I'm good. As far as needing any protection." Undrea tried to smile normally. Nonchalantly. Not like someone who'd just realized that a spell designed to protect a mermaid might not exactly work for her. Seeing as how that wasn't exactly what she was.

Corette frowned. "My dear, we don't know what Nina's capable of. I strongly urge you to let us cast this protection over you."

"It's just that…" She looked at Mattie. "You know."

Mattie shook her head. "What are you worried about?"

Undrea took a breath to calm herself down a little. "I'm just not sure this spell will work for *me.*"

Mattie made a face at her. "It'll be fine."

"I don't know," Undrea continued. "I thought I should *voice* my concerns."

Mattie stared at her a second longer, then her mouth rounded into an O as she got what Undrea was trying to say. The preparations for the spell must have taken over her brain. "Yeah, right, okay. Um…nothing to worry about, though. You're good."

"You're sure?" Undrea didn't want to have the protection spell do something weird just because Corette had built it to work on a mermaid and only a mermaid.

"Positive," Mattie said. "It's a very general protection spell. Male, female, human, supernatural, animal. All covered. You'll be fine."

Undrea exhaled. "Okay. Good."

Pandora was looking at her strangely. Undrea just smiled back and offered the first excuse that came to her mind. "It's just strange to have magic done to me. I mean, I'm already a supernatural. I have my own magic. It seems like the two would cancel each other out. Or worse, do something weird to me."

Pandora nodded like that made perfect sense. "Don't worry. It doesn't work that way. But I can understand thinking that."

For that, Undrea was glad. "Ready when you guys are."

Corette walked around the circle, lighting candles with a thin branch that had been set alight at one end. Undrea had a feeling it wasn't just any kind of wood, but she didn't want to interrupt the spellcasting to ask.

When the candles were lit, Corette joined Pandora and Mattie just outside of the salt circle. They stood equal distances from each other so that Corette was directly in front of Undrea, and Pandora and Mattie flanked her on the right and left. As they spread out their arms, Corette did the same, all of them with their palms up.

Undrea hugged the carrier closer, glancing down to check on the little cat. Bowie seemed fascinated by it all.

Then Corette spoke. "Guardians of earth and air, fire and water, protect this woman, Undrea, and this creature, Bowie. We also ask that you bind a separate spell of protection to this creature for the one who cares for him. A spell to be passed on to him so that he may be protected from the witch, Nina, who means him harm. Guard the woman and the cat within this circle, and the man beyond it who needs protection. Keep them all from danger. Shelter them from dark magic. So mote it be."

"So mote it be," Pandora and Mattie responded in unison.

Corette brought her arms back to her sides and smiled at Undrea. "As you leave the circle, be careful not to break the line of salt. So long as this stays intact, the spell of protection will also be unbroken. It will remain until Ethan is safe."

"Thank you." Undrea stepped over the circle of salt and joined her friends on the other side. "I appreciate you doing that, Corette."

"Of course."

"Now you're going back to researching Nina?"

"I am. Let us know how things go when you return from Ethan's."

Undrea tilted her head. "What do you mean, when I get back from Ethan's?"

Corette touched Undrea's arm. "Someone has to take the cat to him, or the spell can't be transferred. That's why we wanted to protect you too."

25

Undrea hadn't been counting on taking a trip to Ethan's, but then it made sense. How else was Bowie supposed to transfer the protection spell? He wasn't magic. He was a cat.

Seeing Nina, however—that was the fly in the ointment.

Undrea had always considered herself a pretty brave person. But Nina scared her. A little. Mostly because Undrea had no idea what she was capable of. And what she might do if she thought she was threatened.

Although Mattie had pointed out earlier that instead of doing something, Nina had bolted when Undrea had run toward Ethan.

She clung to that idea, to the possibility that Nina might be a little afraid of her, too.

Mattie walked beside her as they headed to the car. "Are you nervous?"

"You bet I am." Undrea looked at her friend.

"What if she zaps me with those same words and knocks me out?"

"Then I'll send Blueberry after her and rescue both of you."

"Yeah," Blueberry said. He was still sitting on Mattie's shoulder, but now he was hanging on to her braid so he didn't fall off. "Then I get cookies?"

Undrea snorted. "Sure, you'd get a lot of cookies for that."

"Hey," Mattie said. "Don't encourage him."

She slanted her eyes at him. "You know I was just kidding, right, Blueberry?"

He looked at her, cocking his little head to the side. "What's kidding?"

Then he slapped his leg and laughed, a tinny, high-pitched sound that had an undercurrent of wheezing breathlessness to it. "Joke!"

She and Mattie both laughed as well, and the lightness of the moment took away some of Undrea's wariness at going to see Nina. Hopefully, she'd get a glimpse of Ethan too. Maybe even get to talk to him.

Maybe even…warn him. Was that possible? Would he believe her? She supposed that all depended just how deep of a spell Nina had him under.

They got into Mattie's Rambler, Bowie on the seat between them, and Mattie drove toward Ethan's.

Undrea stared out through the windshield without really seeing anything. "If I get to talk to Ethan, do you think I should try to tell him what Nina's doing to him?"

"No." Mattie sighed. "As tempting as that might be, do you actually think you could convince him that the woman he's been involved with for the past two years is really a witch and that she's been using her magic on him? That's not a quick conversation."

Undrea nodded. "That's what I was thinking too. It would probably do more harm than good."

"Just get Bowie back to him and let Corette do her research. Once Ethan's protected and we know what kind of power Nina has, we'll make a plan and get him away from her. Then you can have a long, sit-down talk with him and tell him all about things that go bump in the night. And now live next door to him."

Mattie glanced at Undrea. "How do you think he'll react to that?"

"I think he's going to need proof. He's a big thinker but a logical one. And he's an engineer."

"Oh boy."

"Yep." Undrea glanced at Bowie. He wasn't yowling. In fact, he was lying down, looking very much like he was about to go to sleep. Was he worn out from all the excitement? Or had the spell destressed him? Maybe it was protecting him from stress? Interesting. "You know, in a way, he's already seen proof. He just doesn't know it."

"Meaning?"

"Me in the lake being underwater for so long. And my tail."

"Back up. He's seen your tail?"

"He has. He doesn't know it's my real tail, though. He thinks it's a costume, basically." Undrea explained everything that had happened with Bowie scaring her and making her drop her phone in the tub and how Ethan had fixed it, only to bring up the last picture she'd accidentally taken. "Really, it's your fault."

Mattie laughed. "Nope. You do not get to blame that on me." She turned toward Ethan's. "But that's kind of amazing. He not only saw your tail in a photo but came up with his own explanation that sort of makes you look like a weirdo and yet, he's totally okay with it."

"Pretty much."

She shook her head as a slow smile spread across her face. "That man is nuts about you."

"I like nuts," Blueberry said.

Undrea laughed. "You like anything edible."

"I'm going up the driveway," Mattie said. "I'm not parking down by the street."

"Why would you park down by the street?"

"So Nina couldn't see me or my car. But you might need a quick getaway so we're just going to lose that element of surprise."

"I'm fine with that. Especially because if you're not close and she zaps me, you'll never know."

"That too." Mattie pulled into Ethan's driveway. "Although I'd kind of like to see her try. I mean, now that you have a protection spell on you."

"I'll pass on testing that, thanks." Undrea stared at the house. It was late. Almost midnight now. The same blue glow lit the inside of the house.

"She must still be up." Mattie said what Undrea had been thinking.

"Good, because I bet she wouldn't be very friendly about being woken up."

A few feet from the house, Mattie threw the Rambler into park. "What are you going to say to her?"

"Just that Bowie was crying a lot and I thought I'd better bring him home." Undrea shrugged. "Unless you have something better."

"No, that's good. Short and simple. Hand him off and get out of there."

A pang of regret swept through Undrea. She stared at Bowie, nestled in his carrier. "If she hurts him, I'll kill her."

"Ethan or Bowie?"

Undrea looked up. "Either one."

"They'll be safe. Just like you. Corette's spells are very sure."

With a nod, Undrea took the carrier by its handles and opened the car door. The air was chilly, bordering on cold, but they were up in the hills and it was still early spring. Her sweater wasn't cutting it.

She hustled to the door and rang the bell, the tune she'd previously thought familiar playing throughout the house. Then it occurred to her what the song was. David Bowie's "Let's Dance."

She laughed softly, smiling at Ethan's choice.

Then Nina opened the door. Her eyes narrowed. "You."

Undrea stopped smiling. She held up Bowie in his carrier. "Ethan's cat wouldn't stop crying, so I figured I'd better bring him back."

Nina just stared, frowning. She made no move to take the carrier.

Undrea pushed the carrier into her arms, then turned and walked quickly away. She hated leaving Bowie behind, but more than that, she hated having her back to Nina. It caused every little hair on the nape of her neck to go up. Then she heard the door close, and she relaxed.

The job was done. Ethan would be safe now. But then she realized the strangest thing. Her heart ached because she'd given Bowie back. Was that weird? It had to be. He wasn't her cat. And she'd only just met him.

And yet, she missed him. Like she missed Ethan.

She got in the Rambler and stared back at the house.

"You okay?" Mattie asked.

Undrea shook her head slowly. "Not really, no. How can I miss a man and his cat this much after only just meeting them?

"Easy," Mattie said as she drove forward. "You're falling in love."

Ethan woke again in a dark room with a weight on his chest. A familiar weight. One not even his blackout could erase from his memory. He smiled. He didn't need his glasses to know who'd just showed up, either. "Hey, Bowie boy."

He reached up and put his hand on the cat and got a little shock, like a static electricity charge. He yanked his hand back. "Sorry about that."

Ethan put his hand on Bowie again. No shock this time. He pulled the cat closer. "Come on. You know you want to snuggle."

Bowie obliged by flopping over and sinking himself into the crook between Ethan's neck and shoulder. He immediately started purring.

"I love you too, buddy. I'm really glad these stupid episodes don't make me forget you." Ethan turned his head toward the little cat and closed his eyes again. The dizziness seemed to be gone, as was the queasiness in his stomach.

He exhaled, happy to be feeling better. His next inhale brought the scent of salt and sea.

He inhaled again, purposefully this time, and got more of the same. He pressed his face into Bowie's sweater-covered side.

The sweater smelled like Undrea. How was that possible? It shouldn't be. Was he imagining it? He'd never had any kind of sensory side effects with his episodes before.

He lay there with Bowie cuddled up against him for a long time. Long enough for the sky to lighten and chase away the room's darkness. He wasn't tired. But he was comfortable, especially with Bowie's little motor and happy biscuits going on right beside him.

Ethan smiled. "We should get up, buddy. Lots to do." Like find a new place to live. Episodes or not, he wanted to be away from Nina.

Actually, what he wanted was to be with Undrea. More than anything, really. The desire to see her had become so deep, it felt necessary.

His stomach rumbled.

He supposed visiting her could wait until after breakfast. He slid Bowie off so that he could sit up. He sat on the edge of the bed, feet on the floor, and took a moment to make sure the spinning really had stopped.

As he did that, his memory of what had happened began to return. It was the same as it always was. He could remember pretty well until just before the blackout. Then nothing.

This time was no different. He'd been at Undrea's. He smiled. He remembered all of that. Fixing her phone, finding out she liked to pretend to be a mermaid in the tub, the whole thing.

Then Nina had come over. He squinted as the memory started to grow dim. She'd been…outside. And she'd wanted to talk about them.

He shook his head. There was no them. He was sure he'd told her that, hadn't he?

And then it all went black.

Was that what had caused the episode? The stress of arguing with Nina? He tried hard to remember more, but it only made his head hurt.

Bowie came over to lean against him.

He put his arm around the cat. Poor Undrea. She must have been shocked that he'd blacked out like that. What had Nina told her? Everything? That he'd been having the episodes for two years now and there was no cure for them so far?

Maybe that was more than Undrea had bargained for. Maybe she wouldn't want anything to do with him now.

But no, Undrea wasn't like that at all. At least he didn't think so.

Sure, Nina had brought him back here, but then Undrea might have thought that was what was best for him.

Nina could be very persuasive. And this episode would be the perfect excuse to get him back in the same house with her again.

He frowned and scratched Bowie's head. "We need to talk to Undrea."

Bowie meowed.

Ethan nodded. "Right after breakfast."

26

Undrea felt odd as she got ready for work. It wasn't a feeling she knew a name for. Something like sadness mixed with the sense of waiting for the other shoe to drop along with a dash of angry. Maybe a drop of being unsettled. And a big dollop of longing. All with an undercurrent of worry.

She missed Ethan. And Bowie. And she was on edge with not knowing what was going on with them.

Was there a name for that? Worry? It felt like more than that. And as she stood at the kitchen counter slathering a birthday cake Pop-Tart with Marshmallow Fluff to have with her coffee, she wasn't sure she could get through the day feeling like this.

Her ability to concentrate was off. She couldn't focus on anything for more than a minute or two without her mind going back to Ethan. A hot shower hadn't helped. Neither had her first cup of coffee.

Maybe she should have gotten up earlier so she could have fit in a swim at the lake, but she'd been up so late last night.

Just as she was licking a smudge of Marshmallow Fluff off her finger and getting ready to put the lid back on the jar, her cell phone rang. She'd left it in the bedroom, so she ran back to grab it. The ring tone was unfamiliar, but it had probably reset to the factory default after the whole tub incident.

But when she picked it up, there was no incoming call because the ringing wasn't coming from her phone.

The sound was coming from the guest room.

She walked next door and arrowed in on it. Ethan's phone was lying on the bed, half-tucked under one of the pillows. She picked it up. Screen ID showed the call was coming from his mom.

Undrea hesitated, then thought about how worried his mom might be if she hadn't been able to get ahold of him. She answered. "Hello?"

"Well, hello there. You're not my son."

Undrea smiled because she could hear the smile in the other woman's voice. "No, ma'am, I'm not."

"You must be Undrea, because you're not Nina."

Undrea blinked a few times in surprise. "You know my name?"

"I do. Ethan told me he was staying with you."

"Oh, right."

"I'm Constance Edmonds, by the way. In case he didn't tell you that. And please, call me Connie."

"He didn't tell me, but I'm sure he would have

gotten around to it. Nice to meet you, Connie. As it were."

"You too. Is he there?" She laughed softly. "I have a little surprise for him."

"No, he's not, unfortunately. But his phone is. Which is why I answered it."

Connie groaned. "Don't tell me he went back to Nina."

"I wouldn't say he went back exactly…more like she took him." Undrea shook her head. "It's kind of a long story." And not one Undrea felt like she could even begin to explain over the phone to a woman she'd never met and didn't know. Freaking Ethan's mom out just seemed like it had bad idea written all over it.

"Well, why don't you tell me in person?"

"I don't know where you live. And to be honest, I should really go to work today." Plus she had no intention of going anywhere until the Nina problem was solved.

Connie's soft laugh filled the line again. "My little surprise was that my friend Sarah Jane and I are in Nocturne Falls for a visit. Well, the surprise isn't really that we came for a visit; he knew we were going to come. Just not when. That part is the surprise. Say, are you in Nocturne Falls? Or do you live somewhere else?"

Undrea was still smiling. She already liked Connie. "No, I live here. So you're in town?"

"We are. We took a red-eye. It was the cheapest, and when you get old, you don't sleep anyway. We rented a car at the airport and just arrived."

"Do you have a place to stay yet?"

"No, but we'll sort that out. Sarah Jane and I were a little more concerned with breakfast, to be honest. If her blood sugar drops, she can get cranky in a hurry. Can you recommend a good place?"

"I can do better than that," Undrea said. "I'll give you directions and meet you there."

Twenty minutes later and after a call to Whitney to say she'd be in late, she was standing outside of Mummy's diner looking for two older women.

They weren't hard to spot, in part because they were smiling at her and waving.

"You must be Undrea." The woman who had Ethan's smile stuck out her hand. "I'm Ethan's mom, Connie."

Undrea grinned and shook her hand. "It's a pleasure to meet you." Connie had dark, shoulder-length hair with lots of silver streaked through it. She was dressed in mom basics: capri jeans, a striped twin set, and sensible sandals. Her red glasses brought attention to her kind eyes. She was absolutely adorable.

"Aren't you pretty?" the other woman said. She leaned in. "I'm Sarah Jane, in case you hadn't guessed."

"Nice to meet you too," Undrea said. Sarah Jane looked like a distant older cousin of Mattie's, with fully silver hair that went well past her shoulders. Her long denim skirt and embroidered gauze blouse had a bohemian vibe that matched the stack of beaded bracelets on her wrist.

Undrea liked them both immediately. "Come on. Let me show you how Nocturne Falls does breakfast."

They made small talk as they ordered and then dug in, but it wasn't until the enormous cinnamon roll arrived that things got serious.

Sarah Jane shook her head. "Connie, we might have to move here. Look at that thing. I feel like I'm getting emotionally attached."

Connie laughed. "You have an unnatural affection for pastries."

Sarah Jane looked at Undrea. "She's right. I do. Baked goods will be my downfall."

"Why don't you cut it up and we'll all share it?" Undrea asked.

Sarah Jane nodded. "Good idea." She went to work on that.

Connie smiled a little wistfully. "You haven't said much about Ethan and Nina. Would you rather not talk about them? About what happened?"

Undrea took a breath. "No, it's not that. It's just… I don't quite know where to start. She's no good for him. I'll tell you that much."

Connie nodded. "I know she's not. But sometimes men have to learn things for themselves."

"I don't know if he's really learned that yet so much as he's just decided he wants something else."

Sarah Jane gestured with her icing-laden butter knife. "Like you, you mean."

Undrea snorted and shook her head. "Maybe. But it wasn't intentional."

"I don't care if it was," Connie said. "I'm glad you

came into the picture." She reached across the table and took Undrea's hand. "I know you're more than you seem."

Undrea went still. What did she mean by that? "You, uh…do?"

Connie nodded, her eyes filled with motherly concern. "Sarah Jane reads tea leaves, and she saw that a *special* woman would come into Ethan's life a year ago. We've been waiting on you."

Sarah Jane was busy putting pieces of cinnamon roll on their plates but paused to nod. "It's true. I did."

"I know you might not believe in such things, but trust me," Connie said. "There's more out there than you realize. I have a particular gift myself, but we won't go into that because I don't want you to think I'm some crazy woman."

Undrea rolled her lips in to keep from responding too quickly. She needed a moment to figure out how to answer in such a way that wouldn't send them running. Having a little psychic ability was one thing; finding out your son was shacked up with a wicked witch was another. Add a mermaid on top of that and, well, things could get weird.

Sarah Jane frowned at Connie as she licked the icing off her fingers. "She already thinks you're crazy. She thinks both of us are. Look at her, eyes wide like you just grew a set of antennae. Why didn't you do that with Nina and scare her off?"

Connie made a face at her friend. "Because I didn't think Ethan was serious about her, and if I had known—"

"No," Undrea said. "I don't think you're crazy. Not at all. You haven't scared me off one bit." She swallowed. "But we can't talk about all of this here. We can go back to my house, if that's all right with you?"

Connie nodded. "That's just fine."

"Same here." Sarah Jane stabbed another bite of roll. "But this cinnamon bun is coming with us."

27

Undrea drove a little slower than usual so Connie and Sarah Jane didn't get lost as they followed her back to her place. Connie was driving and didn't seem to be having any trouble keeping up, but Undrea didn't want to risk losing her. She was nearly home when her phone rang.

She answered using the truck's Bluetooth connection to stay hands-free. "Hello?"

"Undrea, it's Corette. Do you have a moment? And a safe place to talk?"

"Hi Corette. I have a moment, but I'm driving and you're on speaker. Is that okay?"

"Are you alone in the car?"

She glanced back at the two women following her. What kind of news could Corette have? "I am."

"Good." Corette took a breath. "Nina's not in the American Council of Witches database, which is odd. Odd enough that I did some more research on my own. Message boards and such. Sealed files.

Things like that. I also had to get some other info that Birdie Caruthers helped me with. Like Nina's birth certificate. You know Birdie? From the sheriff's department?"

"Yes, I know her." Undrea was amazed Corette had gone to such lengths but also eager to hear what she'd found.

"Good. That's why it's taken me so long. And I promise all of this is being kept confidential. To our group anyway. But the bottom line is Nina's not a witch."

"She's not?"

"No. She's much worse. She's a succubus. As best as I can tell."

Undrea almost missed her own driveway. She turned suddenly, hoping she hadn't caught Connie off-guard. "A succubus? As best you can tell?" She parked behind Ethan's car and glanced back. Connie was still with her and pulling alongside. Would Connie recognize her son's car?

"Yes," Corette said. "You see, her mother, Elizabeth Willet Hascoe, is a witch. That's probably how Nina found your house. Her mother must have helped her, because I don't think a succubus could do something like that. Elizabeth was a rather powerful up and comer too, at least until she was removed from the ACW for dealing in black magic."

Undrea parked and turned the engine off. "What happened?"

Connie and Sarah Jane were still in their rental. Undrea caught Connie's eye, held up a finger to indicate she needed a minute, then made her thumb and pinkie into a phone and held them to her ear.

Connie nodded in understanding.

Corette went on. "This must remain confidential. No further than our group. Being the coven secretary makes me privy to information not widely available to anyone else. I have access to ACW files that not many do. You understand?"

"Perfectly."

"All right then. Elizabeth's husband's family is old money. Mayflower old. And things weren't going so well. He was caught running a Ponzi scheme that made Madoff look like Robin Hood, and to get him out of it, Elizabeth offered up her soul to some very dark beings. But that wasn't enough. They wanted the soul of her firstborn child, too. And Elizabeth agreed, in exchange for some additional perks."

Undrea's mouth fell open. "She sold Nina's soul to the devil?"

"In a manner of speaking. That pact is why the Hascoe family has become untouchable, but the price for that lofty existence is the constant need for a certain type of sustenance. And not just for Nina. It's possible she's fueling her mother's magic too, now. You see Nina isn't your typical sexually fueled succubus. She requires fame and power and influence."

"The kind she gets from being Ethan's girlfriend?"

"Worse," Corette said. "The kind she gets *from* Ethan. He's the source she needs. And those episodes he has?"

Undrea put a hand over her mouth in sudden insight. "They have nothing to do with anything being wrong with him. It's Nina draining him."

"Yes. We have to deal with her. Now. But it's not going to be easy. Most succubi have a way of tethering themselves to their victims in multiple ways. You may have broken one or two of those tethers with your own magic, but until they're all severed, he'll never really be free of her."

"Just tell me what to do, and I'll do it." Undrea glanced at the car parked beside her and the two women sitting in it. "There's just one little problem..."

Ethan stood by the kitchen window, drinking the cup of coffee he'd just poured for himself. Despite all the sleep he'd had and the coffee he'd drunk, Ethan still felt tired. Just searching his office for his laptop and notebook had worn him out. This last episode had apparently taken more out of him than any of the previous ones.

The severity of his episodes increasing didn't bode well for the future. Neither did his laptop and notebook being missing. They had to still be at Undrea's. He hoped.

Nina walked into the kitchen in her yoga gear and looking like she'd just finished a workout. She was practically glowing. It had to be the sweat, and yet there was something about her. She looked… radiant. She smiled at him. "Good morning. How are you feeling?"

He shrugged. "I've been better."

She nodded, instantly sympathetic. "I'm sure you have been. There was no point in telling you this last night because you wouldn't have remembered, but you had two episodes almost back-to-back."

"I did?" The sick feeling returned to his gut. "Two?" He sank into one of the kitchen chairs. "I don't remember that."

"I knew you wouldn't. I'm so sorry. Maybe it's the stress you've been under lately?"

He took a deep breath, a little anger creeping in because she was undoubtedly the cause of that stress. He changed the subject, although it would probably just make things worse. "How's your search going for a place to live?"

She went to the refrigerator and got out the carafe of green juice. "Do you really think living apart is a good idea? After last night? Who's going to take care of you the next time you pass out?"

Undrea came to mind, but he didn't say anything. He wasn't going to assume. "I can take care of myself."

"Can you? Really? Because you would have been lying on the cold, hard ground all night until you came to. You know that, right?"

"Undrea would have taken me inside."

Nina exhaled through her nostrils, making a short,

sharp sound. "You deserve to know that your fish girl looked like she wanted to run when you went down. I don't think she's cut out for the Nurse Nightingale role."

He turned to see her better. "Undrea saw what happened?"

Nina poured a glass of juice, then put the carafe back in the fridge. "She did. She seemed horrified. I understand. It's pretty shocking the way your eyes roll back and you drop like a dead weight. Not everyone can deal with that sort of event. She took one look at you and went right back into her house."

He turned away again. He refused to believe Undrea had reacted that way. It just didn't seem like her.

Nina went on. "She only opened the door to kick Bowie out, and that was the last I saw of her."

Ethan's jaw tightened in anger. Now he knew Nina was lying. He might not have known Undrea long, but it had been enough time to see that she wouldn't treat his cat that way. He took a breath, schooled his emotions, and as a new plan emerged in his thoughts, he faced Nina with as real a smile as he could manage. "I'm so glad you were there to look out for me. For Bowie too."

Nina smiled back. "Of course, sweetheart. You're my whole life. I hope you understand that."

He got up and faced her. "Seeing you in your yoga gear and drinking that green juice has inspired me. I think I'll go for a run."

"You feel well enough for that?"

"I do." He didn't. But she didn't need to know that. "And from here on out, I'm going to make better food choices, too."

Her smile got bigger. "That's wonderful. How about a veggie stir-fry for dinner? We can have brown rice with it too."

"That sounds great. I'll stop at the market and pick up some things on my way back."

"Perfect. Get some of that baby bok choy if they have it. That's my favorite."

"I'll look for it." He walked over and gave her a poison lips a kiss. "If you need anything else, just text me."

She put her hand on his chest, looking thoroughly pleased. "I will. I assume you're taking the Maserati?" She made a face as if she smelled something awful. "Seeing as how we still need to get your Land Rover back from you know where."

"Yes, the Maserati. We can deal with the Land Rover later."

She patted his chest. "All right. I have to take a shower. You have fun at the lake. Don't overdo it."

"I won't." He watched her leave, his smile vanishing off his face. He was practically trembling with rage.

He waited a few minutes, walking out into the living room to listen for the upstairs shower to come on. As soon as it did, he scooped Bowie up and put him in the carrier that was sitting near the door. Not where it should have been, but there wasn't time to think about that. He held the carrier up so he could look Bowie in the eyes. "Be right back. No yowling, okay? Stealth mode. You got it?"

Bowie pushed his head against the mesh screen, clearly in need of pets.

"Soon, buddy." Ethan set him down by the door, then went to grab the keys to his convertible. The keys to the Land Rover were probably still at Undrea's with his car and the rest of his stuff. Why hadn't Nina brought any of that back? The car he could understand, but why not his backpack?

Keys in hand, he went straight to the garage, picking Bowie up on his way out. He kept the Maserati's top up since he had Bowie along. Ethan didn't want to freak him out with all the air.

As he pulled out of the driveway, his anger dissipated a little, replaced by new determination. Nina was conniving, for sure, but he hadn't become one of the richest men in the country by being dumb.

Bowie let out a little meow.

"Hang in there, bud. We won't be in the car too long."

He'd bought himself some time. Now he just needed to make a few more smart choices. The first one was going to Undrea's.

He'd get her side of the story, then figure out what to do from there. Not only did he need to talk to her, but he was pretty sure his backpack with his laptop, notebook, and cellphone were all still at her place. He needed those.

His laptop and notebook were invaluable. And while everything on his laptop was backed up to his own cloud, the notebook obviously wasn't. He had years of ideas and concepts sketched out in there.

A new thought occurred to him. Was there any chance Nina had those things? And was willfully withholding them?

Maybe. But if stealing his ideas was her game plan, she'd been setting him up for a long time. That couldn't be what she was after. Was it just the fame and fortune of being his girlfriend? And eventually, his wife?

He wasn't sure. And his head still wasn't a hundred percent. Maybe he'd get a hotel room once he had his laptop and notebook back and just sleep for a day. That would help a lot. But that wasn't everything he needed to feel better.

What would help was seeing Undrea. He didn't know how or why, but she felt like the answer to questions that hadn't even been asked yet.

28

Undrea got Connie and Sarah Jane settled in the living room, leaving them to admire the aquarium, then went into the kitchen to put a pot of coffee on. Today was the kind of day that was going to require a lot of it. She could just tell.

Connie had indeed recognized her son's vehicle, but she'd already known Ethan had been here, so it wasn't much of a surprise. Undrea imagined finding out why he wasn't still here would be.

And she was about to tell them everything, so she'd know for sure in a minute.

With the coffee brewing, she went back out to join the women. She sat in the Eames-style chair facing the tank and swiveled to see her guests better. She smiled at them, hoping the next few minutes of conversation went smoothly.

Because the opposite of that was very possible. Especially with what she was going to reveal.

"Go on," Connie said. "I know you have something you want to say."

"I do. It's just finding the right place to start."

"Maybe there is no right place," Sarah Jane said. "Dive in. We'll help you figure it out."

Buoyed by Sarah Jane's choice of words, Undrea nodded. What choice did she have? "Okay. Here goes. I'm not bothered by Sarah Jane's ability to read tea leaves, or whatever gift you might have, Connie—"

"You don't know what it is yet."

Amused, Undrea nodded. "You're right, I don't. But I already know there's very little chance it'll surprise me."

"Oh?" Connie said. And then she disappeared. "Still think that?"

Undrea stared at the place where Connie had been. The place her voice was coming from. "So you can…make yourself invisible?"

Connie reappeared. "Not exactly invisible. The women in my family have always had the peculiar gift of camouflage. Chameleonism, some might call it. If you know what to look for and look closely, you can sometimes still see me. Especially in bright light."

"That's very cool." And it should make what Undrea was about to tell them a lot easier to take. "Ethan knows about this?"

"He does." She smiled broadly. "Where do you think he got the idea for Blnk?"

"Software that helps you disappear online. Wow." Undrea shook her head as the connection became clear. "How about that? I know you said the women of your family can do it, but did Ethan inherit any of your ability?"

"No. He's as human as his daddy." Connie's eyes narrowed ever so slightly. "Back to you. If none of what we shared throws you off center, you must either have friends with gifts or you have gifts of your own. Or both, I suppose. Which is it?"

Undrea let out a breath. She still had to proceed with caution. Just because these women knew a little about the supernatural world around them didn't mean they'd be comfortable with vampires and werewolves and all the other wonderful, interesting citizens of the town. Which meant she wasn't quite ready to answer that question. "Do you believe in...other things? Like witches?"

"Absolutely," Sarah Jane said. Her gaze took on a knowing light. "Family legend says my great-great-great-grandmother was a seer. An actual descendant of one of the Greek oracles. We know there's more out there than what the eyes can see. And what most people understand." She leaned forward. "Why? Do you know a real live witch?"

"I know...several."

Sarah Jane nudged Connie. "I told you the signs were fortuitous for this trip."

"Okay," Undrea said. "I'm just going to lay it all out there. Ethan's in trouble. Nina is a very dangerous creature. She's a succubus. You know what that is?"

Connie slapped her hand down on the arm of the sofa. "I knew she was using him for something. I just didn't figure it was sex."

Undrea held up her hand. "That's not exactly true. Yes, she's using him, but sex isn't her main thing. It's power. The kind of power that comes from Ethan's position in the world. His fame and fortune."

Sarah Jane snorted. "You're saying Nina is literally a fame whore."

Undrea tipped her head back and forth as she thought that over. "I guess I kind of am. Fame vampire, is more like it. Except all the vampires I know are super nice people."

Connie flattened her palms together in front of her face. "My poor boy. What are we going to do? How are we going to get him free of her? Wait. He told me he was done with her." She peered intently at Undrea. "Because of you. What magic do you have?"

"About that… I'm a mermaid." She hated lying to them, but it was close enough for the conversation they were having.

"Get out of town," Sarah Jane said. "Is that why you like fish so much? And do the whole fish tank design thing?"

"It is," Undrea said. She'd told them all about her business at breakfast.

"That also explains why you're so beautiful," Connie said. "But how did you get him free of her? And if he's free, where is he?"

"About that," Undrea began. "Let's go back to the beginning."

And so she did, telling them everything, from how she and Ethan met with a kiss in the lake to what she'd seen Nina do to him. The two women listened with rapt attention right to the very end, where Undrea told them about the protective spell her witch friends had put him under via Bowie. "You can see that Nina has no plans to let him go."

Connie nodded, eyes filled with concern. "Do you think she knows her hold on him has been broken?"

"I don't. She might be getting an inkling of it, though."

Sarah Jane's gaze shifted to something outside. "If she doesn't, I'd say she soon will. Looks like Ethan just showed up."

"What?" Undrea spun around. As soon as she saw Ethan getting out of a sleek, midnight blue sports car, she got up and went to the door.

He smiled as she opened it and he saw her. "Hey. I'm sorry to drop by unannounced when you have company."

She shook her head, smiling. "You're always welcome here. And I think my company will be very glad to see you."

He made a face like he didn't quite understand that.

Until Connie joined Undrea at the door.

His brows went up. "Mom? What on earth are you doing here?"

She laughed. "Surprise! Sarah Jane and I took a red-eye to surprise you."

"Job done. But why are you at Undrea's? How are you at Undrea's? Did you bring Molly?"

Undrea shrugged "Your phone rang, and I answered it when I saw it was your mom. I didn't want her to worry. One thing led to another, and here they are."

"She took us to breakfast at Mummy's. It was fantastic. And Molly's at the neighbors. They love having her."

He smiled. "Mummy's is a good spot."

Undrea backed up. "Come on in. We need to talk."

"Yeah, we do." He started for the porch, carrier in hand. "I hope you don't mind that I brought Bowie with me."

"Not one bit." She grinned and leaned to see into the carrier better. "I missed him, truth be told." She wiggled her fingers at him. "Hiya, handsome."

He meowed back.

She nodded. "I know. I missed you too."

Ethan held the carrier out to the side as he hugged his mom. "How are you, Mom?"

"Better now, sweetheart." She held on to him, gazing at him with such pride that Undrea could feel how much she loved him. "Come say hi to Sarah Jane."

"Here," Undrea said. "I'll take Bowie."

"Thanks." Ethan handed her the carrier.

He and his mom went into the living room to see Sarah Jane. Undrea took Bowie into the kitchen. The coffeepot sat full and hot on its burner, reminding Undrea that she'd yet to serve it. They'd been too engrossed in discussing Nina.

She unzipped the carrier and let Bowie out. He went straight to his food dish, which was empty. "Hi, little man. How've you been? You hungry? Your food is still here. Hang on. I'll get you a new dish. That's a little old."

As she was fixing him a bowl, Ethan came in. "Undrea, I want you to tell me something truthfully."

She turned, the open can of Turkey-n-Gravy still in her hand. "Sure." She dumped it into Bowie's bowl as Ethan went on.

"What happened last night? I know Nina showed up here, I know I passed out, but then what happened after that?"

She put the bowl of food down. Bowie started eating immediately. "Maybe we should sit down. It's kind of a long story."

He shook his head. "I don't mean with me. I mean with Bowie."

She stiffened. Had his mom said something about Bowie having a spell attached to him? Was Ethan mad that she'd gotten Bowie involved in something like that? "Look, he was never in any danger. Those women don't do any bad magic. I promise. I would never let any harm come to him. I adore that little naked beast."

Ethan blinked, looking very confused. "What women? What magic are you talking about?"

"Um…" So maybe his mom hadn't said anything. But Undrea wasn't about to backtrack. It was time to bring Ethan up to speed on the woman he was living with.

"When Nina was here—" He crossed his arms. "Did you physically kick Bowie out of the house?"

"What?" Undrea put her hands on her hips. "Why

would you—you think I would—I would never give him to Nina. And I would never kick an animal. I mean, maybe if like a mountain lion was attacking me but—"

"Nina told me you kicked Bowie out of the house. Her words. Kicked."

"She's a lying liar. I would never hurt that sweet baby. I'd never willingly turn him over to Nina either."

Ethan exhaled and dropped his arms to his sides. "I knew you wouldn't. But I had to hear it for myself. By the way, I am done with Nina. Done. She currently thinks we've made up, but that was just so I could get out of the house without her pitching a fit."

"Her pitching a fit is the least of your worries. But good plan. Because you might not have made it out of the house otherwise."

"What do you mean?"

Undrea pointed at the living room. "Go sit down. I'm going to get a cup of coffee for whoever wants one, and then you're going to find out more about Nina than you ever could have imagined."

29

Ethan helped Undrea find out what his mom and Sarah Jane wanted in their coffee, then he went back into the kitchen with her. Before she could get mugs out of the cabinet, however, he cupped her face in his hands and kissed her.

It wasn't long enough, but there wasn't time for the kind of kiss he really wanted to give her. Not with his mom in the next room. But it certainly scratched the itch he'd been feeling. He broke it off and reluctantly let her go.

Just like that the sick feeling in his stomach and all the residual tiredness from his last episode were gone. She was obviously the best medicine for him.

She smiled at him, a hint of color playing in her cheeks. "What was that for?"

"Because you're amazing and I wanted to. No. That's not true. I needed to. I need you, Undrea. I can't exactly put it into words, but I feel so much better when I'm around you."

She looked away for a moment, like she was suddenly shy or embarrassed. "I feel that way about you too." She made eye contact again. "But we barely know each other."

"Does that matter? Can't we let our hearts do the thinking?"

She laughed. "Aren't you an engineer? Aren't you all about practical and logical and making decisions based on facts?"

"Yes, I'm an engineer. But I'm not a Vulcan. I have emotions." He took both of her hands in his. "What do you say? Let's give us a try. A real try."

"I'm in. But first, we need to have that talk."

"I thought we just did."

She shook her head, and a little of her happiness seemed to fade. "There is so much more you need to know. Not just about Nina either. Come on. Help me with the coffee, and then we'll get into it."

His mom gave him a curious look when they returned. "Trouble with the coffee maker?"

He knew that tone. She was letting him know she was aware of how long they'd been in there and wanted to know why. She'd just have to wonder. "Nope. Just fine." He handed her the mug he'd fixed for her, then took a seat on the ottoman, leaving the chair for Undrea.

She had Sarah Jane's coffee, and once she'd handed that off, she sat beside him in the chair. "Okay. Where to start."

His mom gave Undrea a little nod. "He's a smart man. He'll find his way from wherever you begin. But I'd say start with Nina."

"Right." Undrea took a breath. "Ethan, Nina is using you. As you might have guessed. But it's a little more…intense than you probably could have imagined. She's a type of energy succubus. I don't mean that as a metaphor, either. She feeds off your fame and power."

He stared at her for a moment, trying to process what Undrea had just said. "I realize she can be a little draining but…a succubus? You mean that's a real thing?"

"It is. I know, it sounds crazy, but I promise you, this is all straight up. Those episodes you've been having? We think they're the result of her siphoning off some of your power."

He thought about that. About how he could never remember them happening. About how awful he felt waking up from one. Anger spun up in him. "She's been using me."

"Yes," Undrea said. "Which is why they started not long after you met her."

He was too mad to speak. Almost trembling with rage at what Nina had been doing to him. Then he found his voice. "Do you know how many doctors I've been to? How many tests I've been through? And all the while, she knew exactly what was going on, and yet she pushed me to try new doctors and pursue new therapies and…"

Frustration choked him, and he shook his head, looking away.

His mom caught his eye. "I know, sweetheart."

Undrea reached out and put her hand on his arm.

"The thing is, all those doctor visits probably made news, right?"

He nodded. "No matter how low-key I tried to keep things, the press got wind that something was wrong. Not what, just that I was visiting a lot of specialists."

"So that only served to heighten your fame in a way. The very thing she thrives on. It's no wonder she pushed you to keep going." Undrea sighed. "Don't worry. We're not going to let her feed off of you again."

"How can you say that? She's been doing it for two years. What's going to stop her now?"

"We are. My friends and I." Undrea hesitated like she was searching for words. "Because just like your mom, I have friends with gifts. The kind that can help. In fact, I have gifts of my own."

Today was getting really interesting really fast. "You do?"

She nodded. "Yep. But first I want to say I'm sorry for lying to you. I'm not an amateur free diver. And I don't have a weird thing that involves pretending to be a fish."

"You don't?"

"Nope." She smiled tentatively as if hoping her next few words would make him happy too. "Because I'm a mermaid."

For a moment, he couldn't say anything. The woman he was falling for had just confessed she was a mermaid. There wasn't a set response for that. And nothing he'd experienced so far in his life had adequately prepared him for this moment.

She must have taken his silence for disapproval, because her brows bent and she suddenly looked very concerned. "I realize that's a slightly different gift than your mom being able to disappear or Sarah Jane's tea leaves, but I'm still the same person you went out to dinner with."

"No, you're not." He smiled. "You're even better. A mermaid. Really and truly?"

"Really and truly."

He thought back, narrowing his eyes slightly. "So that pic on your phone of the tail in the tub…"

"Not a filter or a costume. My actual tail."

He put a hand on his head and looked at his mom, then back at Undrea. "That explains a lot. Like how you were able to disappear into the water so quickly. And not need to breathe. Wait, so you can breathe water?"

"I can." She tilted her head and pulled her hair away from her ear. "See? Behind my ear?"

He looked where she was directing. "Gills," he whispered. "My girlfriend has gills. Not to mention a really beautiful tail. Which just sounded like a super weird thing to say."

"Girlfriend?" The corner of Undrea's mouth hitched up.

"Um, sorry. It's early for that, right? I just meant… I don't know what I meant."

Connie cleared her throat. "Yes, you do. You mean that you like her and want her to be your girlfriend. I want that too. But first we need to deal with Nina. I mean really deal with her. A succubus isn't about to just give up her source of sustenance that easily."

Undrea nodded. "Your mom is right. My friends with gifts that I mentioned? They're witches. Pretty powerful ones. And they're working on how to get Nina out of your life permanently."

His eyes widened. "You're going to kill her?"

"Not that kind of permanent. Just no longer your problem."

"Oh. Okay. I'm all for that."

"The process has kind of begun already. It started when you kissed me in the lake and—"

"That was CPR."

"I thought that too, but the universe decided it was a kiss."

"If it was a kiss, it would have gone a lot differently." And lasted longer.

She laughed. "I'm not arguing. I'm just saying it was the start of things. See, men who kiss mermaids often fall under their spell. And the mermaid falls in love with him. Unless they can stay away from the kisser for forty-eight hours. That didn't happen with us."

He grinned. "So you're in love with me?"

"Magically speaking, yes." Eyes full of amusement, she poked a finger into his chest. "Don't get ahead of yourself."

Sarah Jane snorted. "Men." She shook her head. "Go back to Nina. Why didn't the kiss break her spell?"

Bowie sauntered in, licking his chops. Ethan held out his hands. "Hey, boy."

Bowie walked past him and went straight for Undrea, hopping up onto her lap.

Ethan gave his cat some serious eye. "Really? You're going to do me like that?"

Undrea laughed. "I told you he was my boyfriend."

"I see that. But then you do have the distinct advantage of being half fish."

"Probably makes me irresistible."

Ethan understood completely.

She kissed Bowie's naked head as he settled in. "All right, back to Nina and the kiss and all that. Succubus magic is pretty strong. It's like she's got all these invisible tethers connecting Ethan to her. We might have severed the emotional and physical ones, but we have to break the magical one, too."

He didn't want to be connected to Nina in any way. "How do we break that one?"

"I don't know," Undrea said. "That's what my friends are working on. They're calling in some more help. Older, wiser help. They'll come up with a plan. I know they will. But until then, you have to stay away from Nina. Or she will zap you and take you back. Again."

"Even with the protective spell?" Connie asked.

"Hold on," Ethan said. "What protective spell?" His mom was looking at Undrea, so he did the same as he waited for an answer.

"My witchy friends cast a spell of protection over me and Bowie, and gave Bowie another transferrable spell to give to you. That's why I brought Bowie to your house."

He thought about the little spark he'd felt when he'd touched Bowie. "You can do that?"

She shrugged. "It was new to me. Trust me, mer-magic doesn't work like that. But we were going on the assumption Nina was a witch, so I don't know if that protection is going to be quite as useful against a succubus. Maybe a little. But probably not enough. Either way, you need to stay clear of her."

"Then I need to get a place."

Undrea snorted. "No. You're staying here with me." She looked at his mom and Sarah Jane. "You all are. I don't want to run the risk of Nina hurting any of you. Now I know my house isn't the biggest, but I have a king bed in my room, plus the queen in the guest room, and I can put an air mattress in the third room, and there's always the couch. We'll make do. At least until this is solved."

His mom shook her head. "We wouldn't dream of putting you out."

"We're not arguing this," Undrea said. "There is a very real danger out there, and I'm not about to risk Nina getting her hands on any of you. You have no idea what a threatened succubus is capable of. You are all staying here."

He wanted to kiss her again. She was that adorable. "You know I can afford a place big enough for all of us."

"I don't doubt that." Undrea hugged Bowie's loudly purring body closer. "But would that place take Bowie?"

Literally adorable. "Money overcomes a lot of rules and regulations."

She narrowed her eyes at him. "But would I let you take Bowie?"

He laughed. "I was assuming you'd go with us."

"Oh. Well, I don't see a reason to spend money. This will all be over soon. But until then, we do need to stay together so I can keep watch on you." She took his hand but looked at his mom and Sarah Jane. "All of you."

His mom smiled, making it clear what side she was on. "That is so generous of you. But just until this whole thing is sorted. We don't want to be a burden."

"Once this whole thing is sorted out, you won't need to stay here. Then you can all go back to Ethan's chalet because Nina should be gone then." Undrea smiled at him. "Now, let's get their luggage brought in, figure out the rooms, and then I need to call the office."

Ethan wasn't going to fight her. Staying with her was no hardship for him. He never wanted to be away from her. And it would be rude to turn down her generous offer. "Your house, your rules."

She smiled and glanced at his mom. "You really did raise him right."

30

While Ethan helped his mom and Sarah Jane bring their luggage in, Undrea changed the sheets on her bed. She'd already decided that Connie and Sarah Jane would take her room, Ethan could stay in the guest room, and she'd bunk on the couch.

She didn't mind it one bit. The couch was comfortable, and on the rare occasions she was sick or just too lazy to get up when binging some shows, she'd slept out there before. She kind of liked sleeping by the tank anyway. The sound of the water was very soothing.

Bowie helped her change the sheets, although help was a rather generous word. He seemed to think it was a game she'd invented just for him and insisted on skittering around under the fitted sheet while she was trying to put it on, randomly attacking it and then darting to the other side of the bed.

She couldn't help but laugh at his antics, even though he'd turned a five-minute job into one already running past ten. "Listen, you little stinker. I'm trying to put sheets on, not entertain you."

"I see you've discovered one of Bowie's favorite pastimes," Ethan said as he came in with a suitcase in each hand.

"How do I get him out of there?"

"You don't. You're going to have to put him out of the room if you plan to finish without interference." He put the suitcases down. "Come on, Bowie. Get out of there."

"I don't think he's listening," Undrea said. "I'm just going to make the bed right on top of him."

Ethan shook his head. "That's not going to deter him. He loves being under the covers. Face it. You can't outsmart that one."

"There's a joke in there somewhere. A mermaid being outsmarted by a cat."

"You've been catfished?"

She laughed. "Something like that."

He grinned as he went around to the other side of the bed. "I'll grab him."

"Thanks. No sign of trouble outside?" She only asked because Ethan had told her how he'd let Nina believe he was going out for a run, then going to the grocery store, but Undrea knew that wouldn't keep her in the dark for long.

"Nope. I figure I have at least another hour or so before she gets suspicious." He dug Bowie out from under the fitted sheet. The cat meowed in protest as Ethan took him out of the room. "You're not helping, you naughty beast."

Undrea got the bed made in record time after they left, but all she could think about was getting a call from Corette to say they had a plan.

When she'd explained to Corette that Ethan's mom and her friend had arrived, Corette had said it would be best if Undrea brought them up to speed, but that had been before Undrea had known they each had their own touch of the supernatural. She pulled the comforter into place and straightened it, then put the pillows back on the bed.

Probably wouldn't be a bad idea to let Corette know about Connie and Sarah Jane's gifts. And it would be a good excuse to see how things were going. Although maybe she shouldn't interrupt Corette, in case she was in the middle of something. Which meant calling Mattie instead.

She walked into the hall. Ethan was in the guest room, sitting on the bed with Bowie. The contents of his backpack were spread out on the bed. "All clear. You can let him roam."

"Okay." He put the cat down. "My mom is already talking about going to the grocery store to get ingredients for dinner. That's a no-go, right?"

"Right. I just don't think she should risk it. Nina's powers should only work on men, but that doesn't mean she couldn't still do something physical. The last thing we need is your mom kidnapped or something."

He looked a little shocked. "You really think Nina would do that?"

"I think Nina would do just about anything to

hang on to you. Is your mom in the kitchen?"

"Yep."

"I'll talk to her. And then I need to make a couple of calls. Maybe there's a movie or a show they could watch? I know that's not what they came to town to do, but if you hang out with them…"

"Of course." He glanced at the laptop open beside him, then shut it. "I can work anytime. I need to be with my mom. Old habits, you know?" He got to his feet, looking a little sheepish. "Nina used to complain that I worked too much. I guess she was right about that."

Undrea smiled sympathetically. "You didn't get to where you are by taking a lot of time off, but yeah, working later would be good. Although I'm sure you have business you need to attend to. Why not take your laptop out with you, and when they get into the movie, do what you need to do then?"

"No, it can wait. Come on, let's go make sure my mom doesn't already have car keys in her hand."

They went down the hall and into the kitchen. Sarah Jane was at the table making a list, while Connie was standing in the middle of the kitchen dictating said list as she ticked things off on her fingers.

"Heavy cream and Parmesan, too." Connie smiled at Undrea. "There you are. Do like fettucine Alfredo? And do you have a cheese grater? I should probably ask if there's anything you're allergic too."

"I do and I do and I'm not allergic to anything, but we need to back up a step. I understand you think you're going to the grocery store."

Connie gave her one of those motherly looks. "I promise it'll be quick, and if I see Nina, I'll disappear. Literally."

"I know that sounds like a good plan," Undrea said. "But you are not leaving this house. The Shop-n-Save delivers."

Connie frowned. "That's going to be expensive. And I don't think they let you use coupons."

"Mom." Ethan rolled his eyes as he put his hand on Undrea's arm. "I've got this. Go make your calls."

"Okay. Thanks."

"Mom," he repeated. "How many times do I have to remind you that I can afford it? Even without coupons."

Undrea slipped out of the kitchen and down to the basement. It was half garage and half storage. She never parked her truck in here, though. The F250 was too big. And she'd never had the time or need to finish the enclosed part into anything more than storage. Right now it held her bike, a push lawn mower, some other garden tools and a couple of boxes of things she'd never gotten around to sorting.

Wouldn't be that hard to finish the space. Maybe someday. But now she was thinking she should have Ethan put the Maserati in here.

She'd tell him after the phone calls. First, she called Aaron.

He answered right away. "Hey, Undrea."

"Hey. So. Lots going on." She gave him the ten-cent version but, except for her secret, didn't gloss over any of the supernatural stuff. After all, he was one himself.

"Wow. You want me to tell Whitney you're taking a day or two off?"

"That would be great. She can still email me or text or whatever if there are any issues, but I'm sure you can handle most of them anyway."

"So I'm in charge?"

She laughed. "Temporarily. Make sure my maintenance visits get covered."

"Will do."

"Thanks."

"Hey, if you need me for anything, just call."

"I appreciate that. And I might." Hard to say what she'd need, but having a water dragon shifter on your side could be pretty handy.

"And if Nina comes around looking for you?"

"Tell her…tell her I'm out running errands or something. Just don't tell her I'm home." Nina didn't need to know anything about Undrea's location.

"You got it. Stay safe."

"Thanks. Talk to you later." She hung up and dialed Mattie.

"Hey," Mattie answered. "I heard your future mother-in-law showed up."

Undrea rolled her eyes. "Settle down. But yes, she and her friend did. They're lovely. And they're not without their own skills. Sarah Jane reads tea leaves, and Ethan's mom, Connie, can disappear at will. Technically, she blends into her surroundings, so it's not really becoming invisible, but it's pretty similar."

"Now that would be a cool gift to have."

"Agreed. How are things going there?"

"Good and bad. Alice confirmed Corette was right. Nina is a rare breed of succubus called an edax. Corette was right about Nina having strong magical, emotional and physical connections to Ethan too. Your magic might have broken the emotional and physical ones, but the magical one is like Gorilla Glue. He's stuck. And stuck good. If she can reattach the emotional and physical ones again, she's got him."

"There has to be a way to free him."

"We're working on it, but so far the only cases we've been able to find where the edax released her victim was because of death."

"Hers?"

"Yes." Then Mattie sighed. "But also not necessarily. If her victim dies, then naturally being drained by the succubus is no longer a problem."

Undrea's heart sank. "Is that supposed to be the good or the bad?"

"The bad, I guess. Or… I'm not sure. We have more research to do. Obviously. Don't give up hope. We'll figure something out."

"You'd better figure it out before Nina can get her hands on Ethan again. Don't forget, she took him out of my house without entering it."

"That's part of how the edax's magic works. But she won't be able to do that to him again unless she drains him. It's some kind of drawing spell that only works for a short while after the succubus drains her victim. And she can't drain him without being close or being able to see him."

"So keep him inside."

"And probably away from windows. Seriously."

"No point in taking chances."

"Nope. Thanks. Talk soon."

They hung up, and Undrea started for the steps to get Ethan's keys. She wasn't about to let him move that car if it meant putting him in danger. Then a new question came to mind. She stopped and called Mattie back. "Hey, quick question. Am I in danger from Nina? It's just men, right? What kind of power does an edax have exactly?"

"Hang on."

She could hear Mattie moving. Then a door closing.

"Okay, I just had to get somewhere private. She's a lot like you in that her power only works on men. Doesn't mean she couldn't still try to kidnap you and use you to draw Ethan out, but I think she's afraid of you because she knows you're a supernatural but not what kind. Remember you said she bolted when you came out to save Ethan?"

"Right. She did."

"Which is why she's a lot more likely to go after his mom. She has to know Ethan would do anything to save his mother. So even if his mom can disappear whenever she wants, she's still in danger. And I'm guessing she doesn't have the kind of supernatural strength and speed you do."

"I didn't get that impression about Connie, no. But I'm not that fast unless I'm in the water."

"You're still faster than a human."

"Point taken. Okay, go back to work."

"Thanks. Bye."

Undrea started climbing the steps again. If Nina showed up and tried to take any of Undrea's house guests, that succubus was in for a fight. And Undrea had no plans on losing.

31

After Ethan made his mom realize there wouldn't be a trip to the Shop-n-Save, he helped her place an online order for all the groceries she wanted. It was sweet of her to fix supper and honestly, a nice way to repay a small portion of Undrea's hospitality.

Once that was done, he got his mom and Sarah Jane settled in the living room with a movie, then took a seat himself to wait on the groceries.

Undrea took the spot next to him, handing him his Maserati keys. "It already had that little scratch on the passenger's side, right?"

He stared at her, doing his best not to panic. "Um..."

She grinned. "Just kidding. I didn't get it over five miles an hour. Wow, is that a nice car. Maybe when all this is over, you could take me for a drive in it."

"When this is all over, I will do anything you want."

"Anything?"

He couldn't think of anything he wouldn't do with her. "Yep. You name it, we'll do it."

Her eyes narrowed, and she nodded. "All right then."

He snorted. "You're taking this as a personal challenge, aren't you?"

"Maybe." Smiling mysteriously, she stared at the TV without looking at him.

Her sass only made him fall harder and deeper, and it didn't bother him one bit. If he was going to fall for a woman so quickly, it might as well be a woman like her. One worth being in love with. One that wasn't going to take advantage of him.

And one that didn't seem to care if he had money, fame, or power.

An hour later, the grocery delivery showed up. Undrea met the driver at the door and took everything in, putting it on the floor in the foyer and handing him the tip Ethan had given her for the delivery.

Only when the door was shut did Undrea let Ethan come down and help carry things into the kitchen. He'd never had a woman be so protective of him, outside of his mom. Nina had been jealous, but that was something else altogether.

Something that had left him with an uncomfortable feeling. Undrea's actions made him feel loved.

His mom and Sarah Jane went to work putting the groceries away, shooing him and Undrea out of the room after they'd tried to help.

Undrea gave him a look as they went back to the living room. "It is my kitchen, you know."

"Was," he corrected her. "Those two are a force of nature. Better to just stay out of their way."

She shook her head. "I guess I could do some laundry. You could do whatever work you need, if you want."

"I might log on and check emails at least." That gave him an idea. "Hey, you want to see my secret project?"

She grinned. "If you're willing to show me, I'm more than happy to look. Although, fair warning, I may not understand it."

He laughed softly. "I don't think that will be a problem. Come on."

He took her back to the guest room, fired up his laptop and brought up the CAD sketch of the prototype membrane. "This is Freshwater. It's a membrane that will easily desalinize sea water. Mostly to help poorer countries that need drinking water but also to help in disaster situations. Any time or place fresh water is needed in an area with access to the sea."

"That's quite a project. It could be life-changing for some countries. How's it going?"

"It's…going. I can't quite get the membrane right. It either won't hold the ionization or it can't take a functioning amount of water pressure or it breaks down too quickly. Let's just say there have been a lot of hurdles to overcome. But I'll get there."

"When you do, you'll have another billion-dollar sale on your hands, no doubt."

He shook his head. "I'm not selling this one. I'm giving it away."

Her brows lifted. "Really?"

"Yep. I want to do some good in the world. If my name has to be synonymous with something, I'd rather it be for humanitarian work than because of my bank account. Not saying the money isn't fun. It definitely makes life easier. But it's not the end-all. Not for me, anyway."

She smiled. "That's amazing. I love that."

His phone rang. He pulled it out of his pocket and glanced at the screen. "It's Nina. Should I answer it?"

"No. I don't see any reason for you to talk to her."

"Good." He tapped ignore and put the phone away. "Because I don't care if I never speak to her again. In fact, maybe I should block her."

"No, not yet," Undrea said. "Not until this is all completely over. You may still need to get in touch with her."

He frowned. "For what?"

"We might need her in person for whatever plan my friends come up with."

"Oh." He thought about that a moment. "I guess I didn't think about that." He exhaled. "I'm not crazy about having to see her again. Not now that I know what she's been doing to me. And what she'd like to do to me again."

"I can totally understand that. Hopefully, my friends will come up with a plan that doesn't require you to be there. That would be the best, actually. Then you and your mom and Sarah Jane could be out of harm's way."

He glanced toward the kitchen. "I don't want my mom involved at all, if that can be helped."

"Agreed. I don't either." Her phone buzzed. She took it out and glanced at the screen, where a text had popped up. "It's my friend Mattie. She wants me to call ASAP." She looked up at him. "They have a plan."

He backed toward the door. "I'll go help my mom in the kitchen."

"Okay. I'll let you know what I find out." She tapped the screen.

He left her alone to give her some privacy. He and his mom had sort of taken over her house, the kitchen in particular, which now looked like a hub of activity.

He leaned against the framed entrance. "Hey, what are you guys making?"

His mom was measuring flour or confectioners' sugar. He couldn't tell. "Texas sheet cake." She glanced past him. "Where's Undrea?"

"On the phone. Her friends seem to have come up with an idea to deal with Nina."

His mom nodded. "Whatever you need Sarah Jane and me to do, we're in."

"No, you are not. You're staying here. Where it's safe. In fact, I might not even be going. Undrea thinks that's best."

"You sure about that?" Sarah Jane asked. She pointed with the spatula she was holding. "Why don't you ask her yourself?"

He looked over. Undrea was standing just slightly

behind him. He shifted to face her a little more. "Is there a plan?"

She nodded, but he couldn't quite read her blank expression. At best, she looked less than happy. "There is. Unfortunately, you're going to be right in the middle of it."

An hour later, and one of Undrea's friends had dropped off a few key items. He'd also been fully briefed and felt confident in his part. He'd never been much for acting or pretending, but if there was ever a time to embrace a role, this was it.

Now he stood by a bench just outside of Ruffin's Paddleboat Rentals, waiting on Nina to show up. If she didn't buy what he was selling, this whole thing was going to crash and burn faster than the Hindenburg.

He had a single long-stemmed rose in one hand, one of the things he'd been given, and in the pocket of his jeans was the other thing. A little velvet box carrying the very item Nina had been dying for him to give her.

Granted, the engagement ring in that box wasn't a real diamond. The jeweler it had been borrowed from, a woman named Willa, had assured them as she'd dropped it and the rose off that no one outside of a highly trained professional with a magnifier would be able to tell.

Willa was a fae and had used her power to enhance the ring in such a way that Nina would apparently be mesmerized with it. Among other things.

All of this supernatural stuff was so new to him

that he had no choice but to go along and trust that it would work out the way it was intended.

He heard the familiar *click-click* of heels behind him and turned. Nina was walking toward him with a wary smile on her face. "What's this all about?" She glanced at the lake, then the paddleboat dock a few yards away. "Why are we meeting here?"

"Because I have something very special planned. Something I should have done a long time ago." He held out the rose. "For you."

The rose was also enchanted. Or bespelled. Whatever the right terminology was. Willa told him it had come from a witch's garden, a green witch by the name of Marigold who ran the florist shop in town. An apt name, he thought, for such a woman with such a business.

Nina's smile broadened, but he could tell she still wasn't sure about all of this. She took the rose and smelled it.

He almost exhaled in relief. Getting her to smell the flower was important. He'd been told that.

A moment later, her wariness was almost completely gone, but her questions continued. "What are you up to, Ethan? This seems awfully sudden. And considering you wouldn't answer my calls or texts and—"

"Did it ever occur to you I had errands to run? And that maybe I'm trying to do something romantic?" He gave her his best innocent-but-holding-back-a-secret look. "Long-stemmed roses don't just grow by the roadside. And then there was the…never mind." He shook his head. "You'll find out soon enough."

Her eyes narrowed in question.

He held his hand out. "Come on. You'll see. Just go with it."

She took his hand but stayed put. "You know I don't like water."

Touching her repulsed him. Smiling at her and being nice and pretending like he didn't know she was an evil being out to drain his soul was hard enough. But touching her almost made him shudder.

It helped knowing that Undrea wasn't too far away. Her friends were close too. Although he didn't know what most of them looked like, which was good.

Undrea had also warned him that Aaron would be on scene too and that Ethan was not to freak out if he saw Aaron in his true form.

Ethan hadn't made any promises.

"You won't get wet. I'd never do that to you. I know how afraid of water you are." He was counting on that fear. They all were. He tugged Nina forward, leading her toward the rental window, smiling at the man working at the shop. "We'd like a boat, please."

As they came to a stop at the window, Nina laced her fingers with his and hugged his arm against her. "Seriously, Ethan. What is all of this about?"

He took a breath and got his head in the game. Then he smiled and lifted his shoulders in a little shrug. "I made a mistake. About us. And that led to a lot of thinking. You know how I am."

She nodded. "That I do. What were you thinking about?"

"Lots of things. Mostly about you and me and us and our future."

"And?" she prodded.

He hesitated as if what he was about to tell her was something major. "And the conclusion is that I'm ready to move forward."

Her eyes lit up. And he knew he had her.

Maybe whatever spell had been on the rose had kicked in, maybe Nina thought she was about to get the thing she'd wanted most, but in that moment, Nina stopped questioning what he was doing and went along with it.

The man handed them two life jackets. "You don't have to put them on, but make sure these are in the boat with you. Number five is yours. That's one of the purple ones. You'll see it. Have her back in an hour or it's a charge for every fifteen minutes after. Have fun!"

"Thank you." Ethan let go of her hand to pick up the life jackets. He was relieved to have something else to hold on to. He made himself smile at Nina. "Ready?"

"Absolutely."

He'd expected more of a protest, considering the activity involved deep water, but the magic on the rose seemed to be doing its job.

They walked down to the dock and found their boat. He helped Nina in. A fish jumped, sending ripples across the dark water's surface. He stared out at it, running through the next couple of minutes in his mind and losing himself in thought.

"Ethan? Are you all right?"

He shook himself and smiled at her. "Yep, I'm good. Just thinking about the future."

32

It didn't matter how far out they pedaled, just so that they were far enough from shore that help wouldn't be immediate. To distract Nina, he took her hand again and made small talk that he thought would make her happy.

All while making sure it looked like he was having a good time. "It's so nice out here, isn't it? I am really starting to like this town."

She smiled. "I'm so glad to hear you say that. I honestly felt like you weren't giving it a chance."

"I know, and you were right. I just needed to let go of my big-city expectations and realize that a small town like this is just going to be a different experience altogether. And you know, it's actually got a cool vibe of its own. It's still a very creative place. Just in a different kind of way." He meant that, too. Nocturne Falls was a pretty special place.

She looked thrilled. "Oh, Ethan, that's exactly right. And a town like this, filled with such interesting people…how could you not find it inspirational?"

"I'm really glad you pushed me to move here." Another truth. If they'd never come here, he'd still be in the dark about who Nina really was. And what she was doing to him.

The light in her eyes dimmed a little. "I didn't push you. I just suggested it."

She'd pushed. Hard. "I didn't mean it in a bad way." He squeezed her hand. "You just seem to know when I need that kind of direction. And I'm glad about it." He hoped he wasn't laying it on too thick, but then her smile returned.

He kept up the chatter, keeping her occupied on that instead of how far away from shore they were. "What made you pick this town?"

She shrugged. "You know. I did a lot of research. And it seemed like a place with a lot of growth potential." A certain coyness entered her gaze. "A place where we could raise a family. Don't you think?"

What he thought was that having kids would give her another way to increase his fame. What he also thought was that they were far enough away from the dock that it was time to kick the last steps of the plan into motion. He nodded. "You're right. We could absolutely raise a family here."

He stopped pedaling and turned toward her with a look that he hoped she took as earnest intent. "That brings to mind something I've been meaning to ask you."

"Oh?" She stopped pedaling too, instantly captivated by his every move. The paddleboat drifted on the faint current, but it only took them toward the center of the lake.

Unless the boat was moving in that direction because of some unseen help.

Didn't matter. So far, so good, and he needed to focus. The next step was crucial. He reached into his pocket and pulled out the small velvet box he'd been given earlier. It grabbed her attention instantly.

She inhaled softly.

"Nina Hascoe," he began. "We've been through thick and thin." All her doing, but he left that part out. "I can't imagine where I'd be without you, and I am truly grateful for the changes you've brought about in my life." And by that, he meant introducing him to Undrea.

Nina was practically welling up. She had a hand pressed to the base of her throat. "I feel the same way, Ethan."

He opened the box, revealing the phony engagement ring. It glittered in the sun like the real thing, sending a prism of sparks into the air. Willa had definitely provided him with a rock and a half. Exactly the kind of thing Nina would want.

She sucked in a breath. "It's beautiful."

"And it's the perfect ring for you. What do you say, Nina?"

"Yes! A hundred times yes." Her answer almost beat the end of his question. She stuck her hand out.

He took the ring from the box, instantly impressed with the realistic heft of it, and slipped it on Nina's finger. A perfect fit.

She admired it for a moment, then lunged forward and hugged him, causing the boat to rock a little. She stiffened and let out a little yelp, looking around in a panic.

"It's all right," he said. "We're fine. There's no way this thing will tip over."

She swallowed, clearly still freaking out a little. Was that the ring? Heightening her emotions? Making her more afraid of the water than she would have been otherwise? He wasn't sure. But it was working to his advantage, just like it was supposed to.

"Tell you what," he said. "Let's put the life jackets on. There's precious cargo on board. Better safe than sorry, right?"

"Okay," she whispered. "Right."

Good. That was all the opening he needed. He turned in the seat, getting up onto his knees so he could reach into the back and retrieve the life vests. As he did, a flash of iridescent scales slipped past his side of the boat. He smiled for a moment, almost unable to bear the incredible secret Undrea had shared with him. What lay ahead was scary, but he trusted Undrea. He had to. He couldn't keep living this life with Nina.

Eventually, she'd kill him. Better to go at the hands of the woman who actually cared about him.

He grabbed both life vests and stood up. The dragon wobbled, making Nina grab the side.

"Sit," she begged.

"I will, as soon as I have this on, then I'll help you with yours." He unclipped the belt on the vest and turned it like he was about to put it on, anticipating…

The bump came a second later. It felt like they'd hit something. He let out a yelp and fell, as planned, going over the side and into the cold drink.

Nina's cry went with him, the sound loud enough to hear even submerged.

The life vest floated on the surface as he sank. Nina called his name. His chest went tight with the need for air. Down he went.

Until a hand took his.

A swirl of coppery pink hair filled his field of vision, then Undrea's mouth was on his. He closed his eyes. Instinct kicked in and he inhaled.

Air filled his lungs.

He opened his eyes as she broke the kiss. She was grinning. And more beautiful than he could have imagined. Scales edged her hairline and trailed down her neck. Her eyes looked wider, rounder maybe, her teeth pointed and predatory. But he wasn't bothered by it. If anything, he felt honored to see her this way.

Behind her, another shadowy form swam past, long and sleek and deep green-gray metallic that flashed with a similar iridescence as Undrea's tail. The fins were much more angular, and nothing about the creature was remotely human. It disappeared into the blackness of the water.

In fact, it was downright Jurassic. He looked at Undrea. She nodded and mouthed the name Aaron.

Unbelievable. And yet, there was no denying what Ethan had just seen. He shook his head and looked at Undrea again.

She was focused on the surface.

He did the same. Above them, he could make out the bottom of the boat. The life vest had drifted away. Nina was still screaming for him. And for help now, too. He could see her, leaning over the edge of the boat just the littlest bit and peering into the water.

Looking for him.

As if sensing his need for air, Undrea put her mouth on his and gave him another breath. Then she took both of his hands and looked at him with a question in her eyes.

He understood. He knew what was about to happen, and it terrified him, but so did a lot of things in life, and he did them anyway. Without risk, there was no reward. He was Ethan Edmonds. Risk was practically his middle name. He nodded.

Undrea curled her tail up next to her, the fins sheer and silky in the water. She let go of one of his hands. She reached down, selected a scale, and yanked it out.

She grimaced for a moment, checking the boat above them again. Nina was no longer peering over the side.

Undrea handed him the scale. It was paper-thin and iridescent, about the size of a quarter and ever so slightly curved. He'd already been instructed on what to do. He just had to do it.

He glanced at Undrea. She smiled and squeezed his hand. His lungs were aching. There was no reason to wait another second.

He opened his mouth and put the scale on his tongue.

The reaction was immediate. His mouth sealed shut and his lungs burst into the kind of fire created by the horrifying lack of air. Panic sluiced through him. Instinct kicked in, and he stretched toward the sky. Despite everything he'd been told would happen, he couldn't squelch the drive to surface. To fight what was happening to him.

Undrea held on to him. He kicked, trying again to rise. Something cold and leathery latched onto his ankle. A quick look revealed the creature he hoped was Aaron.

Ethan tried to accept what was happening, but it was impossible. He fought harder to break free, unable to stop the instinctual will to live.

Undrea pulled him close and wrapped her arms around his upper body and her tail around his legs.

Blackness edged his vision. His lungs were going to burst. Then the blackness won and there was nothing to do but fade into it, lifeless and limp.

33

Undrea felt the life force leave Ethan. He'd fought, but she'd expected that. She uncurled her tail from his body, still holding on to him tightly. Aaron must have felt it too, because a second later, he let Ethan go as well. She waved at him to thank him and let him know she was going.

What needed to be done couldn't be done here. He nodded back at her, then disappeared into the depths.

Gripping Ethan against her, she kicked her tail and got them moving quickly toward the far side of the lake. She kept going until they reached the shallows, then she kept him under and surfaced to be sure the coast was clear.

It was.

She went back under, pulling him down with her. When the surface was a few feet above them, she put her mouth on his and used every bit of her mermaid magic to break the seal her scale had created and breathe air into him again.

He convulsed as he came to with the same wide, panicked eyes that he'd had when he succumbed, but then he gasped, taking in a mouthful of water, and realized he could breathe.

He went still as he exhaled the water, eyes still wide but now in obvious wonder. The panic was gone. He grabbed hold of her arms, staring at her and smiling as he gave her a little shake. I can breathe, he mouthed.

She laughed, sending bubbles of sound through the water. *You might also be able to hear me in your head.*

His eyes went wider still. *I can. How is that possible? Can you hear me?*

Yes. Magic. But now we need to get air in your lungs or you'll be stuck as a merman. Then she pulled him to the top, and they emerged.

"Are you okay?" Undrea asked as he took his first breath of air again. "I know that was frightening."

He nodded, still taking deep breaths and kicking to keep himself afloat. "It was the scariest thing I've ever experienced. Except for being able to hear your voice in my head. That was amazing. But the panic seems a million years away. Can I actually breathe water now?"

"No, that was a temporary side effect of the magic. With your first breath of air, that ability disappeared. If you'd stayed underwater long enough, it would have remained. But then you would have become a merman, and changing your species isn't something to do without a lot of thought." She let go of him and turned to float on her back, flipping her tail out of the water with a splash. "Come on, let's get to shore and get out of here."

He swam alongside of her. "Are we safe? I assume we're at the other end of the lake."

"That's exactly where we are. Not far from where you first saw me. And yes, we're safe. She can't see us here." Undrea pulled her tail under, her caudal fin brushing the bottom. She shifted back to her human form and put her feet down so she could stand.

Ethan did the same, and together they walked out of the water. Mattie was there to greet them with towels.

Undrea introduced her. "This is Mattie, one of my very best friends and one of the witches who's been helping with the spells."

He stuck his hand out. "Very nice to meet you, Mattie. Thank you for your assistance in all of this."

She smiled, but Undrea could tell she was sizing him up. She shook his hand. "Nice to meet you, too, Ethan." She handed him a towel and his backup glasses. "How are you feeling?"

"Not bad, all things considered." He put his glasses on first since his other pair had fallen off as soon as he'd hit the water. Undrea had promised Aaron would try to retrieve them.

Mattie nodded. "You mean now that you're Undrea's slave for the rest of your life?"

He stared at her. "What's that now?"

Undrea poked her friend in the shoulder. "Quit spinning him up. He's had enough of being enthralled to a supernatural. He's not going to think that's funny."

Mattie laughed. "Yeah, all right." She looked past them at the lake. "Is Aaron coming out this way too?"

"Not sure," Undrea said. "And we don't have time to wait. I need to get Ethan into hiding as soon as possible. Then the waiting begins."

He dried his hair, then pulled the towel down around his shoulders. "I'm ready. I just want this over with."

"We're almost there. And since you technically died, she should have no connection to you any longer."

He tugged on the ends of the towel. "But what's stopping her from coming after me again?"

"For one thing," Undrea said, "there's going to be werewolves guarding my house tonight. No one will get through. Right, Mattie?"

"Right. The sheriff, Hank Merrow, and his brother who's the fire chief, Titus, will be patrolling Undrea's house tonight. For another thing," Mattie went on, "an edax succubus can't attach to the same human twice. For a third, we're already working on a spell to banish her from the town. While you two were having your swim, Pandora let herself into Ethan's house and snagged a few strands of Nina's hair from her brush. We have everything we need to complete the spell now."

Ethan shook his head. "It's a good thing I never got around to changing those locks."

"Wouldn't have mattered," Undrea said. "Pandora's a witch too. She would have just opened the door with magic."

His mouth came open. "My Realtor is a witch? I only ever dealt with her online but— Hey, are there any humans in this town?"

"Most of the tourists," Mattie said with a grin. "Let's go. I should get back to work on that banishing spell."

Undrea nodded. "The sooner that's done, the better. Then you'll really be free." She gave him a wink. "Now get in the car and lie down with the towel over you. I'll let you know when it's safe to get up."

That wasn't until Mattie had backed toward Undrea's garage. Undrea got out and opened the door, then jumped back in the car. "Okay, you can get out, but you're going to have to make a run for it. Mattie couldn't pull in because your Maserati is already filling the space."

He sat up, pulling the towel off. "I really hope this all works."

"It will," Mattie said. "Just give us time to finish that banishing spell. Be patient. And stay out of sight."

"I will, no worries there." He slid out of the car and hurried into the garage. He stood by the side of his car. "Thanks again, Mattie. I owe you. I owe all of you."

"I'll make a note of that." She laughed.

Undrea could already smell something delicious cooking upstairs as she got out of the car, too. "I think your mom's been busy. I smell dinner."

"Me, too. See you up there." He headed toward the first floor.

"And stay away from the windows."

"Will do." He gave her a thumbs-up as he toed off his wet shoes before going up the steps.

Undrea ducked down to see Mattie. "Thanks again."

"You're welcome. I'll let you know how the banishing goes."

As Mattie pulled away, Undrea closed the garage door and followed after Ethan, leaving her shoes behind too. She was happy to see the blinds and curtains were all still shut, the same way she'd left them.

Connie and Sarah Jane hadn't opened a single one. Not that Undrea thought they would. Obviously, Connie wanted to protect her son more than anyone did. Still, it was strange not to be able to look out. They just couldn't risk Nina seeing Ethan.

Undrea found him in the kitchen, hugging his mom.

She was laughing but hugging him back. "You're getting me all wet!"

Undrea grinned. "We both need to change."

Sarah Jane was making a salad. "Dinner will be ready in about twenty minutes, so good timing."

Connie let go of Ethan and pulled Undrea into a hug next. "Thank you for all that you did."

Undrea hadn't expected the hug, but it was nice all the same. "You're welcome. We're not quite done yet."

Connie nodded as she released Undrea. "I know. But we will be, soon. And without you, none of this would have happened." She sniffed, clearly emotional.

"I was happy to do it."

Connie gave them both a little smile. "Off with you now. Get your showers or whatever and get changed for dinner."

"Yes, ma'am," Undrea said.

Connie made shooing motions at Ethan. "You too."

"I'm going." He walked down the hall with Undrea. "Sorry my mom is treating you like she's your mom too."

Undrea shook her head, amused. "No need to apologize. It's sweet."

He stopped at the guest bedroom door. "She's right, though. Without you, none of this would have happened." He took her hand, his expression serious. "This feels like a debt that can't ever be repaid."

"You don't owe me anything. If the situation was reversed, you would have done the same thing."

"You're right. I would have. If I knew how to rescue a mermaid. Which I don't." He glanced down.

She thought he was looking at their hands, then she realized he was looking at her feet. "Checking for webbed toes?"

He shook his head and pointed. "You must have cut yourself on a rock."

She looked. The top of her foot bore a small, fresh wound. "No, that's from where I pulled the scale off."

He frowned. "I'm sorry."

"Don't be. I wouldn't change a thing." She wasn't

going to tell him that it would leave a permanent scar. It didn't matter to her. And it would only make him feel worse. "That dinner smells good, and I'm hungry. We should really get moving before your mom yells at us."

He laughed. "You're not wrong."

"And I want to shower too."

"Same here." He gave her a quick kiss. "See you in the kitchen."

She left him and got straight into the shower, happy to stand under the hot water and soak for a minute. She was a little tired. She hadn't used so much magic in a long time, but she couldn't rest just yet.

Not until that banishing spell was in place and Nina was gone.

Until that happened, Undrea had to stay alert. Even with the wolves patrolling outside. Nina was probably in panic mode. And Undrea had no idea what the succubus would do next.

None of them did, really. Maybe that was why Undrea felt so unsettled. Maybe it was the feeling of waiting for the other shoe to drop.

She tipped her head into the water and said a little prayer that Mattie, Corette, and Pandora didn't run into trouble.

None of them had ever banished a succubus before. Undrea really hoped there was no learning curve. She had a strong suspicion they weren't going to get a second chance.

34

The moment Nina's connection to Ethan had been severed, she'd felt it like a hot knife going through her. But she'd known two truths in that instant. Despite the connection being cut, he wasn't dead. Not really. And there was magic at play.

Neither of those things had stopped the panic and desperation that had welled up inside her as she stared into the lake's murky depths.

Water terrified her. There wasn't a succubus alive who felt differently. She'd only gotten into the stupid paddleboat because he'd given her every reason to believe he was fully under her spell again and about to propose. Which he'd done.

Then everything had spiraled into a nightmare.

When he hadn't surfaced, she'd been sick with despair. The loss of connection with him had left her weak. So weak it had taken the last of her energy to get the boat back to shore. She'd left it at the dock, walked back to the car, climbed in, and just sat there for several minutes trying to process what had happened.

When Ethan had reached out to her earlier, she'd been suspicious that he was just going to tell her again that they were done. She couldn't accept that. She'd put so much time and effort into him. She needed him. Her whole family needed him. Their survival depended on his power and fame and energy.

But he'd been difficult all along.

He should have proposed ages ago, and he hadn't done that. He'd resisted, and so she'd had to make do with the tenuous connection they had. Once they were married, that connection would be sealed by a blood ritual he'd have no choice in. Doing it before he'd agreed to that level of commitment was too risky, so she'd had no option but to wait.

But she'd begun to doubt the proposal would ever happen. Then the fish girl had shown up and things had changed. Ethan had changed.

Nina wasn't sure what kind of supernatural the fish girl was, but she had some power, that much was plain. Nina got a feeling from her that felt like trouble. And not just because Ethan was falling for her, hook, line and sinker.

He'd forced Nina to turn things up a notch. Drawing power from him with such frequency was risky, but she'd felt cornered. She needed him to need her. To believe she was the only one who could take care of him the way he required.

And apparently it had worked, because when he'd

called earlier, the tone of his voice had been full of mystery and promise and she'd found a reason to hope again.

By the lake, he'd been sweet and kind with a light in his eyes she hadn't seen in a long while. There'd been no talk of the fish girl. Just about Nina and their future.

Now that future seemed as far away as Neptune was from Earth.

She'd stumbled into the house and collapsed onto the couch to sleep and heal the gaping wound his disappearance had caused. She felt like a piece of her had been ripped away. Sleep wouldn't cure it, but she didn't know what else to do until she regained some strength.

A thumping sound woke her. She blinked herself out of sleep, groggy and still weak. She was going to have to feed soon or she'd be in serious trouble. This town was filled with tourists. She'd find someone. Just as soon as she had the energy to hunt. She closed her eyes again. The sound came back.

Knocking.

She pulled herself upright. Please let it be a delivery man. Or someone she could drain. Although no delivery man or tourist was going to offer her the kind of energy boost she needed. She needed power and fame and celebrity.

If she couldn't find Ethan and reconnect with him, she was going to have to go back to L.A. or New York. There was just no other way around it. Her family was counting on her.

She got to her feet and opened the door.

Three women stared back at her. One older woman, very put together, with two younger ones. One polished, one a little bohemian. Useless. She needed a man. She started to shut the door. "I'm not interested."

The older woman spoke. "Nina Hascoe?"

"Yes, that's me." If this was some kind of welcoming committee…then she realized the younger polished one looked familiar. She pointed at the woman. "I've seen you somewhere before, haven't I?"

The woman made a slightly perturbed face. "I realize we did most of our transaction online, but I was your real estate agent."

"Oh, right. Penelope something."

"Pandora," the woman corrected her.

"Enough," the older woman said. "We're wasting time."

"Agreed," the bohemian one said.

The older woman reached out toward Nina and spoke a few words.

Nina's body went stiff, and in an instant, she understood that they were witches. And she'd been frozen with a spell.

The older woman held Nina in the spell, pushing her back into the house as the three witches entered.

The other two women lifted their hands toward Nina, too, and the weight of the magic increased. If not for the spell keeping Nina from moving, she would have fallen to her knees with the pressure of it.

The older woman waved one hand over her head, and the front door swung closed. Then she began to speak. "We know what you are, succubus. We know what *kind* you are, edax. And we are here to banish you from this place, from this town, and from the lives of those who live here, including Ethan Edmonds."

Nina tried to speak, but her voice was frozen too. Fools. They would pay for this.

The bohemian one took a handful of powder from a pouch at her waist and sprinkled a circle of it around Nina.

Black pepper, salt, cinnamon, and bay leaf. She might not be a witch, but she knew what things could be used against her. There was a reason she ate her food so plain. The smells rose up around her as the magic grew stronger.

The older woman continued to speak. "*Decedere loco isto non revertetur.*"

Heat wafted off the circle.

The other two joined in, repeating the phrase. "*Decedere loco isto non revertetur.*"

They spoke it a third time, then the older woman pointed both hands at the circle and said, "*Ignis ab igni!*"

The circle flared to life, and flames surrounded Nina. The flames went hotter and brighter and then turned to pitch black, swallowing Nina.

For a moment, she fought, but the blackness overpowered her. It opened a hole under her feet that she was powerless to stop.

And then she fell.

Undrea couldn't remember when she'd had a better home-cooked dinner. Certainly not in her own house. Fettuccine Alfredo with shrimp and broccoli, salad, garlic bread, and Texas sheet cake for dessert, which she'd never had before but would definitely be having again.

When she finally put her fork down, she was as full as she had ever been. Which was saying something for a mermaid.

"That was amazing." She shook her head as she looked at the two women who'd prepared the meal. "I don't know if you two normally cook like that, but you really outdid yourself."

Connie looked pleased. "We like to cook like that, but we don't often get the chance."

Sarah Jane snorted. "Especially since Ethan set Connie up with a meal delivery service."

"Fixing those still qualifies as cooking," Connie said as she looked at her friend.

"It is," Sarah Jane agreed. "But everything is already prepped. You just stir it together and add heat. Pfft. Where's the challenge in that?"

Connie looked at her son. "I love the meal delivery service. The food is delicious."

Undrea put her hands flat on the table. "I didn't mean to start anything."

Connie patted her hand. "You didn't. I'm very glad you enjoyed the dinner."

"I really did. And now I'm going to do the cleanup. You two can go out to the living room and relax, and when I'm done, maybe we can all watch a movie." Undrea felt like it was going to be a long night. She wanted the distraction of a movie. Or something. At least for her guests.

She wasn't sure anything could distract her.

"That's very kind of you," Connie said. "Ethan will help you clean up."

He laughed. "I absolutely will." He got up and started collecting plates.

The doorbell rang, and everyone went silent, looking at each other as if hoping someone knew who'd come to Undrea's house.

She smiled reassuringly, although she couldn't imagine who it would be either. But then, she doubted Nina would ring the bell. "I'll get it. Everyone just stay in the kitchen and out of sight."

As they nodded at her, Undrea went out to the foyer and peeked through the spyhole. It was Mattie.

She exhaled and opened the door. "Hey. Please tell me you have good news."

Mattie grinned. "I do. Nina has been banished. She is *gone*. I mean, literally. A hole opened up in the floor and down she went. The banishing spell worked like a charm."

"Wow." The tension left Undrea's body. "That is fantastic. Does that mean Ethan can go back to his house?"

"Yes, but Corette thinks the house should be

smudged before he returns. None of us knows much about this kind of succubus, so she and Pandora are going to go over in the morning and just make sure there's no residual succubus energy left. If he's cool with that."

"I am," Ethan called out from the kitchen.

Undrea and Mattie both laughed. Then Mattie shouted back. "Can we have your house keys then? It's easier to get in that way."

"Sure," he yelled back. A minute later, he tossed them to Undrea. "Here you go."

She caught them and handed them over to Mattie.

"Thanks. Corette or Pandora will text you when they're done."

"Thanks." Undrea glanced past her friend. "Are Hank and Titus still out there?"

"They are. Even though Nina's been handled, Hank thought one night of protection was still a good idea. He's the sheriff, so none of us argued. Tomorrow, everything can go back to normal." Mattie grinned. "Whatever that means."

"Right." Undrea hugged Mattie. "Thank you. I know I need to thank Corette and Pandora too, but I want you to know how much I appreciate everything you've done."

Mattie hugged her back. "You're welcome. I think Corette would be happy if you just got your wedding dress from her."

"Hush!" But Undrea snorted as she let Mattie go. "He's right upstairs. He's going to think I have designs on him."

"Don't you?" Mattie's grin was wide and mischievous. "By the way, you still owe me a night at Insomnia."

"I'm aware. And I promise to make it up to you."

"I know you will." Mattie gave her a wave. "See you later. Have a good night."

"You too." Undrea closed the door and went back to the kitchen. Most of the cleaning up had already been done. She pitched in, explaining what Mattie had told her as she helped. The good news seemed to motivate everyone, and they finished a few minutes later.

Ethan fed Bowie while Undrea searched a movie to watch. She found an old Doris Day/Rock Hudson picture that Connie and Sarah Jane both said was a must-watch.

They settled in to watch. The movie was great, but maybe it was the day's activity, or maybe it was the heavy meal, but at some point, they all fell asleep.

35

Ethan woke to a cat crying loud enough to be heard over the television, which was now showing a black and white movie he didn't recognize. His mom and Sarah Jane were passed out on the couch, and Undrea was in her chair, also asleep.

The fish tank lights were still on, and Bowie was curled up on the floor in front of it, watching. Or he had been. He was sleeping like the rest of them.

Ethan was on the floor with him, leaning back against the couch. He'd sat there to be close to his mom. He yawned. Maybe he'd only imagined the sound. Or maybe it had come from the movie. It certainly wasn't Bowie.

He got up and stretched, yawning again as he went into the kitchen to turn the lights off. The packets of microwave popcorn were still on the counter. They'd talked about making some, but they'd all fallen asleep before that had happened. All the excitement had worn them out.

As he came back out to the living room, he heard the crying sound again. Definitely a cat, maybe a young one. The sound was plaintive and desperate. And not coming from the television.

There were supposed to be wolf shifters patrolling around Undrea's house. Creatures he knew nothing about. They wouldn't hurt such an animal, would they? He hoped not. But he wasn't sure. They were wolves, after all.

He went to the front door to look out the peephole, but it was too dark to see anything. The threat of Nina was gone. There was no reason not to take a quick glance outside. Especially since the werewolves were keeping guard.

He unlocked the door, opened it a crack, and listened again.

The cry came again, a little weaker this time. It seemed close too. He couldn't help himself, but the sound of an animal in need wasn't something he could ignore.

He slipped outside, pausing a second to let his eyes adjust a little. If there were wolves on patrol, he certainly didn't see them. But maybe that was the point.

He listened, homing in on the cry as it broke the silence once more. Seemed like it was coming from the right side of the yard. Undrea's yard wrapped from front to back around the left side of the house, but part of the front yard was her koi pond.

The farthest side of the pond had a seating area with a bench. Behind it was a lot of shrubs and some willows. It was a beautiful spot, one that he'd thought about duplicating at his house.

The kitten, because he was pretty sure that's what it was, sounded like it could be in the clump of shrubs. It was spring. Wasn't that kitten season? Maybe a mama cat had abandoned one of her babies? Or it had wandered off? He knew enough about cats to know that kittens didn't have a good chance of survival all alone.

Listening close, he went down the porch steps, whispering to it. "Where are you, kitty cat? Are you by the pond?"

The little meow came again. He was definitely closer. He kept going toward the shrubs, working his way toward the pond cautiously so he didn't frighten the little creature off.

"Come on, baby. I'm here to help. Where are you?" He suddenly got the weirdest sensation. Like the air behind him had shifted. Then he smelled sulfur.

"I knew you weren't dead."

And he knew that voice. Unfortunately. He stopped and turned as a pit opened up in his stomach.

Nina stood behind him, looking…different. Her plum-colored hair blew out around her face as if she was standing in front of her own private fan. Her eyes held a slight glow and a touch of something feral. Her body looked more angular and leaner than the last time he'd seen her.

Was this her in succubus mode? He definitely preferred Undrea in her mermaid form.

He straightened, pulling himself up to his full height. Even though he knew what Nina was, he refused to be intimated. "What do you want?"

"What else?" She shrugged. "You."

"We're done. You know that. And you were banished."

She laughed, a sound he'd heard many times before but never with the bloodthirstiness that it had now. "Your little friends did their best, but they were working under some false assumptions."

"Like what?" He took a step back, although he didn't have far to go before he reached the pond. *Undrea, if you can hear me, I need you. Nina is here. Outside your house.*

He had no idea if the telepathy thing was still working, but it was worth a shot.

Nina took a step forward. "By now I'm sure you know what I am."

He nodded. "An edax succubus. You've been feeding off my energy. You're the reason I've been having those episodes." *Undrea, please. Wake up!*

She grinned, a wicked look. "Look at you, all educated on the big, wide world of supernaturals." The smile vanished, and she lifted her chin. "Except you're only half right. Just like they were. I'm a succubus but not an edax. I'm an elara. A much more powerful and higher caste of succubi."

"I couldn't care less."

Her eyes narrowed. "You're about to." She reached her hand toward him, and a bolt of red fire shot forth, piercing him and holding him in place.

The pain was staggering. He knew he was about to pass out. With his last moment of consciousness, he sent a mental plea out to Undrea again.

As blackness overtook him, he had one final, clear thought. The front door had opened. And Undrea had called his name.

"Ethan!" His voice in her head had woken her up, but it had taken her another minute to shake off the deep sleep she'd slipped into. It was nothing unusual. Her body was recovering from the loss of the scale and the use of magic, the latter because she was so out of practice.

But seeing Nina in her yard pinning Ethan with a bolt of succubus magic brought Undrea to life in a way that coffee never had. He hung there as limp as a noodle, impaled by the new connection Nina had sunk into him.

Undrea's hands clenched into fists. "Get away from him, succubus."

Mattie's Rambler screeched into the driveway. Pandora had the passenger door open before the car was parked. At the same time, Sheriff Hank Merrow and his brother, Titus, came running up the drive in their human forms.

Nina laughed and kept Ethan pinned. "He's mine. He'll always be mine. Get used to it, fish girl."

"Not going to happen." There was no time to

think, only to react. And Undrea's gut told her nothing mattered but Ethan's safety. With no concern for the consequences, she did the only thing she could do.

She used her voice. *"Ethan, listen to me. Ignore her. She is powerless over you. All that matters is getting to my side. Come to me, now."*

He straightened. And then, like a switch had been flipped, he turned to look at Undrea.

Nina groaned with the apparent effort of maintaining her grip on him. Through gritted teeth, she asked, "What kind of creature are you?"

Undrea ignored her. *"Come to me,"* she repeated.

Behind her, the door opened, and she could hear the soft footsteps of Connie and Sarah Jane coming outside.

Ethan shook himself, took a step forward. Just like that, Nina's connection snapped, causing her to yelp. Without a backwards glance, he walked toward Undrea.

Nina glared, chest heaving with the effort of what she'd just attempted. Her eyes widened a second later as realization must have hit her. She whispered a word that Undrea had never hoped to hear.

But what was done was done.

As Ethan joined her, Undrea knew what she had to do. She kept her eyes on Nina and spoke to him in her normal voice. "Are you okay?"

He nodded. "My head is killing me."

"Stay behind me."

He nodded again. He had no choice now. He was under her power, and there was nothing he could do about that.

She walked toward Nina. "You shouldn't have come here."

Nina nodded. "I'll go now."

"Too late. You had your chance."

Nina actually looked shaken as she retreated farther. The pond was behind her.

A spark of an idea flared in Undrea's mind. She had no clue if it was wishful thinking or based on something she'd heard or what, but Nina's fear seemed more than just the result of a childhood incident.

Driven by anger and a bone-deep desire to be rid of the wretched woman, Undrea charged. She went straight at Nina, palms out, and hit her in the chest.

The succubus flew back and landed in the pond. Nina screamed in terror, hands reaching up as she sank. "No!"

The water covered her.

A moment later, the pond erupted in violent bubbling as gobs of green sludge boiled to the surface.

"How about that." Mattie stood at Undrea's left elbow. "She turned into algae. Seems fitting."

Pandora, on the other side of Mattie, nodded. "Indeed. And it shouldn't bother the fish too much. Win win, I'd say."

Hank and Titus were on Undrea's right. "How did you know?"

Undrea took a breath. "I knew she was terrified of water. Then it hit me, a story from my childhood, a sort of mermaid fairytale about a terrifying creature that had no ability to swim or float."

"No wonder she was afraid of deep water. And you," Mattie added. "Once she found out what you were."

Titus shook his head. "I never really thought of mermaids as that frightening."

Hank was staring at Undrea. "She called you something else, though."

Undrea swallowed. It was time to come clean. She repeated the word she'd been holding secret for so long. "Siren."

36

Ethan wasn't sure exactly what had just happened. But somehow, Undrea had once and for all gotten rid of Nina.

Despite that, the men who'd showed up, one in a sheriff's uniform, one in firefighter blues, seemed more concerned with a word Nina had used.

The sheriff was staring at Undrea. "You're a siren?"

Undrea nodded without looking at him. "Yes."

"Don't you think—"

"Yes," she repeated. "I should have told people sooner. But then what?" She finally raised her head. "I get asked to leave? Or worse, told? My life is here. My business is here. And I have never hurt anyone. Never used those gifts."

"Until now," the fireman said.

"Hey," Mattie snapped. "She told me."

The sheriff shook his head. "That's not helping her case."

Ethan jogged down the porch steps and went over to where they were all standing. "What's going on? Why does there seem to be a problem?"

The sheriff frowned. "This shouldn't be discussed in front of a human."

Ethan was sure the man had some greater interest at heart, but it was time to get over that. "Listen, I'm more involved in this than any of you, so you can stop with the human business. Besides, my mom has gifts, so I'm not sure I'm completely human anyway. Now can someone explain what the problem is?"

The sheriff shifted his gaze to the women on the porch for a moment, then back to Ethan. "It's not how we like to do things. We try to protect the innocence of our visitors as much as—"

Ethan cleared his throat. "I live here."

Pandora nodded. "He does, Hank. I sold him the house."

"Well, then..." Hank looked at his brother, then back at Undrea. "We might as well go inside and figure this out."

But Undrea didn't move. "Are you going to arrest me? Am I in trouble? I want to know. I've been keeping this a secret since I moved here, always afraid this day would come, and now...now I'm not really afraid anymore. I just want to know what the consequences are."

Ethan couldn't believe what he was hearing. "Consequences for what? For saving me? For turning a succubus into goo? What are we talking about?"

She found her courage and looked at him, giving

him a quick, sad smile. "The consequences of me hiding my true identity. I'm a siren. A potentially deadly kind of mermaid. Basically…a water succubus."

He stared at her. "What?"

After a deep inhale, she nodded. "It's true. Some say that's where my kind come from. The union of a succubus and a merman." She shrugged. "I don't know, and it doesn't matter at this point, but I am a very dangerous creature."

He snorted. "You're about as dangerous as Bowie. Come on, Undrea. You saved my life."

She smiled again. "I'm very grateful you see me that way. What remains is how the powers that be see me."

Mattie slipped her arm around Undrea's waist. "There won't be an issue. We won't let there be an issue."

Pandora nodded and moved closer to Undrea. "That's right."

Hank put his hands on his hips. "I'm sure I don't know everything that's happened, but all I know is the Ellinghams have the last say on this. It's their town. And ultimately, they decide who lives here."

Then he cracked a smile. "If they disallowed those of us who might be considered deadly, there's not a whole lot of us who'd still be living here. If Mr. Edmonds says you saved his life, I don't think you have anything to worry about."

Undrea's mouth came open. "I don't?"

He shook his head. "You've never been anything but a good citizen, as far as I know. And aren't you friends with Delaney?"

She nodded. "Yes, but—"

"Let's call her right now," Mattie said, letting go of Undrea to get her phone out.

"I don't know," Undrea said.

Ethan couldn't stand seeing Undrea so worried. "If this Delaney can ease your mind, then call her."

Undrea blew out a long breath. "Okay. Let's get this over with. I won't be able to sleep anyway."

"I'll do it. Then it'll be official." As Hank got his phone out and dialed, he walked a few yards away.

While he was doing that, Ethan took Undrea's hand and pulled her into his arms. "Thank you. You saved me again. For good this time, too."

"Except you've been exposed to my magic now." She sniffed. "And that's not a good thing, believe me."

"I feel fine, so whatever you're worried about, just stop."

"You don't understand. The sound of a siren's voice drives men to madness. It causes them to—"

"Mrs. Seeley?" Mattie's voice interrupted her. "Hi, this is Mattie Sharpe. I'm a friend of your daughter's."

Undrea whipped around in his arms and hissed at her friend. "Are you on the phone with my mother?"

Ethan wasn't sure why that was a problem.

Mattie nodded. "We need some questions answered about Undrea's powers. Namely how to save a man who's been exposed to—"

Undrea grabbed the phone. "Mom? Mom, listen.

Yes, but—no, I had no choice but to—no." She frowned at Mattie. "Yes." Her gaze shifted to Ethan, and her brows went up. "Really? I actually already did that. Long story that I will explain later. Yes. I promise." She exhaled. "Thanks. Love you too. Soon. I will. Okay. Bye."

She hung up and handed the phone back to Mattie, then stuck her hands in her back pockets. "My mom says that the way to break a siren's spell is for the subject of the spell to ingest one of my scales. And since you already did that, there's no lasting effect to me using my magic on you."

"Yeah?" He still felt ninety-eight percent clueless about what was going on, but if she was happy, so was he.

Except she made a face that held some worry. "Although you're still susceptible to obeying me when I use my siren's voice."

"Meaning?"

"If I tell you to do something using that voice, you have no option but to do it."

He grinned. "Isn't that basically how you got me away from Nina? Your magic was stronger than hers."

Undrea shook her head. "That was just my regular mermaid magic. Apparently."

He shrugged. "Whatever. I can live with it. So long as you promise not to abuse it." He already knew she wouldn't. She wasn't that kind of person.

She gazed up at him. "Really? That doesn't bother you? After spending two years in the thrall of a succubus, you could actually be with another woman who has the power to control you?"

He cupped her face in his hands and stared into her beautiful sea-green eyes. "You already control me, Undrea. You're in my head constantly. I make decisions based on what I think you'd like. Even my cat is madly in love with you. I have been under your spell since the moment I met you, and that had nothing to do with magic."

"But it did. You kissed me and—"

He laughed. "We both know that was CPR. This is a kiss." He pressed his mouth to hers. They fit together as perfectly as if they'd been designed for each other. That was possible, wasn't it? He didn't know. Didn't care. All that mattered was that Undrea was his.

He took a breath. "I can't lose you, Undrea. I couldn't take it. And Bowie would be distraught."

She let out a soft laugh. "Well, for Bowie's sake, I guess we could give it a try." She looked over her shoulder. "So long as I'm not being asked to move."

Hank was walking toward them.

Ethan pulled her close. "If you are, I'll go with you."

Hank tucked his phone away. "Delaney said you have nothing to worry about. And congratulations on ridding the town of the succubus and saving its newest resident. She said if anything, that might qualify you for citizen of the month."

Undrea shook her head, mouth open like she couldn't quite believe it.

Hank put his hands on his hips and tipped his head at the koi pond. "Might want to get that thing cleaned out tomorrow."

Undrea nodded. "I'll, uh, make sure I do that."

"You folks have a good night." He glanced at his brother. "Come on. Ivy will be happy to have me home early."

Titus nodded and started walking. "So will Jenna."

Mattie, who was all smiles, grabbed at Pandora's sleeve. "That's our cue too." She wiggled her fingers at Undrea and Ethan. "Talk to you later."

A couple of minutes later, they were gone, leaving Ethan, Undrea, his mom, and Sarah Jane alone again.

With his arm around Undrea's waist, they walked back to the porch. "Mom, do you have any issues with Undrea being a siren? And with her being in my life?"

"She saved your life." His mom clasped her hands together in front of her. "My only issue would be if she's *not* in your life."

He laughed and looked at Undrea. "Are you okay with my mom being this bossy?"

Undrea snorted. "I'm good with it."

"Ethan James Edmonds, I am *not* bossy." His mom had her hands on her hips now. "But if you don't take that girl ring-shopping immediately, you will be in trouble."

He shrugged and shook his head, happy to see Undrea laughing. "I tried to give you an out."

She nodded. "You did."

"Now you're stuck with me. And her." And the enormous ring he would happily buy her. He'd spend the rest of his life spoiling her, if that's what she wanted.

"Stuck," his mother muttered. "You're a rotten child." She laughed. "I always told you there were a lot of fish in the sea."

He nodded. "I just never guessed mine would be a mermaid."

THE END

Want to be up to date on all books & release dates by Kristen Painter? Sign-up for my newsletter on my website, www.kristenpainter.com. No spam, just news (sales, freebies, releases, you know, all that jazz.)

If you loved the book and want to help the series grow, tell a friend about the book and take time to leave a review!

Other Books by Kristen Painter

PARANORMAL ROMANCE:

Nocturne Falls series:

The Vampire's Mail Order Bride
The Werewolf Meets His Match
The Gargoyle Gets His Girl
The Professor Woos The Witch
The Witch's Halloween Hero – short story
The Werewolf's Christmas Wish – short story
The Vampire's Fake Fiancée
The Vampire's Valentine Surprise – short story
The Shifter Romances The Writer
The Vampire's True Love Trials – short story
The Dragon Finds Forever
The Vampire's Accidental Wife
The Reaper Rescues the Genie
The Detective Wins the Witch
The Vampire's Priceless Treasure
The Werewolf Dates the Deputy

Can't get enough Nocturne Falls?

Try the NOCTURNE FALLS UNIVERSE books.
New stories, new authors, same Nocturne Falls world!
www.http://kristenpainter.com/nocturne-falls-universe/

Shadowvale series:

The Trouble with Witches

The Vampire's Cursed Kiss

The Forgettable Miss French

Moody and the Beast

Sin City Collectors series:

Queen of Hearts

Dead Man's Hand

Double or Nothing

Box set

Standalone Paranormal Romance:

Dark Kiss of the Reaper

Heart of Fire

Recipe for Magic

Miss Bramble and the Leviathan

COZY PARANORMAL MYSTERY:

Jayne Frost series

Miss Frost Ices The Imp – A Nocturne Falls Mystery

Miss Frost Saves The Sandman – A Nocturne Falls Mystery

Miss Frost Saves the Sandman – A Nocturne Falls Mystery

Miss Frost Cracks a Caper – A Nocturne Falls Mystery

When Birdie Babysat Spider – A Jayne Frost short

Miss Frost Braves the Blizzard – A Nocturne Falls Mystery

Miss Frost Chills the Cheater – A Nocturne Falls Mystery

Miss Frost Says I Do – A Nocturne Falls Mystery

Frost & Crowe series

Lost in Las Vegas

Happily Everlasting series

Witchful Thinking

URBAN FANTASY:

The House of Comarré series:

Forbidden Blood

Blood Rights

Flesh and Blood

Bad Blood

Out For Blood

Last Blood

The Crescent City series:

House of the Rising Sun

City of Eternal Night

Garden of Dreams and Desires

PARANORMAL WOMEN'S FICTION:

The First Fangs Club series:

Sucks to Be Me

Suck It Up, Buttercup

Sucker Punch

Nothing is completed without an amazing team.

Many thanks to:

Design & derivative cover art: Janet Holmes using images under license from Shutterstock.com

Interior formatting: Author E.M.S

Editor: Chris Kridler

About the Author

USA Today Best Selling Author Kristen Painter is a little obsessed with cats, books, chocolate, and shoes. It's a healthy mix. She loves to entertain her readers with interesting twists and unforgettable characters. She currently writes the best-selling paranormal romance series, Nocturne Falls, and the cozy mystery spin off series, Jayne Frost. The former college English teacher can often be found all over social media where she loves to interact with readers.

www.kristenpainter.com

Made in the USA
Middletown, DE
08 April 2021

37209848R00195